Lincoln Township Public Library

D0422868

Jack O'Halloran

FAMILY LEGACY

Lincoln Township Public Library
2099 W. John Beers Rd.
Stevensville, MI 49127
(269) 429-9575

Published in 2011 by MP Publishing Limited

6 Petaluma Blvd. North, Suite B6, Petaluma, CA 94952

and

12 Strathallan Crescent, Douglas, Isle of Man IM2 4NR

Published by M P Publishing Limited 2011.

ISBN 978-1-84982-106-3
Family Legacy

1 3 5 7 9 10 8 6 4 2

Copyright © Jack O'Halloran and Overseas & Commercial Management Ltd
Jack O'Halloran asserts his moral right to be identified as the author.

Cover Design by Dorothy Carico Smith

Book Design by Maria Smith

O'Halloran, Jack, 1943-
 Family legacy / Jack O'Halloran.
    p. cm.
 ISBN 978-1-84982-106-3
 1. Gangsters--Fiction. 2. Organized crime--Fiction. 3. Political fiction. I. Title.
 PS3615.H35F36 2010
 813'.6--dc22
                            2010012083

A CIP catalogue record for this book is also available from the British Library

This book is sold subject to the condition that it shall not, by way of trade or otherwise, be lent, resold, hired out, or otherwise circulated without the publisher's prior consent in any form of binding or cover other than that in which it is published and without a similar condition including this condition being imposed on the subsequent purchaser.

The scanning, uploading and distribution of this book via the internet or via any other means without the permission of the publisher is illegal and punishable by law. Please purchase only authorized electronic editions and do not participate in or encourage electronic piracy of copyrighted materials. Your support of the author's rights is appreciated.

BT 11" 30

Part I

Prelude: 1957

Albert Anastasia sat impassively, his broad, muscular frame filling the red leather chair. He wore a double-breasted coat over a crisp white shirt, his fingers resting comfortably on the table. "On Arthur Avenue," Anastasia said gruffly, repeating what the soldier had told him. "Outside the fruit and vegetable store."

Hours later, sitting quietly in the back corner of a bar three blocks south of Anastasia's office, it wouldn't be the mangled corpse of Frank Scalise forcing the next sip of whiskey past the soldier's lips. It would be Anastasia's eyes. The two cigarette burns pressed deep into their gun-barrel sockets bearing down on him, coaxing every last word of the story into the open until the soldier had finally finished his account of what had happened.

Sweat trickled down the long groove of his back. He'd wished he could run a finger around the inside of his collar to let in a little air. Maybe even loosen his necktie and undo his top button. Thin lines of sweat were beginning to snake down the inside of his shirt from his armpits, but his mouth was dry. "Like I said. Scalise always goes to…went to…Mazzaro's."

Frank Scalise had been one of Albert Anastasia's top lieutenants. They went back a long way. That was the reason Scalise had been made underboss in the Bronx. It was also why the two soldiers who had witnessed the murder drew straws to see who would make the trip up to Anastasia's office to break the bad news.

The two giant V's permanently etched across Anastasia's forehead grew darker. "Two shooters?"

"Yes. Brought in from outside, I guess."

"In the head and neck?" The pattern was familiar, the conclusion inescapable.

Less than six weeks ago, Anastasia's lifelong associate, Frank Costello, had been shot in the entrance to his apartment building.

"This is for you, Frank!" the gunman had screamed.

Costello turned his head in time for the bullet to tear from the far side of his scalp to the top of his left ear. The bullet may have missed, but the message was on target. They were getting bolder, and they were getting closer.

Costello, now Scalise. Vito Genovese and his backers were circling closer and closer to the bull's-eye: Anastasia himself. He stood from his chair. "You know what to do."

And the soldier did.

Anastasia was the boss of Murder, Incorporated. For thirty years, he had been the enforcement arm of the national crime syndicate otherwise known as the Commission.

Message delivered. Orders received.

Anastasia followed the soldier out with stocky, purposeful strides and watched him cross to the elevator. The guard outside the office held the door as the boss turned back into his bureau.

"No one comes in till I tell you." And with that, Anastasia closed the door, crossed the oak-paneled room to the rich mahogany desk, and lowered himself back into his chair.

Scumbags like Carmine Galante, the rat who had deserted the Genovese family a few years back to join forces with the Bonanno family, Albert could understand.

But Genovese himself…

Like Scalise, Anastasia and Genovese went way back—to the twenties and thirties, when they had worked alongside each other. Albert Anastasia and Vito Genovese. Tough and fearless, they had clawed their way to the top of the pile. Each man headed one of the five families controlling New York. Their power and influence reached far beyond the city, beyond America.

If nothing else, the boss of Murder, Inc. was a realist. He had stood his ground while support had eroded. Genovese and the rest would have to crush him. Albert Anastasia never budged on what he believed in. He'd be taking those principles to his grave.

Killing was his business, and he was the best. No one disputed it. Anastasia had been watching men die for forty years. Death held no mystery for him. He didn't welcome it, but he didn't dodge it either. His time had come and he accepted it.

This lesson he had learned growing up in Sicily. The code of *omerta* meant more than keeping your silence. *Omerta* was what it took to be a man: accepting your fate without question and without complaint.

And to *omerta*, he now entrusted his legacy.

Pulling the telephone toward him, he put through a call to his private attorney, who had just enough time to answer, "I'll be there in twenty minutes," before Anastasia hung up.

He sat back, squinting into the harsh light bearing down on the Upper West Side. If this was to be the last will and testament of Albert Anastasia, it was destined for worthy eyes.

Closing his own, he allowed himself to savor that thought.

Although his plan had been framed for several years, although he had gone over it and refined it until every detail fell into place, the prospect of finally putting it into play still managed to hold some surprise for him. Temptation lurked, too—a deep-seated desire Anastasia had kept in check for nearly twenty years.

It unsettled him. It excited him.

He opened his eyes and reached for the phone once more. He paused before dialing, then set his fingers to work as if he hadn't skipped a beat. The ring tone at the other end of the line came to him in slow, echoed beats, as if from a dream. Anastasia quickly replaced the receiver once more.

No, not yet, he had decided.

The electric fan hummed. The traffic on West End Avenue kept pace in a constant murmur. The attorney would arrive soon. And then, Albert Anastasia's exile would end.

Chapter One

The team assembled in the changing room an hour before kick-off. Win this and Cooper High would be champions. Though it wasn't just the Colonial Conference at stake. Audubon had players, topped by Jerry Ossler, also aiming for higher things. The scouts would be as interested in them as they were in the Cooper High hopefuls.

Jack tugged on his leather padding and tightened his boot laces around his ankles. Last year's game had been his first run out for the varsity team and the rookie end had shown up well, scything through the opposing team and claiming two touchdowns.

Audobon would remember him.

Outside, the grass field was soggy and already cut up. Coach Sullivan was still upbeat, undeterred. He wouldn't have his players complaining. No time for nerves. No time for questions or self-doubt. All or nothing. They were down to the wire. Finishing second was as good as finishing last.

Each player had his own pre-match ritual.

Jed Freeman, the captain, stood with his back to the bleachers, shadowboxing with a fixed, manic fury—beads of sweat already began to break down the sides of his face.

The quarterback, Lonnie Sherrard, went on a high-kicking jog, his knees crunching up into his chest and pounding back down like pistons, not so much propelling his body upward as pushing the ground away.

Others performed elaborate stretches, bounced up and down—alternately crouching in a squat and springing back up.

Jack sat alone, far removed from the sweeping wave of nervous energy washing over the sideline. At first, his pre-game ritual hadn't gone over so well. The other players were confused and thought it made Jack look soft—something they would quickly change their minds about. By now, the other guys on the team had gotten used to Jack's "air fix," as they called it.

Jack stood far from the others, staring straight through the opposing players as if they weren't there. His routine was always the same: eyes fixed on the opposing goal, a steady rhythm... *breathe deep...hold...breathe out...hold...breathe deep...*

He could isolate himself from whatever was happening around him until he sensed a familiar glow radiating from down inside.

And then he was ready.

"Okay. Gather in." Freeman huddled his team together around their coach.

Sullivan flattened the clipboard to his chest, surveyed the ring of boys gathered around him, made sure their eyes were fixed on his. "Audubon is no pushover. Keep it sharp, you guys. Just concentrate on doing the basics and doing them right. And don't go playing to the gallery. They're way too smart to be taken in anyway." He paused. "You know what I'm going to say next."

"One mistake cancels out three good plays," answered the chorus in front of him.

He grinned in reply, slapped Freeman across the shoulder to send the team on their way. "Keep it tight and let the ball do the hard yards. This one's in the bag...and I've got money on it."

Word had gotten around Haddonfield that Coach Sullivan had something special cooking in his varsity team this year, and the players had grown used to a few dozen unfamiliar faces joining the gaggle of spectators on the decked wooden seats. This afternoon, Cooper High had pulled in the biggest crowd of the season. Row after row, fans hoped to see a memorable victory crown a memorable season clamored in the bleachers.

The game got off to a slow start. The slick field had turned what promised to be a high-flying offense-dominated game into a tough battle for field position. Jack found himself in double coverage for most of the first half, until with thirty-nine seconds left in the second, he got free and found himself behind the secondary. Jack flicked his arm out, hoping Lonnie would find him open down field.

The pass went up.

Jack would have to move if he was going to get under it.

Two long strides and he dove, sprawled out on his right side as the pass came crashing in at shoulder height.

The crowd roared. Jack caught the ball just behind the goal line—the first touchdown in an otherwise scoreless game.

Lonnie came streaking down field, his arms upright, fingers to the sky.

Jack slapped him between the numbers. "Nice pass, Sherrard."

"Just keeping you on your toes."

The offense jogged off the field, the players congratulating one another as special teams got ready to kick the extra point. As Coach Sullivan barked out orders and got the defense ready for the upcoming series, Jack flipped off his helmet and took a long drink of water.

The Cooper High cheerleaders built a pyramid in front of the galley of cheering spectators. The point after sailed through the uprights, though Jack never saw it leave the ground. Instead, he focused on Julie-Ann Peterson, captain of the cheerleading squad, perched atop the other girls. For a second, they locked eyes, and a smile meant only for his eyes slowly spread across her face.

"Pagano!" Coach Sullivan knocked Jack right out of his trance. "Keep your focus, son. Looks like you've got some college folks with their eye on you today."

Jack followed his coach's stare to a group of three men some distance from the rest of the spectators. They sat side by side on the wooden benches, dark overcoats and hats shielding them from the crisp autumn air. Most other people watching the game were clad in mufflers and comfortable winter coats, but this trio stood out from the crowd. Starched collars, neatly knotted neckties, perfectly creased pants, and well-tailored quality cloth set them apart.

It was their shoes that caught Jack's attention. They were highly polished, with no trace of mud. Even from a distance, Jack could tell they were classy. Real expensive shoes weren't worn by football scouts. That much he knew. These three men in the stands had to be something else. Men like that didn't work for football teams—they owned them.

The man in the center of the threesome looked like he might have played some football in his time. He was thickset. His quick eyes moved decisively round the field, taking in details at a glance and filing them away.

From that point on, Cooper High took total control. By the third quarter, Jack's stamina and turn of speed had him cutting holes in the Audubon defense. This one had their name on it, Jack's name on it.

When the game ended, Audubon, deflated and defeated, could only look forward to the 1958 clash. Cooper High had scored a decisive victory. Uncrowned Colonial Conference champions, they rode Jack's four touchdowns and twelve catches for 260 yards to a 48–7 win.

Coach Sullivan, thronged by a cluster of happy, mud-spattered figures, shaking hands, exchanging gags, kept repeating, "My boys…my boys…my boys…" as if to convince himself what had happened was real.

Fans poured onto the field, mostly students, but more than a few parents and siblings in the lot. They thronged round the team. Jack peered through the crowd of smiling faces for Julie-Ann.

She wasn't there.

The stands were nearly empty.

The three smartly dressed men had disappeared too.

Jack shoved the game ball inside his school bag. He hopped on his bike and began to peddle home when he heard the patter of footsteps coming up behind him and a soft, small voice call out, "Easy there. A girl might get the idea you didn't want to be seen with her."

Pulling hard on the brakes, Jack shuddered to a clumsy halt.

"I didn't see you after the game," Jack stammered. "I figured you were…occupied…or…"

The freshness of the late afternoon air had brought a luster to Julie-Ann's cheeks. Her pale blue eyes were wide and bright beneath a fresh layer of mascara. The girl was wearing a neatly tailored dark brown coat. Her neck was swathed in a broad, deep burgundy scarf that peaked through her carefully disheveled corn-colored hair.

"You remember what we talked about the other day after school? About doing some study together?"

"Yeah, I remember." Jack had been able to think of little else the last few days.

"Well, I was wondering about this evening. My dad has a business function to attend in Cherry Hill, some kind of dinner-dance thing, so my mom has to go with him. They won't be back till late. And that leaves me all by my lonesome. Just me and my books." The girl stepped nearer, letting her thigh gently nudge Jack's leg. She laid her fingers over Jack's fidgeting hands. "So how about it?"

Jack didn't answer immediately. A kaleidoscope of images crashed around inside his head: two shadowy figures, limbs twisting round each other, grasping hands, heavy breathing, that ecstatic glow…

She tilted her hair to the side, her hair sliding over her shoulder. "Unless you've run the tank dry after a performance like this morning's, that is."

"Sure," he answered, as if being offered Pepsi in the absence of Coke.

It wasn't the most enthusiastic response Julie-Ann had ever had; still, she treated him to her four-star smile. "My parents will be leaving around six. Let's call it six-thirty?"

"Great," he stammered. "Then I'll see you later."

The girl leant forward and kissed him lightly on the cheek. Then she turned away, tossing a flurry of hair Jack's way, and reminded him, "Don't forget what we'll be doing."

Jack smiled wide.

"*Henry the Fifth*, you dolt. Remember to bring it with you."

And then she strode away, her brown leather ankle boots moving briskly down the sidewalk.

Jack followed the line of her coat around the smooth curve of her hips and the sway of the hem on her trim calves until she turned the corner. When she was gone, he pushed down energetically on the pedals and took off for home, the cold handlebar grips barely registering any sensation.

Chapter Two

Six hours ahead—in Palermo, Sicily—Carmine Galante drew deep on his Montecristo double corona. He savored its earthy aroma before slowly exhaling a steady trail of smoke and watching it disappear into the softly lit atmosphere of the island's most legendary hotel.

He felt pleased with himself. Pleased with the way business had gone. Pleased with the doe-eyed brunette he had bought for the night and left dutifully waiting in his top-floor suite for what Galante found amusing to call "the second coming."

One piece of ass was much the same as another to Galante. Hard against the grimy brick wall of a garbage-strewn alley in Little Italy, or squirming between silk sheets in the Waldorf Astoria—it was all the same to him. Carmine Galante could afford the best there was. The power his money afforded him: that's what turned him on.

He took another swig from the well-filled brandy glass at his elbow and leant back in the deep-cushioned leather armchair to look up at the famous inlaid ceiling of the Fireplace Saloon.

His father had probably never heard of the Grand Hotel et Palmes in Palermo. And even on the off chance that he had, he sure as hell never strolled through its sumptuous Art Nouveau salons. Galante senior had struggled to make a living as a fisherman along the coast in the ancient fortress town of Castellammare de Golfo. In time he joined the growing ranks of impoverished Sicilians who packed up their families and headed out in search of the New World. What he found was the teeming streets and crowded tenements of New York's Lower East Side, where the new arrivals waited to be picked clean like a carcass gnawed by rats.

This environment suited the young Galante. He had made his bones when he was eleven and was the boss of a vicious street gang only a few years later. By the time he was twenty, Carmine Galante had established himself as one of the city's top triggermen. That's when he had come to the attention of Vito Genovese.

When Genovese fled to Italy in 1935 to escape murder charges back home in New York, Galante stayed on to take care of family business. To please his friend and benefactor, Benito Mussolini, Genovese had sent word from exile in Naples at the end of 1942 ordering the killing of Carlo Tresca, the antifascist editor of *Il Martello*. Three weeks later, Galante gunned down Tresca in a Manhattan street and set the seal on his reputation in the city.

Taking another puff at his cigar, Galante indulged himself in a further wave of self-congratulation. Don Vitone was just another name to Galante, who had jumped ship several years back and was now underboss for the crime family headed by Joseph Bonanno—soon to join the ranks of Don Vitone in Galante's rolodex. After the deal he'd struck two days ago, it would only be a matter of time before the heads of the five families were lined up in a row, lips puckered and aimed at Galante's ass.

"Signore Galante," a timorous voice whispered.

Galante swiveled in his chair. He raised his bulbous nose to the face of the bellhop and waited, as if the obvious question would just ask itself.

The bellhop proffered a shiny silver salver, on which laid a white envelope inscribed with Galante's name. "Pardon me, signore, but this message has come for you."

The weasel-faced man shoved the cigar between his teeth, pulled a thick roll of bank notes from his coat pocket, and peeled off a five-hundred lira bill he left where the envelope had rested. The bellhop's footsteps made a soft clapping sound and Galante waited for them to recede into the background noise.

He slid his finger under the flap and tore into the letter.

A single sheet of white paper.

The brief message was enough to start Galante's gut churning. "BINOWHUSKY," it read.

Galante didn't wait for the doorman to hail a taxi. He pushed past the liveried man and turned right down the busy sidewalk. The Via Roma was alive with late-night diners and couples meandering arm in arm to while away the small hours in smoke-filled clubs.

Galante tried to cut through the lines of fast-moving traffic tearing down the Via Bentivegna. An Alfa-Romeo slewed toward the sidewalk to avoid hitting him and rode up on the curb. The driver jumped out and screamed obscenities after the fleeing figure, but Carmine Galante quickly disappeared into the night-time throng.

Two blocks later he came to the Via Cavour. He bustled through the doors of the café and stood inside, blinking at one table after another and adjusting his ears to the wave of animated conversation tumbling over him.

Guidebooks described the Bierreria Italia as the favored haunt of artists, intellectuals, and the aristocracy. Delicacy, or the fear of killing passing trade, omitted to mention it was also the favored social meeting point of the Mafia élite.

Artists, intellectuals, and Sicilian aristocracy certainly flocked to the *bierreria*, but the lure was a glimpse of the lords of the underworld, who dropped in for a miniscule cup of coffee and a quiet exchange with an associate whenever they happened to be in town. At peak times, when the place was heaving, the dark-suited man rubbing shoulders with you at the counter could just as easily be a don as a duke. Only the few odd million dollars separated them.

This was a place to see and be seen. Experience and history showed that no one left the Bierreria Italia unnoticed. Carmine Galante was well aware of this, and the churning in his stomach increased.

A waiter approached. "This way, signore, if you please."

Galante followed through the maze of tables and the warm blanket of smoke.

The man who for fifteen years he had known simply as Husky was sitting at a secluded table near the back. The waiter brought the seated man an espresso and left without taking an order for his companion.

Galante sat down and waited for the other man to speak.

He looked like an insurance broker. A middle-grade banker, maybe. Neatly trimmed hair—mostly gray. Wrinkles weaved across his face like the strands of a spider's web. Husky sipped deeply from his espresso before placing it delicately atop its saucer. "Pleasant weather for the time of year."

Galante reached for the leather case in his inside pocket to draw out another cigar.

Husky leaned against the wooden back of the chair. "Do you mind?"

Galante slipped the case into his breast pocket.

"I hope you feel better for your vacation," Husky continued. "I've always had a soft spot for the old Grand. I trust they've been looking after you well?"

"What are you doing here?"

"I'm here on business. Same as you."

Bonanno, the Maggadinos, and those guys from Detroit, you knew where you were with fellows like that. Galante had been reading their thoughts for the past five days and he hadn't been wrong once.

The same went for the Sicilians: Russo, Greco, and those two from the Porta Nuova family. You could do business with men like that. They spoke the same language.

Not this Husky prick.

"So, what do you want with me?" Galante asked.

"Let's just say we have the same interests at heart. And the same friends." Husky paused to let this sink in. "What's the term I keep hearing? Joint venture? Isn't that what they're calling it when businessmen come together to make a new partnership?"

"Maybe." Galante could see where this was heading. And though he didn't like what he was hearing, he knew he was powerless to prevent it.

Husky slid his fingers around the rim of the tiny cup sitting empty on the saucer. "I hear you may be in need of a partner after your negotiations this week. I'd like to offer you my services."

With anyone else, even Genovese or Bonanno, Galante would have given his trademark sneer and told them to go fuck themselves. Husky operated on a different wavelength. With a different set of rules…and penalties.

"Maybe it would help you to know that our friends here are in complete agreement, Carmine," Husky continued.

This son of a bitch. He takes a cut from the Sicilians, so he wins both ways.

But that's how it always was with Husky. Winning both ways was his stock in trade.

"So, we have a deal?" It wasn't really a question at all. With that, Husky dismissed any idea the New York mobster might have had of challenging his proposition. "We can sort out the details later."

That was it. So simple. So complete.

Galante made to stand up.

Husky lifted his head and a quick sharp look had Galante slumping down in his seat again. "Speaking of details, I believe one other item of business has been agreed. Is that correct?"

"We was unanimous on that," Galante answered, this time with conviction.

Husky gave another smile. "Unanimous? Were you now? I'm glad to hear it's being taken care of." Leaning forward he lowered his eyelids. "When?"

"Soon. When we get back. We have some things to arrange. Then it's done, okay? No problem."

"No problem," Husky repeated. "You sure you can handle this?"

"Are you kidding?" Galante blustered, bridling at the suggestion. "Do you know who you're talking to, mister? Do you fucking know that?"

Across the table the dead blue eyes bore into him. "I know. I know all there is to know about you." Husky remained blank. "That's why I'm asking the question. This is too important to be screwed up. Understand that…and understand it well."

Then he got to his feet and called for his hat and coat, and the check.

"My partner will settle that," he told the waiter, patting Galante on the shoulder as he slipped away.

Chapter Three

Jack pedaled down East Summit Avenue, his face flushed from the wind. Dusk was falling, and a little beyond the intersection on Walnut Street, he had to pull up behind a highly polished sedan parked by the sidewalk and let an oncoming car pass by.

Some of his classmates were discovering the thrill and independence of driving for the first time, but cars didn't mean much to Jack. The kids with rich parents seemed the most excited by the prospect. No shock there.

Jack remembered how Sandy "Dandruff" Doyle had temporarily boosted his popularity when he showed up in a gleaming 1954 Ford Custom convertible finished in dark blue metallic paint. Even Jack privately acknowledged it was a nice-looking set of wheels.

He noticed the sedan parked in front of him was the same dark blue color.

An Oldsmobile.

New York plates. He could think of more than a few schools there where he'd love to play college ball.

There was a flash of light inside the car, a man in the driver's seat lighting a cigarette. Jack glanced through the window as he passed, but the driver's face was turned away, looking down the line of houses set back from the street.

12 Spruce Street was a neat white-painted clapboard house standing on its own, surrounded by a picket fence. Jack dismounted, pushed through the gate, and opened the garage. His mom's black Dodge sat in its usual place and Jack leaned

his bicycle against the wall, its customary spot beneath an old, wooden paint shelf.

He could smell the coffee from the hallway.

"I'm home," he called.

The kitchen door opened abruptly and Jack's mother joined him in the hall, closing the door to the kitchen behind her.

Carmella had put on a different shade of lipstick than usual and swept her dark hair into an elegant chignon. His mom was always well turned out, but today she looked different. He recognized neither the dress she had on nor the broach sparkling with blue and red jewels pinned to her oatmeal cardigan.

Jack figured it must have been one heck of a special event that had kept her from the game.

She fingered the gold chain around her neck and Jack saw that the usual remote, faraway look in her eyes had been replaced by something else. She looked about the room in short nervous glances, as if viewing it for the first time.

And then she began eying her boy, the same strange examination still seemingly in progress. "How was the game?"

"We beat Audubon. We're going to be—"

"Yes. I know." His mom answered so abruptly that Jack wasn't sure she'd really heard the response at all. She took hold of his shoulders and drew him closer to her. "I hear you had a great game."

Jack could hear his mother quietly sobbing. "I'm so proud of you. So proud of the way—"

"We beat Audubon, okay? It's not like I made All-American or anything." Jack shrugged free of his mother's hug and stood clutching her forearms. "How come you know about the game? I didn't see you there."

Carmella stared down at her shoes. "I wasn't at the game. But someone else was, Giovanni. And he's come here to see you now. He's waiting in the kitchen." She turned the wooden knob and pushed open the door to let her son into the kitchen.

Jack wasn't sure what to tell recruiters. Sullivan had warned Jack that they might turn out for the game, but he'd assumed they would want to speak to him there. Maybe with his coach or his mother.

This was unexpected, indeed.

Jack took a second to gather himself, smooth his thoughts out into a long straight trail he could follow. He was always well-liked and made a great impression. His mother had always made sure of that. She'd done quite a job making sure of a number of things in Jack's life and he believed he understood the tears. All this preparation and hard work on Jack's behalf hadn't been easy on her either, and now it seemed it would finally be paying off in the way of a college education.

The Paganos' best china coffee pot stood on a lacquered tray in the middle of the pale-yellow Formica table. A plate of cookies lay beside it. Beyond rested a grey fedora with a broad dark band around the rim. And at the end of the table sat the middle of the three smartly dressed men Jack had spotted in the stands.

Jack's stomach tightened as he felt himself drawn toward the eyes that had followed him up and down the football field. This man did not seem like a scout.

Carmella spoke. Her words barely a whisper. "Giovanni… son, this is Umberto Anastasio."

"Pleased to meet you."

"Giovanni, Umberto is your father."

The man pushed back his chair and stood up, resting his fingertips on the end of the table. "These days, most people call me Albert Anastasia."

The name Anastasia flashed before him from newspaper headlines, from radio and TV bulletins.

Racketeer. Gangster. Underworld boss. The Executioner.

"You're my father?"

Albert Anastasia took another sip of coffee from the Paganos' best china. Didn't bother nodding. He'd said what he'd said, hadn't he?

"But my father's dead. He died before I was born. He died fighting in Italy, or Sicily, or some place in Europe."

Jack's mother remained in the doorway, the frame holding her upright.

"My father was a soldier. A special soldier. A soldier who disappeared in the war. That's what you've always told me, Mother. Isn't it? Didn't you always tell me that?"

Carmella drew a handkerchief from her sleeve and dabbed her eyes.

"Yes," she answered. "It is true, Giovanni. It's all true. It's always been true."

"So how come you kept on telling me my father was dead? How can that be true as well?"

"Your father disappeared. Remember. That's all I ever told you. That's all I could—" She trailed off mid-sentence. Had she completed the thought, it wouldn't have mattered anyway.

Jack's mind was in overdrive.

There had to be something.

A slip over the years. A careless reference.

Something he had missed at the time that had given away her secret.

Hard as he tried, he drew a blank.

"Why didn't you tell me the truth? I thought we had an understanding—with no secrets. Why did you let me think my dad was dead all that time?"

"Because it was easier. It was easier for everyone, for you to believe that. Whenever you asked, I told you…I told you…" Her words gave way to a chorus of sobs. Jack made no effort toward consolation.

The man behind the table continued to sip his coffee. "Your mother told you the same as I told her when you were born. That I had disappeared." He sat back down. "Which I did—until today."

It took Jack a moment to register that the man had just spoken. The man behind the table. The man from the newspaper headlines.

As a kid, Jack had fondly imagined his mother, pretty and carefree, photographed beside a dashing young man in uniform.

These were the kinds of family snapshots he saw in other people's homes. Jack had assumed such pictures were too painful for his mother. Now he understood. There weren't any pictures of his father around the place because they were plastered all over the crime pages of the newspaper.

Jack ran his hands through his hair. "Why now?" he yelled, his shouts filling the silent kitchen. "What's special about now? How come you wait seventeen years before you show up again? Where have you been all this time?"

Still, the black eyes remained fixed on him: cold, analytical, sizing him up maybe.

"Say something, for Christ's sake."

Albert sat motionless at the head of the table.

"And what about Mom? Didn't you ever think about how she was feeling? What it's like bringing up a kid on her own and all? If you didn't care about me, what about what you did to her? Seventeen years," he shrieked. "Seventeen fucking years!"

Carmella shifted her weight from the door frame and moved toward the table, her red-rimmed eyes searching for help in Albert's impassive expression. "Tell him, Umberto. For my sake, tell him. Please."

"I don't come here to be judged, Giovanni. I come to bring you an explanation." The words came even, measured. Without passion and without strain. "I come to tell you why your life has been like it has. And why it has to be the way it is in the future."

"So go ahead. Explain."

"You know who I am. You don't like it. I see that in your face. But you can't do anything about it." Anastasia drew a clean handkerchief from his trouser pocket and wiped his lips. "My blood runs in your veins. It always will. And there's nothing you can change. Nothing. A bond like ours lasts forever."

Albert gestured for Jack to sit down. He poured some coffee and passed it across the table. "Black. No sugar."

Jack reached for the cup and took a long, slow sip. "How come you know how I take my coffee?"

"I know a lot about you. I've known a lot about you for a long time."

Jack looked to his mother.

"It's not what you're thinking. Your mother didn't speak to me once, till I called her back in the summer. That's right, isn't it?"

Carmella nodded, summoning up a smile of reassurance.

Jack cradled the cup in his hands. "What was special about the summer then? Why did you need to speak to Mom all of a sudden?"

"Because the time had come. And because I wanted to see you," he continued, speaking to Jack the way he might if someone had asked him what time it was.

Confusion mounted in Jack's head. He drained his cup, put it on the table, and got to his feet to look out the kitchen window.

"I still don't get it. Why now? Why this summer?"

"That's what I will explain to you. But not today. When we see each other again. Next week. Friday, after you finish school."

This was more than Jack could take. He balled his fist and turned from the window. "Brilliant. Now I have to wait a whole week to find out why my father has suddenly decided to enter my life."

Albert narrowed his eyes. He slapped his right hand down hard on the table. The coffee pot jumped, the half-spilled cups not far behind. "I have had to wait seventeen years. Seven days is no big deal, even for you. Believe me. I know."

A silence settled on the room, broken only by the ticking of the wall clock.

Jack's shoulders slumped as he made his way back to the table. "How will I know where to meet you?"

"You'll find out in time."

Carmella drew Jack in close and brushed a lock of black hair from his forehead. "I know it's hard," she said, his face cradled in her hands. "But you must understand your father had his reasons, good reasons, for staying away."

Albert nodded his head slowly up and down in confirmation.

"You ask where I have been all this time. Yes? I'll tell you. I've been right here, looking out for you and your mother. Not me myself. Good friends of mine have done these things. People I have trusted with my closest secret. And you know what that secret is? It's your mother and you."

His look softened and he gave an awkward, crooked smile that Carmella acknowledged with a smile of her own.

Jack had turned away but his mother's hand on his arm brought his eyes back into contact with hers. "Umberto has important things to tell you," she said. "Things only you must know. Listen to him, Giovanni. Listen well. You have a lot to learn from Umberto. More than you can even imagine."

There was a heavy sigh from her son. He wondered what other secrets his mother might be keeping from him. Worst of all was the possibility that even now she wasn't being straight.

His mother's gaze was steady now. Her eyes had stopped flicking to and fro the way they had when he came home. Her faraway look was back, and for the first time, Jack understood why. She's looking for Umberto, he thought. She wants to find him in me. That's what she's always been looking for.

Chapter Four

Running had always been a release for Jack. Wrapped in the rhythm of his own body, he enjoyed a sense of freedom and isolation that could last as long as he maintained an even, steady gait. With his feet in control, his mind could follow its own path. So when he'd burst from his mother's front door, away from Albert Anastasia and everything he'd just heard, he let his feet choose his route while his mind grappled to make sense of all that had happened.

Familiar sites along the road—the Pioneer Food Stores, Arrow Shirts, the Fisher automobile dealership—drew him along Haddon Avenue, but in the stark shadowy light of the street lamps they had a foreboding appearance.

Anger and bewilderment collided against a gallery of childhood memories. Vacations, Christmases, bedtime stories, early days at school, his first football game, trips to the movies. Every image that swirled through his mind had two principal people: Jack and his mom. The two of them. That was how it always had been. Jack couldn't imagine it any other way. Didn't want to, even.

Not now, anyway.

Sure, there were times as a kid when he wondered what it would be like to have someone else in the house. A dad, like the dads other kids had to play ball, ride bikes. Someone who was good with cars and smelled like motor oil and took them out on the boat. A man with calloused hands who went to work early in the morning and got home just after the sun had set, all just to provide for his family.

Jack had clung to those images. But, like old photographs, they had lost some of their vividness. The color in them had faded. Now, a new image was bumping up against them: Albert Anastasia's.

As the landmarks thinned out and the lighted streets were left behind, Jack entered a new realm of darkness that was briefly punctuated by the dazzling headlamp beams of passing traffic.

On he ran, the South Jersey farmland flanking the road. Toward the edge of Lawnside, Jack ran past scattered houses dotted among the fields: small, cheaply constructed places, little better than shacks, but homes for farm workers employed in the area. As he approached a down-at-heel silver bullet diner, he noticed a group of cars, heavy with chrome, randomly parked outside; there were several motorcycles as well. Through the open door of the diner came the sound of a jukebox.

Jack jogged closer to listen and as he did so he was caught in the dazzling blaze of headlights switched on in one of the parked cars.

"What are you doing 'round here, boy?" a voice shouted through the driver's window.

"Wow, he's the guy from the newspaper!" whooped a girl's voice. "Heh, Charlene, isn't he the one you wet your panties over? You know who I mean? The high-school football star."

Another girl took up the banter. "Oh, Charlene! Who's raising her sights? He does look kind of nice. Be sure to give him a good time, girl!"

A whole group of kids hanging out behind the diner came shifting out into the light. There were a couple of girls there, but Jack's gaze was fixed on the young men swaggering around him.

"Ain't you a little far from your mommy's kitchen?" A ripple of laughter spread through the parking lot.

"Can't you see he's slumming?" answered another girl, mockingly. "He don't want no mommy… "

Jack barely heard her. He barely heard the taunts and jeers coming at him from all sides. The girls never crossed his mind.

Every faculty he possessed was focused on what was about to happen, as if a switch had been thrown inside him and, suddenly, he was being controlled by some external force. He was going through the right procedure; he was confident of that. But everything was happening so smoothly, so automatically, he couldn't be certain that he was controlling his own body or reactions.

"No, no, no." The car's driver stepped out from behind the headlights. "This punk is mine. Isn't that right, Mr. High School Football Hero?"

Jack breathed long and deep. A tall skinny guy, with a well-greased duck's-ass quiff, dressed in denims and a studded leather jacket, pushed through the ring of watchers and stepped toward him.

"Like I said—what are you doing here, son? Have you come to have a little rich-kid fun? Come to rub our noses in the shit like all you rich fuckers always do?"

Jack remained silent.

"Because if you want some action, you've come to the right place. Only there ain't no referee you can run to when things get hot. You're on my football field now—my turf. And I'm going to send you home to mama with something you won't ever forget. You hear me, son?"

"Atta boy, Rick!" a kid yelled bravely from the back of the throng. "You tune that son of a bitch up real good."

Rick strode toward Jack, a cruel leer fixed on his face. But his expression started to change and his pace slowed when he saw Jack moving steadily toward him rather than turning and running.

"Oh, who's a brave boy?" he taunted. "Maybe you won't be so brave when you get a taste of this." He unzipped the pocket of his jacket, took out a mother-of-pearl inlaid handle about six inches long and displayed it in the car headlights so everyone could see it.

Jack knew about flick knives. Knew how to handle all kinds of knives and weapons. He fixed his gaze on the glinting white and silver handle.

When he saw the kid take the handle between his fingers and point it outward, Jack knew there would be no contest. A real knife fighter grasped the handle in his fist with the blade held downwards. This was first-day, step-one kind of information to Jack. Even so, he never let his gaze stray from the handle and the silver button that flicked open the blade concealed inside it.

Rick was close to backing away all by himself. He had seen the change in Jack's expression when the knife came out and now he wished he had left it in his pocket.

"You stick the motherfucker!" shouted another voice.

Rick had to grip the handle tighter and tighter to stop it shaking in his hand.

Jack had approached to within four feet of him by now. His breathing was deep and regular and there was the faintest hint of a smile stretching across his face.

"Okay—you asked for it, asshole!" Rick yelled.

Jack spotted the movement of his thumb, and before it squeezed the silver button in the knife handle, he stepped forward and sent the side of his left hand scything into Rick's throat. The leader of the Lawnside pack dropped the knife. He grabbed his neck and slumped to the dirt, gasping for breath.

To his right, Jack saw a burly youth slipping a brass knuckle-duster over his right fist as he lunged at Rick's assailant. Without breaking stride, Jack angled the instep of his left foot and crashed into his attacker's right knee. With a scream and a thud he had joined the turf leader on the ground.

Jack moved forward toward the ring of stunned faces.

The occupants of the diner had fallen silent, until one of the boys broke away and ran inside yelling, "I'm calling the cops!"

The others stepped out of Jack's range.

They knew who was in control. So did Jack, and he felt a thrill surge through him.

Is this the way Anastasia feels? he wondered.

Everyone around him was at his mercy. He could have laid them out cold—all of them.

Of that he had total confidence.

He watched the muted, frightened group as the look in his eyes caught them one by one before he went back to work. The thrill of it all had captured Jack's senses. The screeching tires and the squad car's flashing lights were entirely lost on him.

Chapter Five

Carmella and Albert sat quietly at the table. Many years had passed since they'd laid eyes on one another. She'd spent many a night wondering how this moment would feel, what would happen. Now that the moment had arrived, she was suddenly unsure of herself.

And what of Jack? What of the devastation? Albert had given her strict instructions, and though she never thought of disobeying or whether or not she could even bring herself to do such a thing, it did nothing to relieve the pain she now felt.

Albert slowly finished his coffee. As Carmella rose to refill his cup, he waved her off. Instead, he pushed the folder in front of him across the table to her. "You can do this one final thing for me, yes?

"You're sure of this, Umberto?" She moved the papers in front of her but didn't look down at them. "Things are bad?"

"Things are exactly as we knew they'd be. I didn't know when, but I knew this day would come."

"He's still so young. You must understand, Umberto, you must. You must understand how hard it is." Tears had begun to gather in the corners of her eyes. "Please give him time."

Though she was sure he had heard her and knew deep down inside that he had considered her request carefully, there was no indication that his mind would be changed. He remained upright, almost rigid in his seat. "Yes, Carmella. I understand. But he must begin to understand me too. That is important. For him, for you, for everyone. And if I could give him time, I would."

It pained her to hear him speak this way. This sense of inevitability had worked its way into her life. It was tough at first, she remembered. But looking back now, in hindsight, with the past so far away, it may as well had been seamless. To see Albert resigned to his fate, and to hear the ease with which he spoke of the future did not have the calming effect she'd assumed it would have.

"We have the boy. We've got Giovanni. What more could I want?" Albert rose, his jacket gathered over the crux of his arm. "I could have asked for nothing greater from you."

She walked him to the door, composing herself for her own sake. For Umberto's, too. A cold chill swept in through a crack in the doorway. The room sat dark and empty around them.

Albert moved closer to her. Her eyes damp, she willed the tears back.

The telephone began to ring.

A half hour later, the car pulled into the driveway. Carmella listened as the engine idled and then died. She had the front door open by the time the door bell chime had faded.

She threw her arms around Jack, drawing him close. For all his confidence during the fight, and for the tough front he had put on down at the station, he did have to admit he was squeezing back harder.

"Go to your room, Jack. Go now."

Without responding he made his way up the stairs and into his bedroom. He didn't close the door behind him. Instead, he stood with it open, just out of eyesight, and tried to pick up bits of the conversation at the front door.

He'd been scared when the cops cuffed him and tossed him into the back of the police car. He'd been even more scared still when they placed him in the holding cell. Now, straining to make out the conversation downstairs, fear had given way to confusion. He'd been in the cell maybe ten minutes when, down the hall, he could hear the cops making a phone call. To his mother, presumably. However, by the time they had returned, something had clearly changed.

At the front door, the two officers were practically apologizing to his mother. He could hear her raised voice more clearly than the two men.

"You arrested my son automatically! Aren't there two sides to every story, officer?" Jack had never heard her sound this way before. "Well? Aren't there?"

A mumbled apology came back in reply, followed by, "A couple of kids ended up in the hospital."

"A couple of kids! How many people jumped my son?"

To this there was no answer. Jack had not even taken the time to make an accurate count, though he was pretty sure the others fled after he began wailing away on Rick and his friend. For as clear as the entire ordeal had seemed at the time, Jack could remember curiously few details of what had actually occurred.

"Please understand, ma'am, that there will be no record. We're terribly sorry for the misunderstanding."

At the bottom of the stairs, the door slammed shut. The click of the cylinder locking into place was followed by his mother's sobs.

Jack moved from his doorway perch and watched as his mother brought her hands up to her face as if hiding. He didn't budge. Instead, he stood watching, unsure what exactly to do.

As Carmella dropped her hands to her sides, she saw Jack standing there. "Would you like to tell me what that was all about, Jack?"

"It wasn't my fault, Mom. I swear. The guy pulled a knife on me. What was I supposed to do? Huh?"

"Haven't I taught you better than that?"

"Sure you did. And you also taught me not to hide the truth for seventeen years." The words hung in the air. Jack cringed, as if their bitter taste still lingered on his tongue. Through all of this, it wasn't really his mother he was upset with, he supposed. No, his anger lay elsewhere. He slowly descended the stairs.

They went to the kitchen. Carmella poured some of the leftover coffee and sat down at the table, Albert's papers still neatly stacked and sitting in their folder. She moved them out of the way.

Jack sat down across the table, where Albert had previously sat. Carmella couldn't help but notice her son's broad shoulders. The way he filled the chair out much the same as his father had.

"The truth, Jack? The truth is that the reason you're standing here right now at all instead of sitting in that jail cell is your father. In all your seventeen years, has anyone given you a hard time before? No. And he wasn't about to let them start now."

"But look at what he is, Mom. Don't you read the newspapers?"

"When I was your age, I learned to make my own judgments. So should you. But, right now, you are condemning Umberto when you know nothing about him, about who he really is."

Jack rose from his chair. "What else do I need to know? What can he tell me that will change the things he's done?"

Carmella held the papers she'd been given. It wasn't time yet. Her son crossed the kitchen and made his way back to the staircase. In the corner of the kitchen, Jack's bag was still half open, the game ball poking out of it. And then she remembered the other phone call she had received that evening. "Jack, before you go to bed. A girl called." She heard Jack stop, though he didn't answer. "She said not to worry—Lonnie Sherrard is helping with her studies now."

Chapter Six

Twelve-hundred miles south, night had fallen over a swampland property in Jefferson Parish, Louisiana, called Churchill Farms.

A prowler snooping around a collection of ramshackle buildings on this 6,400-acre estate would have taken them for any number of run-down sheds and barns left to rot by disinterested owners.

And that was the impression the owner of these buildings intended to give. Stepping inside one of them made you think again.

Behind the rough-timber façade lay a suite of rooms that wouldn't have been out of place in a bank headquarters down the road in New Orleans.

Running the length of one paneled room was a long mahogany dining table flanked by expensive upholstered chairs and lit by a pair of heavy glass chandeliers. A pair of doors led to a fully equipped kitchen, where top chefs throughout the South were brought in to prepare gourmet cuisine; across the room, a matching set of doors led to a well-appointed conference room. To the side stood a fitted office suite with a bank of monitors and telex machines, and a soldier to monitor the incoming telephone calls.

Beyond the conference table, the room adopted a more relaxed air. Two large Italian leather sofas were set either side of a Rococo fireplace, in which a fire was crackling. Between them was a wide, low table inlaid with an intricate pattern of exotic timber, and on it stood a cut-glass decanter of scotch and a matching tumbler—which had already been filled three times in the last twenty minutes.

In the corner of one sofa, close to an alabaster telephone embellished with gold fittings, a portly man whose receding hairline and double chin made him look older than his forty-seven years, had taken up station near the fire. He was dressed in duck-hunting clothes.

Carlos Marcello had other places where he carried out business: the Town and Country Motel in New Orleans, unassuming offices in Baton Rouge, Shreveport, and beyond. Churchill Farms, with its own airstrip, was his most private. Only select associates were invited to this secluded domain. Word had it that Churchill Farms also served as a private cemetery for anyone foolish enough to cross the most powerful underworld boss in the South—or worse still, cheat him on a deal.

Marcello shifted restlessly, stared at the flames and glowing embers.

The Palermo sit-down had gone well. He didn't altogether trust Carmine Galante and the representatives sent by the other New England families, but trust and business had never been easy partners. Besides, the Sicilians there were men he felt comfortable with. They needed Marcello and the heads of the other families to smooth their path.

They would play ball.

It wasn't Palermo that unsettled Carlos Marcello. There was something deeper, still stirring from earlier times.

For one, even Charlie Luciano was going along with the plan. Marcello would have dismissed anyone else out of hand. But not this man. He was different. In fact, he was unique. That's what Marcello was struggling to reconcile.

The soldier monitoring the phone bank approached Marcello. "You've got a call from Tampa, sir."

"Put him through…What's the news, Santo?" he asked eagerly.

"Thursday evening. New York," answered Santo Trafficante, head of the Florida criminal empire he had inherited from his father.

"The three of us?"

"Yeah. That's what we agreed. Us three. No one else."

Marcello reached for his whisky and drank deep. "What about the other prick?"

"He's fixing everything with Barbara."

"I bet he fucking is."

"It's going to be in New York, upstate, out of the way. Somewhere like your place, I guess."

"Cocksucker." The Southern boss shifted again on the sofa, nearly spilling his drink.

"I know how you feel. I feel the same way. But we need those fuckheads to get this business started. When we're rolling, we can kiss them goodbye."

"I'll drink to that." Marcello drained the tumbler and immediately reached for the decanter.

"New York, Thursday," Trafficante repeated.

"I'll be there." Marcello returned the receiver to its cradle.

He hadn't wasted time brooding over little local difficulties when they needed sorting in the past. This was on a bigger scale, however—the drop in the decanter level a testament to that.

Marcello picked up the Confederate army bayonet that acted as a poker and laid the tip in the embers. When it was red hot he lifted it to the nearest log in the grate and carefully inscribed in the bark a continual line with one long, thin loop like a gun barrel, followed by three shorter loops beneath. Heating the poker again, Marcello worked inside the figure, steadily scorching the surface from one end to the other until it was black all over.

He tossed the bayonet into the burnished copper box with the other fire irons, slumped back with his drink and admired his handiwork.

La Mano Nera.

That sign still struck terror in Italian and Sicilian neighborhoods across the country when he was starting out.

New Orleans to Chicago, San Francisco to New York.

These days, you barely got a slap on the wrist from the Black Hand.

Chapter Seven

Cooper Park lay across the Cooper River, flanking the east side of town, less than a ten-minute walk from Jack's home. The autumn tints were fading from the trees, and in a few weeks, the trails would be whitened by the first dusting of snow.

Jack could have walked this route in his sleep. The park was settling for the night as he got to the place where the warning sign had once been.

He checked for movement on the trail: a last walk with the dog, a quick after-work jog. The wind rustled restlessly through the canopy of branches above him.

He was alone.

Beyond the line of bushes, the ground fell away into a steep, narrow gully leading down to the river. Jack pushed through them and moved quietly downhill, toward a second line of shrubs. He crouched low and peered at the base of a small hillock. In the dim light, he could make out a sharply delineated black square set among the coarse grass covering the steep side of the gully. The camouflaged door had been moved aside.

Jack edged toward the dark space, feeling his way cautiously to avoid twigs or anything else that would give him away. He readied himself to go in low and hard, with a lunging forward roll, when a light flashed on and caught him full in the face.

"You'd better come in," a soft Irish voice called.

The harsh beam of light was replaced by a gentle glow. Jack ducked through the low entrance. He pulled the square wooden board fringed with branches and set it behind him.

No one would disturb them. No one ever had.

The Hole smelled of dirt and sawn timber with a feint trace of tar.

Rip Collins set down the electric lantern that illuminated the twelve-by-twelve chamber. Their shadows angled back against the thick timber walls.

The Hole was a log cabin without windows, a giant packing case. Thick scaffold boards tightly butted edge to edge formed the ceiling. Below, the same scaffold boards formed a stout wooden floor, now worn smooth from five years of constant use.

To keep the floor free of obstructions, the ceiling had to be supported by several wire cables fixed to the outside of the hillock by metal plates hidden by turf and bushes. Boring the ducts for those cables had been the hardest part of Jack's six months' work on the Hole.

The most tedious part: getting rid of the dirt. Jack once tried to calculate how many tons he must have loosened, shoveled into burlap sacks, and carried down to the bank of the Cooper River. He soon gave up. The dirt dug out each day had to be dumped before Jack left for home. Some nights, it had been dark as he had struggled down to the water's edge to tip the dirt bags along the riverbank. When rain had turned his route into a slide, he bumped and slipped down to the river, his overalls caked with mud. If anything, the frost and snow were worse. They'd turned the ground to solid stone and left a string of bowling-ball bruises when he lost his footing one time on his way down with a load.

Seven days a week, two hours a day—morning and evening— for six months. The Hole had become a kind of second home for Jack. In spite of the cold and the wet, his aching muscles and raw hands, he never lost the tingle of excitement that charged through him as he approached the warning sign out front: DANGER: BROKEN SEWAGE PIPE — KEEP AWAY.

That was nearly five years ago, and no one had ever come snooping.

Jack couldn't see the eyes hidden in the deep shadows cast by the man's cheekbones. Even so, he could tell his friend was tense. Jack had never seen him like this before. He returned the gaze and waited for the man to speak first.

"I know what's happened," Rip began. "Maybe now you understand things a little better."

"You know about Albert Anastasia and my mother and everything?" The timber walls crept in around Jack. "You know all this stuff about me?"

"Everything, Jack. The whole nine yards," Rip answered.

The workouts Jack did with Rip were different from any of the football workouts Coach Sullivan ran at school. There was no stretching of muscles and tendons, no warming of limbs, nothing violent to get the blood pumping. With Rip, Jack had simply learned to breathe. Steadily, rhythmically, deeply.

At first, it had felt kind of weird; the two of them standing in the center of the Hole, facing each other, their hands at their sides.

"Stick your tongue up against the roof of your mouth," Rip had told him. "It will make you breathe through your nose. Try it."

Jack felt his breath moving deep down in his body and slipping out through his nose.

After five minutes Rip had asked, "How do you feel?"

"Like I've been asleep and woken up."

"Tired, you mean?"

"No. Not tired. The opposite. I feel like I've had a great sleep, Rip. You know the way you feel when you're tired after playing football and then you wake up the next day feeling fresh and sharp? That's how I feel now."

After a few sessions, Rip started Jack on the hand movements, raising his palms upwards as he breathed in and then turning his hands over and lowering them as he breathed out. "Pumping air through your body—this is the best way to get in focus. In most cases, you won't have time for warm-up exercises and all that shit. You've got to be alert and ready to go. This way, everything becomes deliberate. Your reaction time is faster. You move quicker. You're more fluid. Your body is relaxed, but your mind is isolated from all the crap around you. That way you cut out mistakes."

These breathing exercises had been the foundation for the unarmed combat routines Rip introduced as their time together training in the Hole had moved on. With five years of judo and karate training under his belt, Rip's pupil had become a formidable opponent.

The two of them stood facing each other. Jack pushed his tongue up against the roof of his mouth and took slow deep breaths.

"I've never lied to you," Rip told him. "I've been straight with you all along. Don't you ever forget that, in spite of what you may be thinking. You must remember that."

"My mother said the same. She thought I was going to get mad with her."

"But you do feel mad with me, right?"

Jack kept the answer to himself. He'd never thought of Rip as any kind of substitute father figure, but the man had been around for half his life, for Christ's sake. "Why now? That's what I can't figure out." Jack paced over to the wall opposite the entrance. "How come this stranger shows up today to tell me he's my father?

"He tells me my mother has known him for twenty years. And now you. After everything, Rip. Building this place in secret, working out here. The mind training and all. You knew what was going on the whole damned time and you never told me a thing.

"What is it with you people? Don't any of you trust me? Didn't I have a right to know the truth, to know I still have a father?" A dull thud reverberated through the room as Jack slammed the base of the wall with his foot. "All the time I've had this picture of him as some hero who disappeared fighting in the war. What do they call it? Missing in action?"

Rip wiped his brow. "I see how it must look that way. I'd feel cheated too. But you're no dumb dog, Jack, and I've never treated you like one."

"How come you know Albert Anastasia, anyway?"

"There's no secret now" Rip sighed, taking a seat on the metal trunk by one wall where Jack had once kept his working clothes and digging tools. He looked down at the floor, his hands on his forehead, "Your father and I have known each other for thirty years. We met soon after I came to America. We have a lot in common. We both came to America to find something, and, you could say, we started working together."

"It seems like I have a lot of catching up to do." Jack spit the words out, as if holding them in his mouth might make him sick.

"That's right, actually. Your father has things to say that he would only tell you and maybe two or three other people." He let Jack absorb this for a moment. "It's not just me who thinks you're special. Albert has been laying out these tracks for you for a long time. He's the only person who can tell you why. Take this from me. You're the son of a very powerful man. You may not want to believe it, but it's true. I've never lied to you about your future. It is unique, as you put it. But you'll have Albert to thank for that, not me.

"Try to see it this way, Jack. Nothing has really changed. Just because you didn't know about Albert doesn't mean that he wasn't really there. You have to understand what's happened. You've lost the imaginary dad of your childhood dreams, sure you have. But he wasn't real."

Rip leaned back against the wall. Jack could see the strain in his face.

He wasn't finding this any easier than Jack.

"Go see Albert. Take a few days' break from here. You've got some thinking to do. We'll pick up the workouts later..."

Jack bent down and pushed open the door. Outside, the air was damp and chill.

"Yeah. See you around, Rip." And, with that, he disappeared.

Chapter Eight

Albert Anastasia was up early. The morning was crisp and bright and while he was waiting for his driver he took a turn around the garden.

He'd had the yellow stucco house built to his own design ten years earlier. It was a large Spanish-style place, set on the very edge of the steep cliffs of the Palisades, overlooking the Hudson River toward Upper Manhattan and the Bronx beyond. A seven-foot barbed-wire fence ringed the other sides of the property, and at night, the sleek dark shapes of Dobermans growled and their eyes tightened when strangers passed by.

The car arrived with Tony Coppola at the wheel. Tony had placed his boss's newspapers on the back seat. This morning, however, Albert preferred to look out the car window as they crossed over the George Washington Bridge, which joined New Jersey to Manhattan. It was twenty-six years to the day since New York Governor Franklin Delano Roosevelt had officially opened the bridge to traffic for the first time, Tony informed him.

Full of all kinds of useful facts, ain't ya? Albert thought.

He tried to remember what he had been doing on October 25, 1931. That must have been around the time Capone had been sent to jail, he thought to himself. Yeah, that was it, six months after Luciano had sent Anastasia to Coney Island to take care of Joe "The Boss" Masseria. Joe Adonis and Bugsy Siegel had been shooters with him on that job.

So had Vito Genovese.

He and Anastasia had come a long way since then. They'd had it made. Every one of the five families did. Now it was all being shot to hell. Genovese was headed down the wrong road and the others looked like they would follow. Anastasia warned time and again it was a dead end, but was anyone listening? After his meeting the night before, he could see the answer was an irrefutable, "No."

Anastasia knew that Trafficante was already steeped in the shit.

Marcello? He'd hoped the pedigree of the man who owned New Orleans might have swayed him, even at the eleventh hour, but money talked louder than loyalty.

The two men from the South had tried persuading him that Luciano was backing the deal. So why did *he* still have a problem with it?

"Charlie speaks for Charlie," Anastasia had answered. "Like he always does. Me…I speak for myself."

They tried to convince him that this was some kind of licensing agreement. The Sicilians would be doing all the work, taking the risks, paying their dues.

"We just take the dough." A beaming Marcello had smirked as he said it.

Wearily, Anastasia had repeated the mantra they had heard many times before. "If we touch it, our children will touch it, and it will be the downfall of our families."

Across the bridge, Tony joined the Henry Hudson Parkway as it followed Riverside Park down as far as 72nd Street. Below the park began the piers, jutting out into the river like the teeth of giant zipper fastener. This was Albert Anastasia's domain. Vito Genovese would never get his hands on it.

At 57th Street, Tony turned left for five blocks and took Seventh Avenue past Carnegie Hall. He pulled up by the sidewalk at 55th Street and opened the door for his boss outside the Park Sheraton Hotel, where twice a month Anastasia liked to have his hair cut.

It was a quarter after ten. Three floors above, checked in under an alias, Santo Trafficante finished his second cup of coffee.

Mr. Anastasia was popular with the hotel staff. He gave generous tips, and for most of the hired hands on the Park Sheraton payroll he was very much the gentleman. Warm, familiar words greeted him as he strolled down the hallway and turned right to push open the glass doors of the barber shop.

In the near corner, Arthur Grasso, the shop owner, looked up from the cashier's stand and greeted Anastasia with a smile.

"Haircut," the broad-chested man called over to Joseph Bocchino, who held down chair four, facing 55th Street.

Bocchino wiped the chair with a towel while Anastasia hung up his top coat and stripped open his white shirt. He was dressed entirely in brown: brown shoes, brown suit, brown tie.

Taking his place, he sat bolt upright facing the mirrored wall. The barber draped a cloth around his thick neck and swirled the sheet into place over his shoulders. He pulled the electric clippers from the locker. Anastasia's hair was thin in the front but it grew thick and lush at the back and down his neck.

Overhead, the fluorescent lights gave a cheerful glow.

Joseph Bocchino had been plying the clippers for a couple of minutes when a group of men muffled in hats and overcoats pushed open the doors behind where Anastasia was seated.

Scarves covered their faces, and through his veil, one of the men snarled at Arthur Grasso. "Keep your mouth shut if you don't want your head blown off."

The shop owner went sickly pale, but his lips stayed closed. He slowly stepped away, his trimmer barely dangling in his half-opened hand and his lips to slack to make words even if he'd wanted to.

The new arrivals crossed to the manicurist's cabinet. If Anastasia's eyes had been open, he would have seen them in the mirror...seen them drawing handguns and pointing them directly at him.

As it was, he sat relaxed and oblivious until the first bullets thudded into his well-built frame. The shots came in short bursts and all hit their target.

Anastasia leapt forward. His heavy feet kicked the footrest and wrenched it away from the chair. Staggering upright, he swung toward his attackers. He slapped out, his arms trying to slam down across theirs, to pivot the guns downward.

He'd miscalculated. In the confusion of the gunfire and as the screaming wound ripped open in his side, he'd spun toward the glass—the mirror images of his attackers, safe from his attack.

The second volley sent him crashing into the glass shelving in front of the mirror. The firing continued until the final shot, the *coup de grâce*, dispatched the boss of Murder, Inc, leaving an exit wound on the opposite side of his head.

His heavy body turned before slumping to the floor two chairs away.

Guns still in hand, the gunmen strode to the door without a word, leaving the barber shop staff frozen with terror.

Outside, their gunfire caused pandemonium. A stream of frightened hotel staff and guests crowded the glass doors in the outer vestibule, desperate to make the street.

Constantine Alexis, owner of the flower shop next door, watched in amazement as the crowd surged past his window. He watched as a knot of four or five men fled down the subway stairs, pedestrians scattering to either side of them in heaps.

"Somebody's gone crazy in there!"

The florist dialed the police. In a few minutes, radio cars had converged on the Park Sheraton. A doctor had been called from nearby St. Clare's Hospital.

Neither law nor medicine could help the man lying sprawled on his side on the barbershop floor between chairs two and three.

The doctor applied his stethoscope, though it was little more than standard procedure. Nobody in the room awaited any confirmation, any indication of what they already knew...

A crowd swarmed the sidewalk outside the barbershop. Santo Trafficante quietly checked out and left the Park Sheraton unnoticed. A few blocks away, Carlos Marcello left the hotel where he had stayed the night and was driven to La Guardia airport, where his private plane was waiting to take him back to Churchill Farms.

Chapter Nine

The blue Oldsmobile was at the rendezvous when Jack arrived. The Century picture house at Kings Highway and White Horse Pike boasted "ample convenient free parking space." In the late afternoon, no one hung around its draughty expanse.

Jack secured his bicycle and hurried toward the car. The rear door opened and he stepped inside, grateful to be out of the cold.

Alone in the backseat, a newspaper lay folded beside him. The rear of the car was fragrant with hints of leather upholstery, eau de cologne and expensive hair oil. It was otherwise empty. Two men wearing broad-rimmed hats occupied the front seats.

"Are we meeting Mr. Anastasia someplace?" Jack asked.

Marco Reginelli's eyes shifted momentarily toward the driver.

"No," he answered. "I guess you ain't heard what's happened."

Jack didn't understand. "What do you mean? What's happened?"

Reginelli nodded toward the newspaper.

Jack unfolded the evening issue, the stark bold lettering of the headline caught his eye immediately, followed by the photograph below: rows of barber chairs and a man's body draped with white towels lying sprawled on its back behind them. The man's bare chest had been left uncovered for some reason, and jutting toward the camera from the open cuff of a white shirt was a hand, its fingers curled upwards. Thick fingers. Strong fingers. Fingers that had pounded Jack's mom's kitchen table less than a week before.

"The cowards shot him in the back," Reginelli muttered with disgust. His account was brief, but it contained details not available to journalists. Albert Anastasia's killers had been brought in from outside. They weren't known in New York, that much had already been established. And because they weren't known, no one could yet be sure who had commissioned them.

Shooting Albert Anastasia was no random killing.

It was a well-crafted assassination. "A fucking conspiracy," as Reginelli termed it.

Albert Anastasia's son felt cheated.

He hadn't asked for this meeting. He hadn't asked for the childhood picture of his father to be rubbed out so cruelly. But after the mangle he'd been put through, he had a right to know whatever it was Albert Anastasia needed to tell him.

Now that gruff voice was silenced.

Those black piercing eyes that had tracked him on the football field had been closed for good. All week, Jack had been playing hide and seek with them in his mind: in class, in the locker room, in school hallways, behind trees in the street. Albert Anastasia had been haunting him, taunting him.

It was even worse at home.

"Does my mother know about this?" Jack placed the newspaper carefully on the seat beside him.

Reginelli gave a thin smile of reassurance. "She does. And I promise: Carmella, she knows how to take it."

Jack slumped back, stared blankly out the window. Cars whipped past, drivers purposefully gripping their steeringwheels with eyes fixed on the road ahead. In the still of the blue Oldsmobile, they were nothing more than flickering shadows.

"You'd better take a look at these, too." Marco turned farther in his seat, making sure he had Jack's attention. "Your old man spent a lot of time working on stuff for you. Albert never put nothing on paper, so it's got to be important. You take good care of this."

Jack slipped his finger under the gummed lip of the brown envelope he'd been handed and tore it open. Inside was a sheet of typed business paper headed with the name and address of

Albert Anastasia's private attorney. It was dated June 25, 1957, and carried a single paragraph.

To Whom It May Concern

We the undersigned state and confirm that Giovanni Pagano also known as Jack Pagano born August 23 1940 is the true son and rightful heir of Umberto Anastasio also known as Albert Anastasia of Fort Lee in the state of New Jersey and of Carmella Pagano of Haddonfield in the state of New Jersey.

Below the paragraph were three signatures above three typed names: Frank Costello, Albert Anastasia, and Meyer Lansky.

Jack held up the piece of paper. "What's this?"

"Your passport," he answered. "Your health insurance."

"And these other names?" Jack's eyes returned to the slip of paper. "I've seen them in the newspapers. Didn't someone shoot this Costello guy a few months back?"

"Albert and Frank have been together a long time," Reginelli added. "Same as Meyer. Back to Atlantic City in '29."

"What happened then?"

Reginelli reached forward and came back with another envelope. "You read this, too."

The second envelope contained another sheet of paper. Like the first, it came from the office of Albert Anastasia's private attorney, though this was dated a few days earlier, June 17, 1957.

(Dictated by Mr. Anastasia and transcribed in his presence)

For My Son,

If you are reading this, Giovanni, it's because I won't be speaking to you again. Today, men who want me dead killed a dear friend of mine. Six weeks back, the same people tried to kill another dear friend. I see my own time coming. I don't know when. But I know it will happen.

So now is the time for me to tell you things—very important things that will change your life. Your mother, God bless her, has papers for you from me. Read them. Read them good. Think about what they say, because they will not make sense at the beginning.

Two of my friends will help you understand what I am leaving you. One of them is Frank Costello, the one they tried to kill because of who he knows and who he controls. My other old friend is Meyer Lansky, the smartest businessman you will ever meet. These friends of mine will become your friends too. They are powerful men, but they do not let power go to their heads. They are rich men, but they do not let money control their lives. They are not Sicilian, but they respect the things we respect in the famiglia. That is why I trust them to look after you when I am gone.

Show them the same respect. Learn from them. Then you will come to know your father and respect me better than I think you respect me now. This is my hope.

> *Umberto Anastasio*

Jack looked closely at the signature at the bottom of the page. It was a scrawl. Not the hurried, easy dash of a man who signs his name so often no one needs to read it. The fingers that wrote this signature were not comfortable with a pen. There was a raw earnestness about the way Albert Anastasia signed his name.

"Do you mind if I go?"

"Will you be okay?"

"My mom…I should be with her, shouldn't I?"

"Carmella would like that," Reginelli told him, trying to sound reassuring. "So would Albert."

Carmella Pagano was alone in the parlor when Jack came home. In other houses down the street, lights were being turned on, fires lit, family meals prepared. When Jack pulled up outside, Number 12 was dark.

He let himself inside and called her name, but the house remained quiet. Jack checked the kitchen. His mom's handbag was on the table, her car keys beside it. He called again and this time an answer came from across the hall.

"I'm in here. Come see me, Giovanni."

A lump rose in Jack's throat.

An uneasy truce had settled on the house since Albert Anastasia's visit. He could tell that his mom had been choosing her words carefully when they spoke to each other. Jack had to admit that he hadn't been home often and he hadn't made conversation easy for her.

Football practice, long lone runs, sudden demands of school work in the library, and a few early nights had limited their time together—deliberately. Now he felt ashamed of the way he had behaved. Nervous, too, about how she would react.

Carmella sat beside the empty fireplace, hunched over like she was seeking warmth from the cold grate.

The door clicked shut as Jack closed it behind him.

He stood quietly, waiting for the words to come.

Without looking up, she held out a hand for him to take. "Thank you for coming back."

Jack had never seen her look so vulnerable, so lost and alone.

His mother's hand clutched a white handkerchief. Her long elegant fingers were curled around it and pointing upwards. The newspaper picture from the barber shop flashed through his mind.

Jack knelt beside the chair to hold her hand and place an arm round her shoulders. "Geez, Mom. I'm so sorry."

Carmella turned to face him. She was dressed entirely in black. "Thank you," she said again, dabbing her eyes with the handkerchief. "I hoped you would understand my feelings even if you couldn't find it in your heart to understand your…your father." Jack gave her shoulder a squeeze. "I knew this day could come. Umberto always warned me something like this would happen. Was I so wrong not to care that it might? For all those years he was gone, I knew he was always there for us. In a way I hoped I would never have to hear his voice again, because I knew when I did, the end would not be far away. But nothing can prepare you for this emptiness, this pain."

"I know," he lied.

Carmella kissed his check and he felt the warm tears on her face. "Umberto had plans for you—has plans for you. Be true to them, Giovanni. That's all I ask of you. Be true to them and you will be true to me and him."

"So, you know about all that stuff?"

His mother raised her head and got to her feet. "I know your father, and I was taught the same as him. When the *famiglia* loses a member, it gets stronger, not weaker, like new shoots growing from an old plant. This is what Umberto wanted—why he planned things the way he did. Now he's gone and your time has come."

"Reginelli gave me some things from Albert."

"Umberto told me about them."

"One of them says you have papers to give me from him. Is that right?"

Carmella took a cigarette from a gilt box on a side table, lit it with a silver lighter, and inhaled deeply. "Umberto gave them to me when he came last week. I've kept them upstairs, ready for this day."

Jack's throat was dry, but he tried to make his voice sound gentle and consoling when he asked, "Would you mind giving them to me? I'd like to have them, if that's okay."

"Of course." A thin smile spread across Carmella's face. She stubbed out the cigarette, leaving it bent and smoldering in the ashtray. "I'll get them now."

Jack listened to her footsteps disappear up the stairs and return a minute or so later.

She handed him three brown envelopes like the ones he had brought home in his school bag. "Take your time. Umberto would not want you to be hasty."

Then she left the room, switching on the light before closing the door.

Chapter Ten

(Dictated by Mr. Anastasia and transcribed in his presence)

I was seventeen when I came to America. That was in 1916, at night, over the side of a ship off Brooklyn. But my story goes back to other people who came to this country on other ships. So you should begin there too, Giovanni.

When I was your age, ships didn't just bring things to America. They brought immigrants, too. Hundreds and thousands of people from all over: Russia, Sweden, Poland, Germany, France, Scotland, Ireland, Italy, and Sicily. They came from Asia, too, from China.

People have been shipped here for three hundred years because America was the New World. America was so big, it wasn't a new country, it was a new world—a whole new world just waiting for its time. And when the time was right, people started coming. As if someone had turned on a faucet and out they flowed, ship after ship full of people.

Now think about who these people were. Were they the rich people from the Old World: the bankers from Europe, the old merchant families of China, all the old money that had been making those people richer and richer for hundreds of years, could be a thousand?
I don't think so.

No. The people who were shipped here were poor; they were hungry. People told them this New World was like the Promised Land in the Bible, with streets paved with gold.

Some of the dumb fuckers believed that, they really did.

Okay, they didn't find gold in the streets, but they did find they could do things in the New World that they couldn't do back in the Old World. Jewish people found they could own property. Irish people found they could lay down the law and run cities—check how many Irish cops there are, you'll see what I mean. People who had never known power and never been seen as important, they found they could be something in the New World. You heard about the American Dream? That's what these people thought they'd found.

Maybe they started with a handcart, selling things in their neighborhood. But they weren't stuck with a handcart. Pretty soon they might have a stall, then a store. They made more money, so they moved to a better neighborhood. They made more money so they spent more money. They had more children, they bought new clothes, they ate better food. This American Dream had no end in sight. These people making it good in the New World, they looked back at their fathers and grandfathers in the Old World and they wondered why they had been poor for so long. How come they were making it in the New World when the people back home hadn't?

But here's the pisser. Because the only thing they thought about was finding new ways to make money and new ways to spend money, they didn't see that nothing was really different after all.
If you don't have money, how can you spend money, right? But if you have never had money before and now you

suddenly have more money than you have ever known, what do you do with it? You spend it. It makes you feel good. You think other people will respect you, because everyone you know respects people who have money. Okay, you ask, where's the problem?

The money. That is their problem. It always has been and it always will be. These people, who make all this new money, they find there is never enough money. So they work harder, they get more tired, and life doesn't look so good any more. They need something to make it better again and in this New World of America there are plenty of things to make it better: booze, gambling, whores and everything else money can by. That's so long as you have the money.

And what do you do if you don't have enough money? This is a dream, remember. Do you want to wake up and lose it? No. That's the last thing you want. Who wants to look at all the shit in the real world when you can live in a dream? So you find the money any way you can because this money is now like a drug: you need it, you can't live without it.

Greed. Human greed. That's what it is. It's as simple as that. You can give it any name you want. You can try to cover it up and describe it a hundred different ways, but when you cut it to the bone you find that's the basic instinct of survival—greed.

Now get this. You've got a New World and it's being filled with people with one thing on their mind—to get on and make money: greed. But there is no money in this New World. Did the Indians have money? Fuck me, no. They didn't have shit on a stick. So where could the money come from?

*From the Old World. People said America was the land
of opportunity, but what good is opportunity if you
can't do anything with it? And to do anything you need
money. So someone turns on another faucet and out flows
money—millions and millions of dollars. Money to build
the railroads, money to mine coal, money to make steel,
money to make oil—money to make all the things you
ever dreamed of. But see here, who makes these things?
Who does all this work?*

*The hungry people. The people who are greedy for money.
They do the work and they get paid for it with money from
the Old World. This is how the dream comes true for them
in their eyes. So what do they do with this money?*

*They spend it. Suckers. They spend it, so they need even
more money. They have to work harder. Life gets harder.
Again they need more money, because this time they are
spending money to try to make life better. Only now they
don't think about anything but getting that money. What
they don't see is where the money they spend is going.
Maybe they have to borrow money. So where does the
payback money go?*

*Maybe they like to drink, to make their worries go away.
Where does the booze money go? Maybe they think
screwing whores will make life better. Where does that
money go? Not to the poor fucking whores. Maybe they
think they will get lucky at the race track or playing cards,
rolling dice. Where does all that money go?*

*Those dumb fuckers, all they look at is how to get money
with one hand. They don't see where it goes from the
other hand. It gets taken back, right to where it came
from, to the Old World. The money that comes from the
Old World is like it's on a roulette wheel. Only when it*

goes back it takes all the money from this New World with it. The old money of the world has given life to this beautiful, young country and now it rapes it—for its pleasure, for its greed.

The same deal has worked every place else; right around the Old World, all through history. Look at every so-called civilization the world has seen: the Roman Empire, the Chinese Empire, the Russian Empire, the British Empire. Why not here? America is the new playground. Always follow the money, then you find the answer.

I'll tell you all I can about my business, but my business is just one part. There are other men, dear friends of mine who will help you. So you will learn the whole business from the men who know it all. I sent Rip to get you started. Now I tell you what I know. These other men, they will do the same. Understand that this is not something you can learn from one man alone.

Back home, in Sicily, there are many ancient mosaics, beautiful pictures made by Greeks, by Romans, by the Moors, by most people who have come to Sicily. So believe me when I tell you, I know about mosaics. But in a mosaic you only see the picture when you look at how all the little stones fit together. When you look at just one little stone, it don't mean nothing. Look at just part of the picture, that don't mean nothing, too. To see the whole picture, you got to see how the whole mosaic fits together. That's what you must learn, looking at the mosaic.

This mosaic tells everything about us, like it's a living part of us—a smell, a skin that surrounds us. When I look at a person, I see their mosaic. I see everything about them: where they come from, who their parents are, how they feel about themselves, what makes them feel good,

*what makes them feel bad, what makes them scared—I
look at their mosaic and I see all the shit in their lives. I
see it right to the bottom line truth. And you know how I
can see this mosaic? Because I know my own mosaic; I
know it better than anyone else.*

*This country has a mosaic as well. Think about these
people who come to the New World to make their fortune.
Their greed drives them on. They grab land, stealing it
from the Indians, stealing it from each other. Someone
finds gold, they rush to find gold, too—fighting over a
scrap of dirt and finding nothing. And what follows them?
The booze, the gambling, the whores—all the things that
help to make life better and all the things that take back
their money. Easy, isn't it?*

*But this is just chicken shit to the people who send the old
money. When they are ready, they set down a plan, a big
plan like a framework. This plan, it doesn't happen quick.
It isn't meant to happen quick. This plan was started over
a hundred years ago. It hasn't finished yet.*

*First they send people to America, people who have
one thing to do: make babies in America, so that these
babies grow up to be Americans. These are special
people though, people who can be trusted to keep their
eyes open and their mouths shut. They settle all round
the country: New York, Providence, Boston, Buffalo,
Cleveland, Detroit, Chicago, Milwaukee, Kansas City,
New Orleans, Tampa, Philadelphia. They settle, and
when they are ready, they go to work, like their families
have worked for centuries. They know how to lend
money to people who need it. They know how to get the
booze for people who need it. And the whores and the
gambling and all the other shit. They know these things
because they understand greed.*

But these people understand something more important than greed. They know the power of fear. Look in any history book, you find the same sort of people doing the same things. How do you think those kings in Egypt built the pyramids—because the people loved them so much they wanted to sweat in the desert all their lives? Who kept the emperors in power in Rome, or China, or any place else? It sure wasn't John Doe in the gutter. No—it was the men who knew how to use fear. They've been doing it pretty good for thousands of years, so why shouldn't they be doing it good still and why shouldn't they be doing it good here—right now?

It's not like they teach you in school. I didn't learn such things at school. That's why my friends must tell you about their business. Not me, because each business has its own place in the framework; only the man who has that business can really tell you about it. But when you listen to them, listen good and you will hear some things like I am telling you now.

If you understand what I tell you, then you must also understand we all exist in a business. This business, it controls our lives: your life, Frank's life, Meyer's life, and my life. So when a life has to come to an end, it's business—nothing else. And that is my second reason for telling you these things now. My life must end. I have lived my life the way I have because of what I believe in. I cannot exist in the world I see coming. I am a powerful man, believe me when I tell you this, but even I can't change what must happen.

My death is not to be talked about. And it is not to be avenged in the wrong way. Look at the mosaic, read it good. The people who take my life will not come from my own circle, from my own city. You are a man, and you are being educated as a man. I was a man when I was twelve. So were my friends. If we could carry this knowledge, so can you, because you come from us.

There is no price tag on my soul. There is no price tag on yours. That is why I need you to work with me after I am gone. Follow the money. Go find who is building this drug business. But do it smart. Don't show yourself. Remember that no one knows who you are, so keep it that way. My friends know what is to be done, but they need you to unlock the door. Work with Frank and Meyer. Help them and you will be helping me. I understand you better than you will ever know, Giovanni. Now it's your turn to understand me. As you read the things I have left for you, please remember this...

Chapter Eleven

The Ambassador liked to receive memos.

Maybe they helped preserve the self-importance he clung to, the picture he still had of himself as a man of consequence on the world stage. Predictably, these were no mere trifles: one of the richest men in America, the nation's representative at the Court of St. James (the most socially prestigious posting in the U.S. government), confidant of the president himself, the shrewd judge of international affairs, the investor who backed a resurgent National Socialist Germany to cut a victorious swathe through vassal states—the Ambassador had enjoyed his moment of glory.

That had been seventeen years ago and his public star had waned since then. But he still liked to receive memos. James Lovall understood this, and it amused him to pander to the old man's foibles. Lovall knew well enough that his proposals could be implemented even if the Ambassador had not been there to receive them. The old man was a pawn, but it was convenient to have him as a front—to let him take the credit for whatever Lovall decided needed doing.

Lovall had come to the Ambassador's attention in the spring of 1945. The clean-cut, blue-eyed, sandy-haired young intelligence officer had been attending the founding of the United Nations in San Francisco, which the Ambassador's eldest surviving son, Jack, was covering for the *Chicago Herald-American.*

Joe Kennedy was an affable guy, who enjoyed a good time and didn't take himself too seriously. One weekend break from that heady international assembly, the two of them had flown up to join Jack's father at the Cal-Neva Lodge, Lake Tahoe's "jewel of the North Shore."

The Ambassador had been a regular visitor to Cal-Neva since its opening in 1926. In recent years he had been spending more and more time at the high-class hideout nestled between the cobalt blue water of the lake and the emerald green mountains. He enjoyed the seclusion of the private chalets tucked away behind the massive log-clad edifice of the main hotel building.

Lovall quickly surmised that it was the two-sided character of Cal-Neva as much as its isolated location that appealed to the Ambassador. The lodge straddled the state line dividing California and Nevada, which explained its name. The story ran that the card tables in the famous gaming room were pushed back and forth across the line, from one state to the other, depending on which legislature's police had shown up to bust the place.

It was a good yarn, and the Ambassador clearly got a kick relating it. James Lovall smiled and chuckled indulgently, even if he wasn't entirely convinced. He knew perfectly well that Cal-Neva Lodge was generous in paying off state officials on both sides of the line; police raids were rare, and Cal-Neva's clientele was seldom disturbed.

Lovall was a fixer.

He got the right results. That's what the Ambassador believed he was paying for when he bought James Lovall's contacts, drive, and expertise.

The last two years had worked out well. Lovall had a right to feel pleased about that. Jack Kennedy had achieved modest national recognition as an award-winning author when he walked off with the Pulitzer Prize for his biography, *Profiles in Courage.* But Jack didn't have the time or inclination to write all of it; much of the work had been delegated to Kennedy minions. But James Lovall had made sure that the youthful senator had received the plaudits for the prize-winning book. Lovall had also persuaded the Ambassador to buy thousands of copies to ensure that Profiles in Courage retained its high rank in the best-seller listings.

At the Democratic national convention a few months later, the Ambassador's son staked his claim in the political consciousness by damn near walking off with the vice-presidential nomination as Adlai Stevenson's running mate.

In Lovall's view, coming a close and gracious second was better than winning. Stevenson would never wrest the White House from Eisenhower; Lovall had that on the highest authority. As a sop to win the Catholic vote, Jack Kennedy would have been blamed for the defeat.

This way, he got maximum exposure for minimum loss. Earlier in the proceedings, the *New York Times* had reported, "Kennedy came before the convention tonight as a movie star." Not a bad return.

The Ambassador certainly approved.

Ironically, losing the nomination gave Jack Kennedy a platform to build on.

Lovall ran his eyes down the page in front of him searching out a name: Estes Kefauver. It was Kefauver, the two-bit senator from Tennessee, who had clinched the nomination as Adlai Stevenson's running mate ahead of the Ambassador's son.

Kefauver was a nobody, a nonentity. What interested Lovall was how he had gotten where he had.

In Lovall's judgment there were two straightforward reasons for this: organized crime and television.

Wittingly or not, Kefauver had hit a home run seven years earlier by bringing these two together. Over a period of ten months, beginning in the summer of 1950, TV viewers across the nation had been tuning in to follow the proceedings of the Senate Special Committee to Investigate Crime in Interstate Commerce, chaired by Senator Kefauver.

In city after city, those called to testify either took refuge behind the Fifth Amendment and refused to answer the committee's questions, or they revealed details of greed, corruption, and murder that gripped and horrified the millions glued to their small frosty screens.

Lovall had watched in fascination. Within a few months, the drawling senator from Tennessee had become a folk hero—a virtuous "everyman," pitting himself against the sinister forces lurking in the shadows.

Organized crime and television had elevated Kefauver. And if Kefauver, with his modest assets, could achieve so much, how much more could a Kennedy achieve?

Lovall felt particularly pleased with himself when Jack had been elected to Harvard's Board of Overseers. That was a nice touch. The old man had crowed about it for weeks.

Less prominent, but in Lovall's design perhaps the most telling move, had been placing Jack on the McClellan Committee. Like the Kefauver Committee before it, it was investigating the link between organized crime and labor racketeering.

Jack wasn't the only Kennedy on Senator McClellan's committee, of course. His younger brother, Bobby, had been serving as its chief counsel and ran the proceedings with all the grit and vehemence of a scrawny terrier hunting cunning, bloated rats.

For Lovall, Bobby Kennedy was the perfect foil. What he lacked of Jack's easygoing charm, Bobby made up for in humorless devotion to duty. Union bosses hauled in front of him were browbeaten for hours on end as the chief prosecutor warmed to his task.

Thanks to Bobby, the Kennedy brothers took on the mantle of Estes Kefauver. Once again TV audiences were treated to the sight of villainously corrupt leaders of organized labor being hounded from their lairs by the messianic zeal of the chief counsel. It was his crusade, and Bobby Kennedy was nobly carrying the standard of decency and justice into battle.

This is what people would remember, Lovall reflected. Meanwhile, Jack could follow in his younger brother's wake and gather in the spoils of public adulation.

There were risks—serious risks—in pitting his sons against the dark forces ranged against them, he had warned. However,

Lovall had detected something deeper in the Ambassador's opposition to going after the mob than merely safeguarding his boys. It had taken hours of patient probing before he uncovered the reason for the old man's reluctance. But that had been time well spent. What James Lovall had learned confirmed hints and rumors he had been gathering since before he and Joseph P. Kennedy had ever met.

James Lovall laid aside the folded copy of the *New York Times*, poured himself another cup of coffee, and spread a little orange marmalade on a slice of crisp golden toast. He had acquired a taste for Cooper's Oxford Marmalade during his time in London at the end of the war.

The murder of Albert Anastasia filled the page in front of him. Lovall studied it with interest, as he knew the Ambassador would. The boss of Murder, Inc. may have been dismissed in the popular media as a piece of particularly violent waterfront muscle, but Lovall and the Ambassador knew otherwise. Anastasia had served a useful purpose. Lovall's regret was that it had been necessary to dispense with his services prematurely.

An hour later Lovall drew a neatly typed sheet of paper from his typewriter and read it through for final approval.

MEMORANDUM

To:	**Ambassador Kennedy**
From:	**James Lovall**
Date:	**October 26, 1957**
Subject:	**Organized Crime**

You will be aware, sir, that the official line taken by the present administration and every one of its predecessors is that organized crime does not exist in the United States. FBI Director J. Edgar Hoover is on record stating this fact. Despite revelations to the contrary that surfaced in the hearings held by the Kefauver Committee seven years ago, the American public remains almost totally unaware of the presence and power of a nationally orchestrated criminal network. This is something we will soon rectify.

The presence of your sons on the committee chaired by Senator John McClellan guarantees that they will benefit significantly from the publicity our actions will generate. Please be assured that these actions are also designed to cause considerable disquiet in the FBI and law enforcement agencies nationwide, the majority of which will be shown to be not only impotent, but frequently complicit in their dealings with organized crime.

I appreciate that you take a close personal interest in these matters, sir. So I trust you will understand it when I say that revealing the scale, wealth, and influence of what may perhaps be termed the enemy within will draw the attention of the above-mentioned agencies away from investigating cases of, say, twenty or thirty years ago. Public opinion alone will ensure that the official focus on criminal activity will be on those identified as the leading criminals of the present day.

I need hardly remind you, sir, how similar publicity advanced the political aspirations of Senator Kefauver. I have complete confidence that Jack will benefit in the same way from what is about to unfold.

He figured that would be enough to get the old man's juices running. He smiled at the image of the bright eyes shining with malevolent pleasure behind the round lenses. Skeletons in the Ambassador's closet had started to rattle recently. Lovall could see he was on edge, but he hadn't yet figured out why.

Chapter Twelve

"Like I told you, we couldn't take any risks." Carmine Galante pushed the tangled cord from the telephone around the corner of his desk. "What do you mean, 'Do it some place quiet with one hitter?' Look what happened with Costello. We needed two to take out Scalise, for Christ's sake."

"And these men are secure?" Husky asked.

"As tight as a nun's pussy."

"Let's hope they are. Remember what we discussed in Sicily. No mistakes."

"Yeah...no mistakes," Galante answered, trying to mask the resentment in his voice. "We done the job, didn't we? Like you asked. Right?"

"Let's hope so," the voice repeated.

"So what about the other business?"

"Now that this local difficulty has been taken care of, we can proceed as planned. Everything is in hand."

"You mean they're all going to be there? From Chicago and Los Angeles and Tampa and all?"

"Yes. Why shouldn't they be?"

"No reason. Getting everyone together like this, that don't happen too often."

The voice in the earpiece sounded cold and mildly irritated, "Precisely. It happened in 1929. Don't you think this is just as important? Or maybe you are getting a little out of your depth, my friend? We wouldn't want you struggling if you can't cope."

"What do you mean, struggling? If you've got any worries about anyone struggling, how about Genovese and Barbara?"

"Take it from me—I have no worries with them. Barbara is doing just fine. Rooms are being booked. Even the menu's fixed. Do you think it's every day Armour & Co. in Binghamton gets an order for…wait a minute, let me tell you exactly…yes, here it is: 207 pounds of steak, 20 pounds of veal cutlets and 15 pounds of luncheon meat. Some barbecue, huh? And everything is as it should be for Genovese. All the pieces are moving into place. There's no one to stand in his way now, is there? He can step up and take his seat at the head of the table."

"Yeah, if you say so," Galante grunted.

Fuck you, he thought to himself. It was bad enough to have Don Vito, his old boss, on a roll, but Husky held the winning cards in this deal like he did on every other one. Only Lansky and Costello had stayed out of the game. All the other serious players had agreed that Anastasia had to go. So none of them could bitch about it afterward and cause trouble. Drawing on the talent of Genovese's number-one enforcer from way back had been a smart move. Galante's involvement made it look like his present family was getting close to Genovese. Maybe the Bonannos were? In the quicksand of shifting alliances that Galante walked, he was cautious of every step he took.

"No mistakes. Do I make myself clear?" snapped the voice down the line.

Galante agreed and listened as the telephone was hung up at the other end.

Husky adopted a very different tone in the telephone call he made a few minutes later.

"We have a conclave," he announced modestly when he was put through.

"And will all the cardinals be present?" he was asked.

"The ones that matter."

"I see. And are we sure the smoke will be the right color?"

"God has spoken to the faithful; they will not fail him."

"I am very glad to hear it."

"So, is it time for the guardian angels?"

There was a pause. "Yes, I think it is. Send the word my good and trusted servant."

In less than five minutes, a telephone was ringing in the Vestal police station in upstate New York.

Chapter Thirteen

Rip Collins had come to the Hole as usual every morning and every evening after Albert Anastasia's visit to Jack's home, though Jack hadn't joined him since that day.

The young man needed time. Rip knew that. One week Jack had a dad who'd suddenly stepped into his life from behind a curtain where he'd been waiting all along to make his entrance. The next week, the curtain had become a shroud and the young man would never see his dad again. After the turmoil of that week, he figured Jack might need his routine in the Hole—something familiar he could take refuge in, a foundation to build on. And so Rip had spent many lonely hours waiting for him.

Early Sunday morning, a few days after the shooting at the Park Central Hotel, Rip was sipping a mug of hot coffee from his thermos flask when he detected movement outside. He set down his mug, stood up, and moved silently to the wall beside the opening where he had put the camouflaged door back in place.

He listened, but the movement had stopped. It had been faint.

A minute passed.

Ninety seconds.

Then the door moved swiftly aside. A shaft of daylight sprung through the opening and then quickly disappeared again as a dark form ducked inside.

Rip's hand shot down to grab the intruder, but his arm was parried before he could get a hold. The force of his lunge propelled him off balance and lifted him over his assailant. He crashed hard on the wooden floor, a loud thunk sounding as he collapsed.

Rip twisted free and was on his feet immediately and braced for attack.

"Do you want to carry on, or shall we talk?" Jack asked from the shadows.

"You choose," Rip answered. "I have coffee and bagels."

"Sounds good."

Rip poured the coffee. Jack replaced the door, fitted the electric lantern with the freshly charged batteries Rip always brought with him, and turned on the light. When he was finished, they sat together on the tin trunk cradling the hot cups in their fingers.

Jack blew across the surface of the dark liquid. A thin veil of vapor rose and melted into the damp air. "Have you talked to my mom?"

Talking to his mom had been difficult for Jack, but it was even harder with Rip. Jack looked around the stout wooden walls, trying to remember what it had felt like, hacking out the dirt, hauling in each railroad tie and setting it in place. Five years, more than a quarter of his life, had been spent working here.

"Did you know all that other stuff? About government and business working with crooks and all?" he asked Rip.

"I think you should be careful how you use the word 'crook.' Men like Albert, they aren't hypocrites. He had some hard things to do and he did them—right across the board—wherever he was needed. One thing you've got to understand is that the people he worked with, in the government and in business, they did exactly the same kind of things, only no one ever pointed a finger at them and called them crooks. This is what Albert's told you, right?"

"Yes, that's just what those papers say, only…"

"Only you don't believe him?" Rip sat down beside him again and patted his leg in reassurance. "You've got to try and detach yourself from what Albert's telling you. This is his world he's talking about, not the world he put you in to keep you safe and out of sight."

Jack studied his coffee cup as if some mystical answer lay hidden inside.

Rip offered him a bagel. He took a bite out of his own, none too eager to be done chewing, maybe. "Albert didn't expect you to see things his way straight off. But he did want you to know how to begin to look at things the way he did. Your head's all mixed up right now. Pretty soon it will start to clear. And when it does you'll see how the work we've put in is going to help you split the light the way Albert split it."

Rip unscrewed the cap of the thermos and refilled their cups.

"You remember the way we started with that memory game?"

"Of course I do,"

"Then it got harder, with the radio and TV and the telephone calls. Well, Albert wanted your mind to get sharp and agile and strong, just like your body. He saw for himself at the football game what you and I have achieved here physically. Now he's gone, it's time to let your mind go to work as well.

"Albert's done what he can to help you. You know I'm here. Soon you'll meet the other people who are ready to help you too. We can turn on the light, Jack. But only you can learn to look at it like Albert does."

Jack blew on his cup again. "Why me, Rip? How come I got chosen? No one asked me if I wanted this. We were doing fine, Mom and me, and then Albert Anastasia shows up out of nowhere and it's a done deal. Everything I've known for as long as I can remember is kicked aside and I find I got a dead man running my life."

This was the challenge Rip had been anticipating when Anastasia set him to work training his son. It was a tough call. After all that time, he still wasn't sure he had the right answer.

"Albert needed someone he knew would come to care about these things as much as he cared. He gave his life defending what he believed in, but he didn't want anyone else to be put in that position. He was living in a nightmare, he knew that, but it was his choice. He never wanted you to get sucked into that kind of life. That's why he kept you outside it. Sure, he needs you to burrow into it, to find out what's going on. The difference is you'll be working from the outside. No one knows who you are. All they'll see will be a regular Joe, with no history and no links to your old man or his associates."

"What about his other son? I read about him in the newspaper. How come Albert didn't choose him?"

"Listen to what you just said," Rip answered. "Sure, Albert has another son, and he's given him his own name: Umberto Anastasio, Jr. Now ask yourself this: how could anyone with that name ever do what Albert has chosen you to do? Everyone who reads a newspaper knows about that son. But they don't know about you."

"I don't have a choice, do I?"

His old friend breathed in deeply and ran his hand through his cropped, graying hair, searching for the right response. "It's not a question of choice, Jack. For a man like Albert, it's your destiny. Your reason for being here. Like I told you, although you didn't know it, Albert's been looking out for you and your mom for your whole life. Now it's your turn to repay that by looking out for other people—more people than you can ever imagine."

Jack didn't answer immediately. For the first time in as long as he could remember, he wanted to shut his brain off. He wanted to turn his thoughts to something else: a life filled with football and scholarships and awkward conversations with girls like Julie-Ann. He wanted to run home and see his mother smiling again, not whimpering and crying, a faraway look on her face and a box of tissues at her side.

And what was this talk of help? His mother had done everything for him, and he'd only ever needed her. But Rip seemed to have a different idea. And while it was easy to push the papers away—at least at first—it was much harder to argue with Rip.

"Albert Anastasia is a stranger to you," Rip continued. "He knew you would need time to get to know him. That's the reason he wanted to spend time with you—and perhaps more importantly, he wanted you to spend time with the people he trusted after he was dead. Not just me, but people who play in a bigger league: Lansky and Costello. They'll take care of you, just like Albert did. What they want is information. They'll know how to use that information when they get it. And for this they need fresh eyes and ears. That's what you're going to be. Somebody to move about under the radar, to watch and listen without being seen."

Jack pushed back on the tin trunk and got to his feet. For whatever reason, Rip had been good to him, there was no denying that. Things he'd been saying since they first met were falling into place as well—even if it wasn't in the way Jack had been expecting.

He slid the soles of his sneakers across the smooth-grained floorboards like he was skating. "Do you know Mr. Lansky and Mr. Costello?"

"I met them a few times, with Albert. But we operate at a different level, if you know what I mean."

"So how do I get to meet them?"

"They'll send word," he told Jack, "when they think the time's right. What happened to Albert is kicking up one hell of a storm. Your old man kept everyone in line for thirty years. Now he's gone, it's like a volcano erupting. All the families will be tumbling over each other trying to get the biggest piece of the pie. Lansky and Costello will let things settle down first. They need to give the big players time to show themselves. Then you'll get to meet them."

There was a strange pull, this feeling of helplessness gnawing at him. He wasn't disappointed at having to wait. Well, not entirely, anyway. Why should he care what Lansky and Costello need?

Jack couldn't answer these questions. He knew Rip couldn't either. Wouldn't even try. Rip, like the others, had done what was asked of him, and now it was up to Jack what to make of this

Albert Anastasia. What to make of these newspaper names. For all Jack knew last week, "Frank Costello" and "Meyer Lansky" were just letters on a page. Albert Anastasia, too.

"How long will it be?" he asked. "Until I meet them."

"We'll both just have to wait and see."

Chapter Fourteen

Carlos Marcello was in his office when the call he'd been expecting came in from Santo Trafficante. He switched off the TV to take it. For the last two days, the Apalachin bust had been headline news.

"You back home now?" he asked.

"Yeah, no thanks to that Genovese, and the other cocksuckers in New York." Trafficante sounded real steamed up.

"Joe said the cops picked you up." Marcello had been represented by an underboss, his brother Joseph, and understood all too well the seriousness of what had happened.

"We didn't have no place to go. I made it into the woods, okay, but how the fuck were we going to find our way out? The cops were all over us, like fleas on a dog. Soon as I stuck my head out they were after me. Firing guns in the air to make us stop, like in the movies. What do you expect us to do?"

Marcello tried to picture the scene. It would have been funny if it hadn't been such a disaster.

"They say the cops made sixty of our top guys. Sixty, for Christ's sake! What the fuck did Genovese think he was playing at?"

"So now he sees why Chicago wanted the sit-down on their patch. With Giancana and Rosselli running the show for Accardo, nothing like this would ever have been allowed to happen. All those New York cops had to do was block one lousy road and wait for us. We was like rats in a barrel."

Marcello grunted in sympathy. "But it screwed Genovese real good, am I right?"

"You bet your ass it did. Some of the guys are ready to kill him. You know what beats me, Carlos? That fucker really believed he was going to make himself 'boss of bosses.' He seriously thought that guys like us and Lansky and Costello were going to let him start telling us what to do. Then there's Charlie. I wouldn't want to be Vito Genovese when Charlie gets to hear about this."

There was silence at the other end of the line. Marcello was uneasy. "This is bad, Santo. Real bad. Now all this 'Mafia' shit is flying round, some people are going to start getting real heavy. And the Feds, this don't make them look too smart. Hoover's going to have to do something or he can kiss goodbye to the Bureau."

"What do you think's been on my mind since Thursday? We got everything nice and sweet down in Cuba. Business is good all over till Vito fucking Genovese starts to play his sneaky little games." Then something surfaced from the back of his mind. "What's with this 'Mafia' thing?"

"Search me. Maybe someone took Meyer for real when he said each city should have its own name for business."

"Well, the whole goddamn country's talking about the mafia now and that ain't good for anyone's business."

"Some dirt's going to be turned up when they start digging. You know how many of our guys they picked are on police files?"

"Yeah, well that don't mean jack shit…"

"It didn't used to, Santo. When things were running like they should, police files didn't mean fuck all. This is what I don't like: things are changing. People are starting to open their mouths. People are stepping out of line. And there ain't no Albert around no more to knock heads together. There's going to be some serious heat put on us. I'm starting to feel it already. You know what I mean?"

Trafficante knew all right.

It echoed across the South when his name made the news bulletins. He could just imagine what low-level soldiers would be thinking when they saw their bosses get busted in a dumb meet like Apalachin. Then there was running through the woods like rabbits, throwing away wads of dough so they wouldn't be caught with a whole load of cash they couldn't account for. Some had even thrown away guns. Respect didn't come easy, but it was real easy to lose.

"Thank Christ we still got Cuba," he told Marcello. "That Batista, at least he knows how business should be run."

"I say 'Amen' to that."

Chapter Fifteen

Three days later, word had come from Frank Costello.

It was a bright fall day, crisp with a chilly edge to the wind. His mom had told him to dress smart. "Your father's friend is always immaculate," she explained. "He'll notice things like that."

So Jack boarded the train at Camden feeling like a college student headed for a big city interview. He'd made the journey to New York often enough to be familiar with the route, but there was still a tingle of excitement as the train pulled through the reedy tracts of scruffy marshland toward the Hudson River and the serrated skyline of Manhattan.

Less than two hours after buying his ticket, Jack was standing on the sidewalk outside the echoing columned concourse of Pennsylvania Station, looking across noisy Seventh Avenue to the towering monolith of the Pennsylvania Hotel.

"Jack Pagano?" asked a man in a well-cut double-breasted suit. "I think Rip Collins told you I'd be here."

Jack was on his guard. He knew from newspaper photographs that this man was not the celebrated "rackets boss" he was expecting to meet. "I don't understand. Who are you and what do you want with me?"

The man smiled. "You have a meeting at the Sherry Netherland. My car is this way."

The driver led him to a highly polished Lincoln and showed him into the rear seat before taking the wheel and pulling out into the traffic. Swinging past the Empire State Building at 34th Street, the driver turned onto Fifth Avenue heading uptown. The neoclassical façade of the New York Public Library slid by the car windows on Jack's left, the Gothic spires of St. Patrick's Cathedral on his right. Just above Grand Army Plaza at the foot of Central Park, the driver pulled over behind one of the Fifth Avenue double-decker buses to let Jack get out opposite 61st Street and the entrance to the Sherry Netherland Hotel.

"Second Floor. Room 242," the driver told him.

"Thanks for the ride."

"You're welcome."

The Lincoln slipped away into the line of traffic.

Crossing Fifth Avenue, Jack strode through the heavy glass-paneled doors. Every step echoed through the well-polished lobby. Jack felt out of place.

He wasn't inferior to the people traipsing through the lobby. Anastasia's name or not, that was never a concern. But he imagined he could see himself from above. As if he were floating above the room or peering in on closed-circuit cameras.

Jack checked his watch. A couple of minutes before twelve o'clock.

He found Room 242 and knocked on the door.

A thick voice called from the other side of the door. "Come in."

Jack let himself into a deep-carpeted room overlooking Central Park, an endless sea of green sprawling across midtown and out toward the horizon. An oblong table stood in the center of the room surrounded by a dozen gilt chairs upholstered with red velvet.

Approaching him was a man in his mid-sixties, dressed in a light gray two-piece suit, a soberly patterned silk tie, and a pristine white shirt fastened at the wrists by a pair of discreet gold cufflinks.

"Pleased to meet you." The man extended his hand. "I've heard so much about you."

The man grabbed at an overcoat draped over the nearby chair.

He led Jack out of the room and over to the elevator, up to the roof garden atop the Sherry Netherland where they could be alone and speak freely. On the rooftop they stood by the perimeter rail high above Fifth Avenue, looking toward the cluster of skyscrapers stretching away toward Wall Street and the harbor. The boats passed slowly from this height, as if they were barely moving as they approached the docks.

Jack felt the cool rail beneath his fingers. He wasn't a fan of heights, never had been. But at this moment, the thought of betraying even a little bit of his reluctance did not suit him.

They shared the view for a moment before the man spoke. "Your father called me Frank. I'd like you to do the same."

"Thank you," Jack replied.

He drew closer. "I know what he has left you, and I know it ain't easy for you to take in everything that has happened, but he said you can handle it and I have to believe what he told me."

"There's a lot to read. I've hardly made a dent."

"That's because it is very important," Costello replied.

"He knew he was going to be killed, didn't he?" Jack asked. "My father, I mean." The words had rolled off his own tongue but still managed to surprise him.

Walking across the rooftop garden, Costello took the cigarette from his lips and examined the comfortable residential districts of the Upper East Side. Then he moved back in the opposite direction, down toward the East River, to the low-rise tenements of the Lower East Side, where immigrant families struggled to find a foothold in the New World.

"Some people thought he was standing in the way of progress." He stubbed out his cigarette, walked back to the handrail, and lit another. "Albert always said the same thing: if we touch drugs, our children will touch them, and that will be the downfall of our families."

"He mentioned that in his papers." Jack remained fixed on Costello. "Those same exact words."

"That doesn't surprise me. Those words cost him his life, and that is why he needed you to understand all this, needed someone to carry on his fight."

"Don't I have a say in any of this? Suppose I don't want the fight. It got him killed—"

"He also protected you all your life. Don't you think you owe him the chance to make his case? To assemble all the facts?" Costello took a long drag from his cigarette, though the floor was clearly still his. "Isn't that what you learned from Rip?"

Costello went silent, his eyes fixed on some distant point squarely in his own mind.

Jack peered over the edge of the rail, down at the ants below, scurrying down the sidewalks and through the avenues. "He said things are changing."

"That's what Apalachin was all about. Vito Genovese called together bosses from all over the country to lay out his master plan for a nationwide heroin business. It's why so many of the big players were there—and why we stayed away. Meyer and me, I mean. You remember what your old man told you, and now watch what happens."

Costello checked the time on his gold wristwatch. Taking Jack's arm, he walked him to the door that led to the elevator. "Your father has brought us together—okay? Meyer and me will know whenever you need us, just like your father would know. Don't you ever forget that."

He reached out and took Jack by the hand, then drew him closer to kiss him on both cheeks in farewell.

Jack was still waiting. Still waiting to find out what it was that Costello wanted from him.

Rip had mentioned Jack's help would be needed, but Jack still wasn't sure what to do. He still didn't know what carrying on Albert's fight meant, never mind whether he wanted to do that.

"My car will be waiting outside in ten minutes to take you back to Penn Station."

"Thank you."

"No—it is me who should be thanking you. And your father. I'm sorry for the reasons that made us meet, but I am very pleased that we have. Can you find your way to the lobby?"

"Sure."

"Then I'll say goodbye for now. Wait here for five minutes before you leave," and he made his way toward the elevator, lighting another cigarette as he left.

Chapter Sixteen

Uptown, in a noisy tenement in the Bronx, Mario Sapienza took a long drag from the cigarette he was smoking and passed it across to his brother, Bernardo.

They had to share cigarettes. In fact, they had to share most things. Money was short and living in New York was so much more expensive than back home in Ponte Sagana, a village fifteen miles inland from Palermo.

Three weeks ago, the Sapienzas had never set foot outside Sicily. Here, they found themselves surrounded by people who spoke a different language, ate different food, and lived by a different set of rules. Instead of mules and donkeys and the occasional beaten-up truck they were used to at home, the streets roared with traffic. Though, already, Mario and Bernardo were acquiring a taste for the smooth ride and sleek upholstery of expensive automobiles, like the one Bruno Pafundi—Vito Genovese's underboss and the man they served—cruised his sector of the city in.

Brought up to be loyal to their *famiglia*, the Sapienza's never questioned the instructions they had been given. When they had been told by a senior member of the Porta Nuova family to pack their bags for America, they did so immediately.

The don told them they had been chosen to spearhead a new venture in New York. Mario and Bernardo knew that powerful Sicilian families had clan members well-established in the US. This was their chance to do something for the Sapienzas—the opportunity to lay down the foundations of a business that would secure their relatives and associates power and wealth.

Don Vito Genovese, a man they had known by reputation and respected since they were children, had endorsed this new business. Members of the families set up in America had flown to Palermo recently, where plans had been set in place. Carmine Galante, once Genovese's key lieutenant (and still rumored to be his hit man of choice when a particular need arose) had been among them. Now that Mario and Bernardo had found their feet, they were becoming aware of Galante and his fearsome reputation in the city.

They were less sure about Don Genovese.

Word spread that he had recently been the cause of serious trouble for a number of family bosses from across the country. Even the newly arrived Sapienzas recognized the names of several men taken in by the police someplace near the state line with Pennsylvania. Mario and Bernardo didn't know the details, but in the world of constantly shifting alliances and betrayals they had grown up in, they were used to reading the way people behaved. And from what they picked up on the street, one thing was clear: questions were being asked about Don Genovese.

From Bruno Pafundi, to whom the shipments from Europe were first delivered, to the street-corner pushers, who sold small glassine-enveloped "pops" of heavily diluted heroin at a few dollars a bag, rumors were radiating that Don Genovese might no longer be the all-powerful, all-controlling narcotics boss he had set himself up to be twenty years earlier.

For young men like the Sapienza brothers, stories like this were unsettling. Working midway between the "receiver" and the pushers, they were the wholesalers, or "connections," brought in from outside because they were fresh to the turf and would operate without the distractions of existing allegiances or prejudices. Presented with a crew of established pushers, their job was to control and regulate supply. In practical terms, this meant further diluting the heroin they received to make the shipment go further, cutting it with whatever white substance they could lay their hands on—harmless lactose powders if they were available, more sinister and lethal chemicals if they weren't.

However, the Sapienzas were investing their future and the future of their family in Don Genovese's new business. So what were they to make of these doubts that were starting to be raised about him?

Far from home, and with few friends, powerless and bewildered, they waited and worried and shared pack after pack of cigarettes.

Chapter Seventeen

Albert Anastasia was buried in Brooklyn during a private ceremony. Of course, neither Jack nor his mother could attend, though Jack had given Frank some flowers to take on his and his mother's behalf. While Albert was being laid to rest, Jack studied his father's letter—in the library after school and in bed before he fell asleep. Slowly but surely, Jack was determined to understand the importance of what he was being told.

Then, the Saturday of Thanksgiving weekend, Jack boarded the train at Camden again. Folks were at home for the holiday and the station was almost deserted. Jack made his way toward the railroad yard. He wasn't sure when it had begun, but after a minute or two he had become aware of a slightly built man, no more than five feet five, walking beside him. Nobody had mentioned any companions to him.

His pulse raced. The cops. They must know. Must have seen him coming and going from the meetings. The fancy hotel, all of it.

Worse. It was the government. The federal agencies had Jack Pagano on their radar. They were keeping a file on him, on his family. They watched his mother as she cooked dinner and cleaned the living room. Jack hadn't been back to the Hole, but somehow they must know about Rip too.

Even worse still. Vito Genovese was on to him. He'd heard that Albert Anastasia had made some peculiar stops before that fateful morning that found him closed-eyed in a barber chair. This man was a hired gun. He'd sneak up close to Jack. Shove the heavy gun between his ribs and fire, using Jack's body to silence the blast. He'd do it in a quiet corner, where no one would see them.

Beads of sweat began to trickle down Jack's back.

"I think we should have a cup of tea." Jack turned his head and instantly recognized the face he knew from newspaper photographs.

Together they walked in silence, Jack allowing himself to be led to a small café in the train station, where they found seats on either side of a table in the corner and ordered tea. When the waitress had gone, the little man reached out his hand and said, "Let me introduce myself. My name is Meyer Lansky."

"Jack Pagano. I'm pleased to meet you, sir."

Lansky smiled and sat back in his chair, stretching his legs beneath the table. Jack guessed he was around Anastasia's age: mid-fifties. His nose was prominent like Frank Costello's, but his eyes and mouth were larger, making his face appear more open, more approachable somehow. His dress was less distinctive than Frank Costello's as well. Where Costello could have passed for a swanky Midtown attorney, Meyer Lansky looked like a regular commuter. One of the thousands who travelled the railroad through New Jersey to New York weekdays. Dressed in a white shirt and white T-shirt, the only thing that set him apart was his suit. Well-cut, it was made of high-quality cloth; Jack could tell that at a glance.

"I understand you're a very open-minded young man, with the ability to listen well. I'll lay the rules down right now so there is no misunderstanding. We'll meet just like we did back there. You'll never call me direct. I will give you certain telephone numbers to leave a message that will reach me—but only if it's an emergency. We do not have casual chit-chat, you and me. We will not infringe on each other's world. Just know that you are never alone."

"Okay," Jack answered. "I know what you mean, Mr. Lansky."

"I think you understand that this is purely business, don't you? And that you don't ever let anything mess with business. You see that too?"

Jack nodded as he sipped his tea.

"That's good. And save the Mr. Lansky deal. You call Frank, Frank. So call me Meyer, okay?"

"Sure."

Jack snapped a cookie in half and put a piece in his mouth.

Meyer Lansky took a sip of tea, placed his cup back on the saucer, and leaned across the table once more to tell Jack, "You know how this whole world plays, son? When you boil this world down it runs on two words: money and fear. Not fear of what I can do to you with a weapon, but fear of what I can do to you with my money. Because my money is much stronger than any weapon you can ever have. If you have a gun, I can use my money to buy a bigger gun. If you have a bomb, I can use my money to buy a bigger bomb; isn't that what Hiroshima showed the world? This whole ball of wax, kid, runs on those two words: money and fear. Don't ever confuse it. Money is really nothing. It's a commodity like oil and railroads. It changes like the wind. But respect it and understand it if you're going to use it. Because if you respect money and you understand money, people will fear you."

Jack leaned closer and lowered his voice. "Can I ask you about something Frank said to me? I guess money and fear comes into it."

"You can ask. I can't promise I'll answer, but go ahead."

"He said you could explain how narcotics fit into all that stuff Albert left for me."

Lansky kept his voice low. "Drugs and arms sales, that's how money is going to keep on growing. I know, because I see it happening already in Cuba, in Uncle Sam's backyard."

"Albert wrote about Cuba."

Cuba was Lansky's special domain. Listening to the little man describing how he had built the casino business on the island over thirty years, Jack began to understand more fully how men like Lansky and Costello had established financial empires from gambling without ever being put away for it.

Lansky had been controlling gambling in Cuba since the 1930s, he told Jack, and there was real pride in the way he described the casinos and the shows he financed. "Batista has been on the payroll since he became dictator down there in '33. He mans the front desk so we can get on with business out back. I've had a lock on the casinos in Cuba for over twenty years and no one has ever muscled in on me. So, what do they do? They look for other businesses: drugs coming into America and weapons going out."

Jack hesitated to interrupt. "This is where Albert saw the danger, right?"

Lansky seemed pleased with that question and nodded.

"You've heard about Atlantic City, right?"

In fact, Atlantic City had taken up quite a bit of Albert's notes. Jack nodded that he was somewhat familiar with the subject.

"It was about stopping the wave of greed that had been gaining momentum," Lansky continued. "There was to be no more fighting between families, between cities, between anyone in business together. And after Atlantic City, Albert was going to see to that by any means necessary—he really excelled at that sort of thing. There was some serious money coming from bootlegging and gambling, and everyone could see the fortunes to be made from war and weapons."

The tea in Jack's cup was cold, but he drank it slowly; his mouth felt dry. He told Lansky some of what he remembered from the notes. Albert had written that though the meeting was definitive, there were still some smart-asses who thought the rules didn't include them. They thought if they were away from New York, away from Chicago, that they could do pretty much whatever they wanted.

John Bozzano was like that, Albert said. By the time they finally found Bozzano he was rolled up in a carpet and left in the gutter with twenty-two ice pick holes in him, his tongue cut out, and his mouth taped shut.

"Albert said that each of these was a sign," Jack concluded.

"Exactly." Meyer Lansky smiled at the memory. "Remember this, kid. Your father knew it well. The right sign and the right signal can make any message stick."

Jack wondered what exactly the signs had meant, but he didn't ask. He suspected their meanings were fairly obvious.

"Anyway, we went down to Atlantic City around this time of year. Early May, 1929. It was a crazy time. No respect for money. All the high rollers came in from New York: bankers, industrialists. Chicago pulled in all the other heavy money. Chicago sent Joe Kennedy, too, because this was going to be the kind of stock deal that Joe used to work in his sleep.

"The plan was to start selling short in the third week in October. When the market had dropped low, the money guys would move in to clean up the stock, make a killing, and take control of key industries."

"That was the plan. Only things changed when they saw what was happening. Men like Joe Kennedy, who'd been down this road before, saw their chance to hit the jackpot big time. Instead of going back into the market like it had been planned, they sat on their hands and watched it fall like a stone. By October 24, Wall Street was out the plane without a parachute. Billions of dollars were wiped off share values. There were eleven suicides in New York alone that day. And when the markets hit the bottom, Kennedy and the others moved in like vultures and swallowed up everything right across the market: manufacturing, banking, insurance—you name it, they had it, and for a bargain basement price, too.

"But see here, it wasn't only the fat cats who took a beating. What Kennedy and the others who worked the Crash did hit all the small investors real hard. Some people lost everything. Worse still they lost their independence, their freedom to choose to live how they wanted. Sure, the government stepped in with soup kitchens and welfare handouts, but they bought and owned those poor suckers just like they own them still.

"That ain't the way business should work. You want more from somebody, you don't squeeze them dry so there ain't nothing left. You put another loaf of bread on their table. They like you because you make life better for them. You give them bread, so they work harder, work better. They make more money, so you make more money. It may take a bit longer to find its way back, but you get your money in the end and you get a whole lot more besides, because when you put a loaf of bread on the table, that money keeps on flowing."

When he spoke again there was softness in his voice. "Albert wants you to follow your own path, Jack. He doesn't want you getting involved with crews. He wants you to stay clear of the bullshit on the streets. That way you can be your own man, walk your own line. You've got what it takes to stay on the tracks he's laid down for you. I can see that; Frank can, too."

Jack lowered his voice again to ask, "And what about this stuff for you and Frank Costello? How do we work that?"

Meyer Lansky raised an eyebrow. "You have a very direct way of asking questions."

Jack apologized, anxious he had overstepped the mark.

"I'll take it as a compliment you feel you can say things like this to me. Only be very careful about the people you speak to in that way. Never let anyone see what you are thinking unless you trust them with your life. Take that as a first lesson from me."

"I appreciate it." Jack summoned up a smile of reassurance.

Lansky looked at his watch. "I think there's a train back to Philadelphia in six minutes."

Jack took his cue and got to his feet. Lansky stood so they could shake hands.

"Thank you for my tea," Jack told him, squeezing out of the table and making his way out of the café.

"You're welcome," came the reply as the door swung shut behind him.

Joe Kennedy. Meyer Lansky had uttered the name with such disgust. Jack didn't know quite how he fit into all this yet. There were pieces, sure. Plenty of pieces of the mosaic Albert had written about, but the picture still hadn't quite come together. But Jack could start to see the outlines, the basic framework. And all those pieces that didn't quite fit, Jack carefully filed them away, keeping them always at the back of his thoughts.

Chapter Eighteen

After the Apalachin debacle back in the fall, Bruno Pafundi had worked hard to keep a lid on things on the street.

Beat cops who used to be content to pocket their weekly payment and leave Pafundi's men to go about their business had started to become leery. They never refused the money, but for a while some of Pafundi's boys were picked up when they shouldn't have been; from what he heard from other parts of the city, the same went for every borough. Apalachin had turned the spotlight on business everywhere, and everyone caught in its glare was feeling the heat.

If anything, the situation was worse on the waterfront, where state and federal narcotics agents were swarming like rats through the holds of ships arriving from suspicious ports in the Middle East and Europe.

This interrupted supplies right down the line.

"If we cut this shit any more, we'll be selling flour," Bernardo Sapienza had complained to Pafundi in a colorful burst of Sicilian. "And Mario and me didn't come to America to be bakers."

On the street, the price of junk had risen rapidly. As addicts became desperate, they had resorted to mindless, reckless criminality. In Pafundi's patch, one of the regular junkies had been shot dead in the futile act of trying to steal money from a Western Union office armed with a broken bottle.

Pafundi had done what he could to smooth things over. He'd slipped Bernardo an extra hundred bucks to keep him sweet. He arranged with a pimp who operated with his permission to let the Sicilian boys enjoy a pair of his hookers at a generous discount.

Genovese's underboss had shown his face around his turf, glad-handing it with the cops, dropping by coffee shops and diners to spread reassurance and good cheer. And when a couple of wise guys from the neighboring patch had tried muscling in on Pafundi's numbers operation, they woke up with cracked ribs and faces so bruised nobody recognized them when they turned up in hospital beds.

All the same, this was no way to carry on business. Vito Genovese was keeping his head down someplace outside the city. Pafundi spoke to him by telephone, but Don Vitone was guarded in what he said. Maybe he was worried there was a tap on the line, Pafundi didn't know. What he did know was that the voice on the other end was seething with rage, but he didn't have anything constructive to say.

"We ain't a fucking charity," Genovese had berated Pafundi when the underboss had complained that his crew was having a hard time as a result of Apalachin. "Tell those assholes to get out there and get working," Genovese ordered. "They'll be happy enough when supplies pick up as usual. We ain't got no production problems. Everything in Sicily is running as smooth as silk. You tell them that. And tell them to cut out the whining."

Pafundi had absorbed the message and passed it on. But even he was starting to wonder how much longer Vito Genovese could hold his sprawling empire together.

Chapter Nineteen

With the end of high school came the college selection process. Jack liked to think that he owed the succession of enticing offers to his football prowess, but he couldn't be sure about that. His father's associates pulled strings everywhere. Judged against that, what value could he place on his own abilities?

Coach Sullivan had persuaded Jack to look at several prestigious schools, all of which were eager to offer Jack football scholarships. But Jack already knew that he would be enrolling at the University of Miami. The Hurricanes, the University of Miami football team, had an enviable reputation and presented a natural destination for a player of Jack Pagano's skill. Though, in truth, this was Albert Anastasia's choice.

No questions. No discussion.

Meyer Lansky's business interests in the state and the close proximity to Cuba made it the only school on Jack's radar.

He made his first visit to Florida as Cooper Park was still shaking off its winter cloak. Stepping out of the airplane into the dazzling sunlight and tropical breeze wafting over Miami International Airport, the contrast with grey, cloud-covered Haddonfield had him blinking with surprise as he adjusted his eyes.

Frank Costello and Meyer Lansky were staying at the recently opened Fontainebleau Hotel in Miami Beach, where a room had been reserved for Jack as well. "You can take some time to look around your new school," Lansky had explained, "and Frank and me can spend some time with you, too." It would be Jack's first meeting with the two of them together.

Meyer Lansky had told him that almost anyone seeing Miami Beach for the first time was amazed. "Forty years ago it was nine miles of beach and swamp islands. Today, you got nearly four hundred hotels, the most expensive and luxurious you'll find any place. On Lincoln Road, you got a mile of Fifth Avenue shopping. Top quality golf courses. Sun, sand, and the ocean. But I tell you," Lansky had continued, "the best thing about Miami Beach is that it only exists because it gives people what they want. It's like Las Vegas on the beach."

Lansky hadn't exaggerated. The view was breathtaking. The taxi turned onto Collins Avenue running beside the beach for the full length of the island, a golden stripe disappearing into the distance, flanked by the ocean darkening to a deep blue as it stretched away to the horizon. On the other side of the road resort hotels flashed by in dazzling white, pink, and pastel green, fronted by palm-shaded pools and lush tropical gardens.

The taxi lurched to a stop next to the wide curve of a white building that was more glass than not. The driver took a crumpled wad of bills from Jack, who nodded, as if to say he wouldn't need change.

Inside, men in panama hats, sandals, and heavily patterned tropical shirts worn outside their pants drifted about with women in voluminous summer dresses. There were sunglasses everywhere. Jack checked in nervously and took the elevator to his room with its stunning vista over the twenty-acre tropical garden and the wide expanse of the ocean beyond.

Frank Costello called on the house telephone twenty minutes later. "Come on up," he said cheerfully. "There's someone Meyer and me want you to meet."

Jack didn't waste any time.

Costello greeted him dressed in a lightweight pale blue suit and matching shirt and tie. "Three-letter guy," he told Jack quietly at the door. "He's okay, but you should know." Then he let Jack in and said in a louder voice, "Meyer's outside." He waved his hand toward a wide balcony decorated with tubs of exotic flowers, low tables, and steamer chairs. He offered Jack a drink.

"Can I have a Coke, please?"

"With a dash of rum?"

"A Coke will be fine."

Costello fixed himself something from the well-stocked cocktail bar and led the way outside across the deep pile carpet.

Meyer Lansky was lying against the striped cushions of a steamer chair wearing a long-sleeved cream-colored sports shirt buttoned up to his neck, yellow cotton pants, white socks and sneakers. There was another man in a light beige linen suit standing at the rail with his back to Jack, looking out to the ocean.

"Miller, this is our young man." Lansky turned to Jack. "I'd like you to meet an old friend of ours, and your father's."

The man at the rail turned to face Jack with a smile. Miller wore wire-framed sunglasses, the kind Jack had seen worn by pilots.

He offered his hand. Jack shook it firmly.

"I've heard a lot about you," Miller told him. "I'm very pleased to meet you at last."

"Nice to meet you too, sir," Jack told him. There was something about him that made Jack think of Rip Collins. His build perhaps? This man must have been about Rip's age. He had the same trim physique. His hair had the same salt-and-pepper coloring as Rip's.

Lansky gestured for the men to sit. "So, was I right about Miami Beach, or was I right?"

"I'd say you were right on the money. I've never seen anywhere like this."

"Wait till you see our places in Havana," the little man told him. Lansky then reached for the tall glass of lemonade on the table beside him. "I got a penthouse in the Riviera that looks like a palace."

"I should say," Miller answered.

"Miller and Frank and me have been working together in Cuba since the thirties," Lansky explained. "Your father, too, Jack."

Miller removed his glasses and patted Jack's arm. "It was terrible what happened to Albert. Pointless and wasteful. A great loss to us all."

The men all smiled and nodded, and Jack did the same.

Miller continued. "Your father and I got to know each other well during the war. There was a lot of high-level intelligence being leaked to the Germans. The OSS, the government agency detailed to handle it, needed a break, and it was your father gave it to them. Courtesy of Meyer."

Lansky lifted his glass in a toast that Miller returned. "What are friends for?"

"Albert and his brother, your uncle, Tony Anastasio, had the inside track on everything that moved in and out of the harbors. They gave us the leads we needed. They persuaded Charlie Luciano to help out. And those leaks dried up pretty quick."

Jack tried to recall Albert Anastasia's account of the same event.

"We worked together in Europe and Latin America, as well as here in the States. We had a lot of common interests. That's why I feel sore about what happened to Charlie. They made a deal with him and they cheated on it."

"We all know who to blame," Costello told him. "Those schmucks in Washington. They'd sell their grandmothers if they thought there was something in it for themselves."

"I guess you're right," Miller replied. "But it still doesn't make me feel too good about what happened."

"Maybe helping out with this narcotics business will let you set the record straight," Lansky added.

"Let's hope so." Miller breathed on the lenses of his sunglasses and wiped them clear with a handkerchief. "Things are starting to get serious. Real serious. You know there are over three hundred thousand American tourists streaming into Havana every year. You're the numbers man. You tell me how many potential carriers that is. And that doesn't count what's being shipped into New Orleans and Galveston and who knows where else."

Frank Costello returned with a freshly filled glass that he placed on the table beside Miller.

"I know you believe Batista has got everything back under control. But my sources tell me that this Castro guy is no slouch. Okay, he's tried twice in the last six years to get rid of Batista and failed both times—but he's a determined fucker, and Batista don't have many friends in Cuba. You know what I mean?"

"No," Costello responded. "You think we're going to let go of our greatest asset? You think we're going to let some Commie hobo from the hills take it away from under our noses?"

"That's not what I mean, Frank. Don't you think I know you better than that? Where would Castro be if Meyer wasn't making proper arrangements? You don't buy guns and feed an army with fresh air and mountain hooch. You got too much to lose in Cuba. Of course you're putting money Castro's way as well as Batista's. It's good economics."

"Well, I'm glad we're agreed about that," Lansky said, unable to keep himself from laughing.

Nobody else joined him.

Miller held up his hand in acknowledgement and also to finish what he was saying. "What worries me is what will happen if Cuba becomes real unstable. We can see already what's happening when you lose the kind of control Albert had—and that's in our back yard. Cuba could be a hundred times worse. Genovese is building up his operation from Sicily. Here's another island, just off the mainland—like Sicily—and a whole lot closer to the United States. Add to that the cocaine business coming up from down south. Tell me if I'm wrong, but it seems like Cuba is the perfect way-station for narcotics shipments into this country."

"Of course, you're not wrong," Costello answered glumly.

Meyer Lansky sat up and set his glass back on the table. "This is why we need to get to work." He turned his gaze to Jack. "It's why we need this young man to help us."

He felt uneasy with all three of them looking at him. Before, as they bickered back and forth, it felt like it was all just an act.

This opulent penthouse suite, the shining sun, the expensive cars rolling along the streets below—it felt like a stage. Now the actors were staring back at him, waiting for him to deliver his lines, and he wasn't sure he'd even read the script. "I'll do what I can, but I don't see how I can be much use to you gentlemen. I mean, well, you know people in places I've never heard of."

"It's not people like that we need right now," Lansky told him. "We have to find out what's happening across the board, what's really happening. You understand?"

Frank Costello picked up what his friend was saying. "It's like I told you already, Jack. We can point you in the right direction, but we've got to have someone invisible and someone reliable to do the looking and listening." He paused to take a sip from his glass, watching Jack's reaction. "Now you've met Miller. You can see this game is serious and you can see who our partners are—just like Albert told you. Am I right?"

Jack felt his throat tightening. "Yes, Frank."

Miller's replaced his sunglasses and turned to face Jack "We know what use you will be to us, as you put it. The question is, how much do you have to convince yourself?"

That went to the core of Jack's dilemma. And gazing out across the ocean under the warm Miami sun, he honestly didn't know.

Chapter Twenty

Barely a week after school had ended, Jack found the answer.

Miller was in Philadelphia and telephoned to say he'd like to get together, that there was something he wanted to talk over with him.

Jack was intrigued.

Lansky and Costello were becoming familiar; but Miller was an enigma. Jack had listened with fascination as the three of them had talked and Miller made no attempt to disguise his work in U.S. intelligence, which Jack found reassuring and mildly flattering. Miller clearly regarded him as someone who could be trusted with sensitive information. Lansky and Costello had vouched for Jack's integrity and that had been enough for this "three-letter guy" to be completely open with him. He was Albert Anastasia's son and that had been all Miller needed to know. This was an endorsement Jack hadn't sought or expected, and yet, there it was. Here was another man who had great respect for Anastasia, another man like Rip who was prepared to hold the son in the same high regard.

But if Jack got a secret kick out if it, it was also deeply troubling. Miller was a government man. Someone on the other side of the law. Jack wasn't entirely sure what to make of him.

Miller suggested they meet at Philadelphia's 30th Street Station. The morning rush had passed and they found a quiet corner of a coffee shop where they could talk undisturbed. Miller took the corner seat, which gave him a clear view of the entrance, the bar, and the passage through to the washroom. Sitting in the corner seat meant his back was covered, too.

They talked about high school and college. Miller showed interest in Jack's football plans, remarking that travelling to Hurricanes' games could provide a useful cover for other trips he might need to make.

Jack registered that. Miller was a pro and was grooming him accordingly.

The conversation switched to other aspects of college life. How much did Jack know about the business school he would be attending? Had he fixed his accommodation yet? Miller's questions were probing, but courteous. They invited Jack to open up and answer freely. Being with Miller made him feel comfortable, though he realized later that he'd found out almost nothing about the man himself. Jack didn't even know his first name. Lansky and Costello referred to him simply as Miller and Jack had simply followed their example.

They got a second cup of coffee and Jack had nearly finished his when Miller's tone changed. "There's something every one of our sabotage teams goes through right before they get sent into the field, Jack. They can have all the training and planning, but that can't prepare them for the way they're going to react when their lives are on the line. So this is what we do. We send them on a mission with blank charges. Everything else is like the actual mission: reconnaissance, infiltration, installation, and withdrawal. And the thing that makes it for real is that they get sent into some place where the guards are trained to kill on contact. When our teams go in, they know the guards won't have any prior warning about what's happening. As far as they're concerned, our guys could be the first wave of a Soviet strike. If they're found, the only way out is in a body bag. That's what gives those missions the edge—for them and for us.

"When it comes to their business, Meyer and Frank are the best," Miller continued. "There's no one to touch them and I've met some heavy operators, I assure you. But these things they may want you to do—Frank and Meyer ain't done stuff like that for years. They forget what it's like. They don't know the way things have changed. And you? You don't know what it's like at all. But in this game nothing can be left to chance. Albert was careful. You have to be too. And there's one way to be sure."

"What's that?" Jack asked, unsure that he really wanted the answer.

"Go on a real-life trial."

"Like the ones you were just talking about?"

"Not exactly," Miller answered, "but something to show you how well you can move in, get what's needed, and clear out without being detected."

"So how does this work with me? What kind of test have you got in mind?"

Jack could see the point, but he couldn't see himself sneaking up to some high-security installation with a backpack filled with dummy explosive.

Miller leant forward in order to speak quietly. "First, let me ask you something. How much do you know about the investigation into Albert Anastasia's killing?"

"Only what I read in the newspapers."

"Okay. How much is there in the newspapers now about that case?"

"Not a lot, I guess."

"Don't you think the police would be making a big deal about it if they were on to something? Wouldn't they want to make a big splash in the newspapers if they knew who they were looking for? The police don't know who to go after. It looks like whoever it was shot your old man is going to go unpunished, unless someone else finds them. And that would have very serious consequences. Anyone who could take out Albert Anastasia and get away with it might think they could do whatever they want to whoever they like. Do you follow what I'm telling you?"

"I think so."

"Good. Because I've got a lead on the men who did the hit on your old man."

In a way, Jack wasn't surprised by what Miller had said. That was the kind of work he did, after all. The shock that surged through Jack came from the idea that Miller was expecting him to go after them—to kill these men in the way Murder, Incorporated used to deal with its targets.

"Look, this is not anything I should be doing. It's not what Albert wanted, and it sure as hell isn't what Frank, or Meyer, or Rip would ever think of asking."

He pushed back his chair and made to leave, but Miller grabbed his arm. "Steady there. You got me all wrong. A job like that is the last thing I would ask you to do. Can't you see that? What do you take me for, Jack? Some greenhorn? No, that has to be a professional job. More importantly, it's got to be seen to be a professional job. So don't go jumping to conclusions that ain't there."

"Then what is it you want me to do?"

"I need to be sure. I've got to know that this information is one hundred percent accurate before anyone does anything."

"Why do you need me? Why can't you check this out yourself?"

Miller leaned closer so their heads were almost touching. "You remember Vito Genovese—the man Meyer, Frank, and me talked about in Miami Beach?"

"Yeah, I remember. Meyer has talked about him, too."

"My information is that Genovese ordered the hit on Albert, but he wanted to make it look like it was another narcotics boss. Have you heard of Carmine Galante?"

The name meant nothing to Jack.

"Genovese knows me as well as Albert did. Genovese had to take time out in Italy before the war. He was running the black market in Naples when I caught up with him. Mussolini's foreign minister, his son-in-law—that guy, Ciano—relied on Vito Genovese to keep him fixed up with heroin. So we borrowed those contacts, and made good use of them after the war when it looked like Italy might go communist. Genovese got to come home, so everyone was happy."

He sat back to let Jack digest what he had said. "Now do you see why this has to be done by someone else?"

"Sure, but I still don't know that I…"

"You won't be alone. There's a guy I have in mind to go along with you. A street guy, someone your father knew. He'll take care of everything. I just need you to watch and listen and then tell me what you see and hear. If the names stack up, then we can decide what needs to be done. But first I have to have that information."

Miller's proposition was starting to look more reasonable, but Jack had serious misgivings. "What about Frank and Meyer? Do they know about this?"

Miller shook his head. "No. And they mustn't. That's part of the test. I want to see if you can move in and out of this without either of them getting to hear about it. If you can do this kind of operation and without them knowing, that proves you're able to operate pretty much anywhere. This is why I need Joe to go along with you."

"Joe?"

Miller reflected for a moment and then gave Jack his partner's name. "Joe Gordon. He's the one who'll be with you. Joe worked with your old man. He was one of Albert's best boys. Sharp as a razor, cold as steel. Albert sent Joe to help out with some government work that needed handling quietly with no fuss. He did it all right. That's how I met him. Joe stuck to Albert like glue. He'd have died for your dad, if Albert had asked him. That's why I want Joe to be with you. Remember what Frank said about your back being covered every place you go? Here's the proof. Albert didn't trust too many people to know about you, but Joe Gordon was one of them."

"What about Rip? And my mom?"

"You'll tell them you're spending the weekend in New York with a friend. You'll be in and out of Detroit inside thirty-six hours. You and I will meet in New York, at Penn Station, and then you'll catch the train home. Mission accomplished."

"Detroit? Where does Detroit fit in?

"My information is that Genovese brought Albert's killers in from outside. They came from Detroit."

"And all I have to do is a reconnaissance job with this guy Gordon?"

"I need names and identification, Jack. That's all. Joe and I will take care of everything—don't you worry about that."

Jack tried to get clear in his head what Miller had told him. Was this what the training with Rip had been building to? Jack had been told he'd never be alone. From Albert, from Rip. Frank and Meyer had made the same promise too. Am I really going to flunk the first test? How would Rip feel about that? And Miller? Here's a hotshot CIA man trusting me with a critical assignment. Would he really be doing that, if I'm not up to it?

But it didn't add up, couldn't. Why couldn't anyone know?

There was a cacophony of voices shouting at him, urging him to do this or that. But, steadily, one voice grew louder, rising above them all. "My blood runs in your veins. It always will," Albert Anastasia was repeating to his son.

Chapter Twenty-One

It wasn't difficult for Jack to convince his mother he was going to New York for the weekend. He'd been making private visits like this for the past few months, and she knew better than to ask too many questions; the same went for Rip.

Early in the morning, three days after meeting Miller, Jack was back at the 30th Street Station skimming through the *Philadelphia Inquirer* with one eye glued on the coffee shop.

Five minutes before they were due to meet, he saw Miller cross the echoing concourse. Walking with him was a scrawny-looking man in a crumpled suit and a hat that had seen better days. He looked like a pickpocket walking in lockstep to the police car with an arresting officer.

Joe Gordon greeted Jack with a furtive sideways glance. "How you doing?"

Somehow, Jack had it in his head that Gordon would be younger. With his hat removed, he could have been Rip's age. Gordon's hairline receded almost to the top of his head, made his face look narrow and pinched.

Over coffee, Miller outlined their itinerary with clipped precision. After taking the train to New York, traveling in separate cars, they were to make their way to a private airfield near Teaneck, New Jersey—across the Hudson River from upper Manhattan. A light aircraft piloted by a contact of Miller's would fly them west to Buffalo, New York, where the Magaddino family held sway throughout northern New England, Ohio, and Ontario. A car would be waiting for them, courtesy of Stefano Magaddino himself. Magaddino would also ease their passage over the border into Canada, where they were to take the road west to Tillsonburg and then north to hook up with the highway linking Toronto with Windsor, Ontario, and Detroit. Gordon seemed familiar with the details and simply grunted along as if bored by the conversation.

Miller checked his watch and got to his feet. He handed Jack a ticket. "Time for your train. See you Sunday, in New York."

Gordon slapped his hat on the back of his head, picked up his bag, and answered through a smile lined with crooked teeth, "See you around, Miller."

Joe Gordon didn't have a lot to say for himself: a few mumbled directions in New York City, a shouted comment above the noise of the airplane engines to explain Jack's presence to the pilot at Teaneck, and an exchange of wisecracks with Magaddino's wheelman, whom Gordon appeared to know.

Most of the journey passed more or less in silence, which suited Jack. If he'd had any objections to the plan, he couldn't bring himself to mention them. Any uncertainty had been drowned out by thoughts of Albert Anastasia, by thoughts of his father. Now, he waited quietly, running through what was about to happen in his mind.

He envisaged the two of them cautiously staking out the address Miller had given, taking clandestine photographs perhaps, maybe tailing Miller's suspect on foot, hoping he would lead them to the other men who had killed Albert Anastasia.

Would they operate together?

Separately, Jack decided. They made an incongruous pair.

Dusk was falling as they crossed the bridge over the Detroit River and drove back into the US. The man they were seeking lived alone in a nondescript apartment in a street you could find in any industrial city. Miller's details had been brief and to the point. The target's name was Louis Reggio. He worked as a line foreman at Goodyear Tires, and the address Miller had given them turned out to be in a blue-collar district close to the factory.

Gordon parked a few blocks away and the two of them walked casually through the darkened streets. He'd told Jack to leave his bag behind, though Jack saw him take something from his own when he lifted it from the trunk. To Jack's amazement, they walked straight to the address Miller had given them.

Gordon pushed open the door into the hallway and made for the stairs. "Keep your mouth shut and your ears open."

Reggio's apartment was on the third floor. Reggio kept his address private; he didn't have casual visitors.

Jack could hear the muted mumble of a television on the other side of the door.

Gordon knocked.

This was not the quiet bit of eyes-and-ears work Jack had been expecting. No, he suspected this was something entirely different than what Miller had told him he'd be doing. Certainly they couldn't just walk up to the apartment door and ask the man what they wanted to know.

"What do you want?" Reggio wasn't yet eying them through the peephole, but Jack was sure he would be soon.

"Union business," Gordon answered. "Fitzsimmons could use a little help."

The names meant nothing to Jack. He hadn't heard this part of the plan and didn't know if Gordon was just improvising or had hatched this part of the scheme with Miller.

The man who opened the door was in his mid-thirties, five foot nine, and going fat beneath his stained T-shirt, though his broad chest suggested he might have been powerfully built in his time. He checked the two ends of the hallway. "So Fitzsimmons sent you?"

"Yeah," said Gordon, swaggering inside ahead of Jack, a hand pressed into his coat pocket. "It's about the shipments down to Akron. Fitzsimmons thinks those tires should be going by truck. He'd like some help to arrange that. He don't like to see the Teamsters losing business to the shipping companies."

Jack marveled at what was happening, hardly able to keep the look of surprise from his face.

Reggio closed the door. "Is that so? What do I get out of it?"

"This." Gordon whipped around, punching Reggio viciously in the groin. Reggio sank to his knees, gasping in agony. The light of the naked bulb hanging from the ceiling momentarily flashed on the glinting knuckle-duster before a crunching blow to the skull sent Reggio sprawling onto the thin carpet.

Jack was paralyzed. Rip had taught him what a blow like that could do. For all he knew, Gordon could have just killed Reggio.

But the Goodyear foreman was tougher than his bulging gut suggested. Before Reggio had time to react, Gordon grabbed him by the hair, pulled back his head, and shoved the barrel of a .38 into his mouth. "Don't give me any bullshit. I don't have time to play."

He wrenched Reggio's head around toward Jack. "I brought you a little surprise," he snarled. "Take a good look at this kid, a real good look, because you may see a family likeness."

Gordon thrust the gun barrel deeper into the man's throat. "No?" Gordon mocked. "His old man was Albert Anastasia."

"What the hell are you doing?" Jack yelled. What would Miller say, let alone Lansky and Costello?

"Shut it, kid." Gordon dragged Reggio to his feet. "Me and this punk have some business to conclude. I worked with your old man since I was your age. I owe him this." With the gun pressed against the roof of Reggio's mouth, he pushed him into the bathroom and crashed backward into the tub.

Gordon sneered at the terrified man. "I don't need you to see nothing no more, but maybe this will help loosen your tongue nice and quick."

From the doorway, Jack watched in sickened horror as Gordon jammed his left thumb into the corner of the Reggio's right eye and pushed down until the eye popped out of its socket and dangled against his cheek.

"Take your last look, asshole," Gordon said, leaning over him. Then Reggio was sent writhing and thrashing in agony. Gordon crushed Reggio's eye like a grape. He drew a knife from down by his ankle and held it in front of Reggio's good eye, then laid it against his neck, and pulled the gun out of his mouth. "Are you going to tell me who set you up to whack this kid's old man?"

"Galante, Carmine Galante," answered the man in the tub.

"I don't think so. Try a different name." Gordon slowly increased the pressure of the knife blade. "How about the real name, for instance?"

"The real name? I don't know the real name," Reggio wailed. "Nobody does. This fella don't use no real name. Ask...H... Hus...Hussss...Askee..."

Louis Reggio's speech gave way to gurgling. Gordon threw a towel over his face and pushed the blade through Reggio's throat.

Jack saw the bright red stain spread through the towel.

The violent contortions of Reggio's body sent his arms and legs flailing into the wall. The thick wet sound as he tried to scream nearly made Jack vomit. If the man didn't bleed out, Jack was sure he'd likely drown. "What are you doing? What about the others? How are we going to find them now?"

But Gordon's only concern was in finishing with Reggio. He turned on the faucet and sent the clear water pink and red as it circled the drain and disappeared into the pipes and sewers below. Then he started cutting the dead man out of his clothes. Jack was ordered to take Gordon's bag into the back room at the end of the passage and open the window onto the fire escape.

"Throw me the small bag and the hammer and chisel," he shouted to Jack. "Get the body bag ready and make it snappy. I want out of here."

Jack was in no position to argue. The image of Reggio's blood-smeared face and the raw red hole of his eye socket kept flashing through his mind. Where was the precision, the craft, the skill? Gordon might as well have started emptying the revolver into Reggio the moment he entered the door for all the information he had extracted.

Something wet thudded onto the floor beside him. He heard Gordon's angry voice up the hallway. "What the fuck are you playing at? Put the clothes in the little bag. Get the big one ready. And throw me the tools to break his fucking teeth, okay?"

The bloodstained towel and T-shirt and the newly soiled underwear nearly had Jack retching. His head was still spinning as the hallway began to rattle with a crashing and splintering burst. Gordon was shouting, but his voice was drowned out by other voices yelling louder. Jack caught isolated words.

"Police!"

"Bathroom!"

"Gun!"

And then a volley of shots that would be accounted for in the official report as "suspect killed resisting arrest" rang out in the tiny apartment.

More shouts and footsteps. An eruption of noise as the bodies piled through the shattered doorway. From somewhere beneath came the sounds of doors being kicked open and rooms being searched. There was an urgent hiss.

He heard someone call his name.

In the open window was a familiar silhouette.

"Miller? Is that you?"

Chapter Twenty-Two

It was a good five minutes before Jack's thoughts came back into focus. His recollection of what had happened came as a series of brief flashes. There was Miller's arm pulling him through the open window, the rattle of their feet as they raced down the fire escape, the sound of a car engine revving below. Voices shouting above, something blunt and heavy smashing against his leg as he dove into the back seat and slammed the door shut. The roar of the engine and tires screeching as the car sped away, a hail of bullets in its wake.

Jack sprawled out on the back seat breathing heavily, being flung from side to side as the car rolled and pitched around corners and darted across traffic-filled streets.

Jack elbowed himself upright. "What are you doing here, Miller?"

An arm shoved Jack back down into the seat. "Stay down. It's thanks to me you're still alive. Don't get your fucking head blown off now."

A few blocks later, the car slammed to a halt in the bowels of a narrow alley.

The rear door burst open and Jack was pulled out and bundled into the back seat of a dark-colored sedan parked farther down the alley.

Miller didn't bother looking back at Jack. "The plane's waiting for us. But you keep your head down until I tell you."

With his face pressed against the seat cushion, Jack soon lost sense of direction.

He closed his eyes, but burned into his brain was the tortured image of Frank Reggio's face drained of blood, the deathly white skin damp and rubbery and the gory red hole above his cheek sagging open.

Jack struggled to wind down the window. "I'm sorry, Miller."

A blast of cool air brushed his face followed by a gob of warm sticky fluid as he vomited into the Detroit night. Jack pulled out a handkerchief to wipe his face and blow his nose. He felt soiled and tarnished. He let the wind blow through his hair, as if it could somehow clear away everything that had happened with Joe Gordon.

Albert Anastasia's son had taken his first steps into his father's world and failed almost immediately. Worse than that, he had disobeyed one of his father's specific warnings. Jack recalled the words with a shudder: *My death is not to be talked about. And it is not to be avenged in the wrong way.*

"What are you doing here, Miller? How come you showed up at that apartment? How come Gordon killed that guy?"

The man in the front exploded with anger. "That son of a bitch! You say he killed the fucker?"

"I thought that's why you got me out."

"I wish it was. But it's a whole lot worse than that. Don't ask me how, but the cops must have had a lead on him. When I saw those cars arriving, I knew you were in deep shit."

"But you're supposed to be in New York? What are you doing in Detroit?"

"Just be glad that I am, kiddo." Then he added, "I don't want to think about what Costello and Lansky will say."

Jack didn't care to either.

Instead, he slept on the flight back to Teaneck. Once or twice the cold woke him and he saw Miller silhouetted in the glow of the instrument panel up by the pilot. If they were talking to each other, whatever they were saying was drowned out before it reached Jack. There was little to see out of the window. No lights shone up from the ground to mark their route back east. There was no horizon to draw them on. Jack fell asleep to the pounding throb of the engines.

Chapter Twenty-Three

In the dark, Jack recognized little of the drive to the city. Miller crossed the George Washington Bridge and followed the river downtown. Then he turned left for a few blocks before pulling into a street where he parked. The two of them entered an apartment building and had taken the elevator to the eighth floor, Jack remembered that much. The apartment Miller let them into seemed more of a hotel room than a home. Comfortably furnished and well appointed but soulless somehow, the rooms pristine and undisturbed.

The next morning, Miller was dressed and wearing the same clothes as the previous day. Jack followed the smell of coffee into the kitchen. There didn't seem to be anything to eat in the apartment.

Miller was sitting back in an armchair. He gestured for Jack to take a seat. "You want to talk me through what happened?"

A night's sleep had made it easier for Jack. He tried to stick to the facts—repeating word for word, as best he could, what Joe Gordon had said to him. He described the evening's events accurately and without emotion.

Miller listened intently. He didn't show any reaction when Jack described what had happened to Reggio, nor when the police broke in and the shooting started.

"That's when I heard you at the window," Jack finished.

Miller went over what Jack had told him. "Stupid, stupid fucker. Why didn't I see it coming? Revenge: that's all Joe was interested in. He didn't give a flying fuck about the others who killed Albert. All he wanted was to get one back for him."

"How did you think the police knew someone was in Reggio's apartment?" Jack asked. "And why did they break in? It's like they knew someone was going to be attacking him."

Miller shrugged, hardly acknowledging the question. "Lansky and Costello will not be happy with this. It's all my fault."

"It's not your fault Gordon went berserk. Surely they know he was one of Albert's top men. They'd probably have chosen him to go with me, just like you did."

Miller didn't look convinced.

The prospect of what could have happened if Miller hadn't been there made Jack's gut turn every time he thought about it. If the cops had found him in the bathroom with the body, he could be as dead as Joe Gordon, lying in some Detroit mortuary, awaiting identification. Miller had no way of knowing what Gordon was going to do, he reminded himself, as he ran through events from the first time Miller had suggested the practice run in Detroit.

They finished their coffee in uneasy silence. A little before midday, Miller dropped Jack outside the apartment building where Costello had told him to meet them,

"Good luck," he said with little conviction.

"Thanks," Jack answered. "Thanks, you know, for coming to get me out of there and all."

"What else could I do?"

Jack found Frank Costello and Meyer Lansky in an airy apartment. He wasn't expecting a comfortable reception, and he didn't get one. There was no shouting, no time wasted on recriminations. It was analytical. Dispassionate, businesslike.

Jack went through the same debriefing he had given Miller, acutely aware that, to his own ears, the story was becoming little more than words. The emotional, visceral connection was already beginning to wane, and this disturbed Jack, how easy he was finding it to get lost in the events slowly unravelling around him. He was careful to stick to the same script; he was certain that the two versions would be compared closely later.

His father's two friends heard him out in silence and looked noncommittal when he finished.

"You had to have a good reason for doing what you did," Costello said. "Miller has explained that it was his idea to send you into the field, so you could put your training with Rip to the test in a real situation. But this is not what your father would have wanted, Jack. We know that, and you know it as well."

Jack knew this was coming, but hearing it from someone of Lansky's experience and standing made the weight heavier to bear. He didn't try to put the blame on Miller, though. Jack understood why he had been sent to Detroit in secret. He had to be given a taste of the kind of action he had been trained for.

"This is why Albert has been careful to keep you out of all this street shit," Costello said, barely keeping his tone of annoyance in check. He pointed his finger at Jack. "So perhaps you understand better what he was getting at. Why your father kept you out of the way like he did. Why he got Meyer and me to watch over you when he wasn't around no more."

"It was wrong," Lansky added. "Okay, Miller should not have involved you in any of this eye-for-an-eye revenge stupidity. And he showed disrespect to Frank and me."

Jack stared at the pattern of the carpet, followed it across the room until it ran smack into the wall. He couldn't look either man in the face. They had made their point.

Frank lit a cigarette and walked over to the window, standing with his back to the room. "You had a close call last night, but you got away with it. That's what matters." Jack looked up and saw him brushing his fingertips over the side of his head where Gigante's bullet had left its telltale scar beneath his well-groomed hair.

Meyer Lansky leaned toward Jack. "Men like Miller don't take many hostages. They're pros at this game. That's how they've gotten where they have—how they've stayed alive. It may have been Miller's idea for you to go to Detroit, but you agreed to it. You were willing to take the risk as much as he was.

It's lucky for you he didn't leave anything to chance and pulled you out before the cops got to you. You owe Miller and don't think he'll let that go, because he won't—and you will answer for that when the time comes, rest assured."

The two men exchanged glances. It seemed implied that Miller was also lucky he hadn't left anything to chance—for his own sake.

Costello stubbed out his barely smoked cigarette and pulled up a chair to sit beside him. "Okay, maybe me and Meyer have had to reschedule things, but that's business. You know what people say when you fall off a horse—that you have to get right back in the saddle again. So this is what we think you should do—in Sicily."

"Sicily?" Jack repeated with surprise. "Sicily is…so far away."

"Of course it is," Costello said. "It needs to be. We've got to get you out of this country and quickly. A scuffle with some kids outside a diner, that's easy enough to make disappear. A murder though? Jack, you have to understand. This is no small thing. Right now, for you, Sicily is the perfect place. You have family there who can look out for you. Your old man had always planned for you to go visit the family. So now you can."

Jack's mind was racing. "How long will I need to be away? I have to start college in the fall."

Lansky waved his hand dismissively. "We've covered every base. Come back at the end of the summer; everything will be taken care of."

"Does my mom know?"

"She knows Albert wanted you to go back to your roots, sure she does. But she'll understand why you need to go now."

"So you're going to tell her what happened yesterday?"

"No, no, we don't need to worry her with that," Frank answered.

Hearing that brought Jack considerable relief. Facing Costello and Lansky was enough of an ordeal, but explaining things to his mom was something he had really been dreading. Even so, doubts remained. "But how are you going to explain why I'm suddenly disappearing to Europe for the summer?"

Frank Costello gave him a reassuring pat on the arm. "It's time for you to go to work, Jack. Your mom will understand that. No problem. But for you, it's your chance to get straight back in the saddle. We don't have all the pieces in place yet, but it won't be long. And when they are, well…let's just say, you could make yourself useful out there. Real useful."

"By the time you get home today, your mom will know what's going to happen," Lansky said. "Do not worry, Jack."

Jack was having difficulty keeping pace with what was happening. "So, when do I leave?"

"Tomorrow," answered Costello. "On the Rome flight from Idlewild. A driver will collect you tomorrow afternoon."

"Tomorrow?" But I don't even have a passport."

"You will. You'll be given it at the airport with your ticket." Frank Costello gave a thin smile. The kid was young, he reminded himself. He still had a lot to learn. "What do you think me and Meyer have been doing all morning? Eating brunch?"

"Everything's taken care of," Lansky assured him. "You fly to Rome. Then you fly down to Sicily, to Catania. There you'll be in the safe hands of a dear friend who won't be too much of a stranger to you, even though you've never met him." He paused and started to smile. "Dominic Pagano is your mother's cousin. Nothing happens in the eastern half of Sicily without his approval. But you'll find that out for yourself."

Jack still looked uncertain.

"This is for the best, Jack," Costello told him firmly. "After what happened yesterday, it's good to do something your old man wanted, so you listen good to what Pagano tells you. Do what he tells you. You're family, remember—he don't take no risks with family."

Part II

Chapter Twenty-Four

More than eight months in New York had convinced Mario and Bernardo Sapienza that the business they had come to America with such high hopes to build wasn't rolling out the way they had expected.

They tried to stick to the plan laid down for them, but the pushers they supplied proved unreliable. Bruno Pafundi seemed to be losing interest in them, too. At first, he had been helpful. The Sapienzas still giggled together about the hookers he had laid on for them. But recently, Pafundi was distracted. He was late for meetings. One time he hadn't shown up at all.

"This city is like a jungle," Bernardo told his brother. "Everyone is like a wild animal, out for what they can get for themselves."

"Isn't that what we want too?"

"Of course it is. What I'm saying is—we aren't getting it. We haven't been getting what we want since we arrived."

Mario shrugged his shoulders. "Maybe. But what is there we can do about it?"

"We can be like the beasts in the jungle." Bernardo tapped the side of his nose with his index finger. "No one here gives a shit about you and me. I say the time has come for us to go our own way. We know the business. We know the customers. All we need is one big shipment, Mario. If we clean up on that, we can take the money and get back home before anyone here can do anything about it."

For a moment, his brother sat in silent amazement. Bernardo had never spoken so forthrightly before. This was what America had done to him. It had made him bold and fearless. Had it made him foolish as well?

"How could we do this?" Mario asked. "How could we get what we need to make so much money so quickly?"

"Everyone is thinking like me. They all want to make more money for themselves. I say we make it look like we are helping them."

"But how do we do this? Who do we help, as you put it?"

"We find a new supplier—in secret. We do a deal with him for a bigger share of his shipment than we get from Pafundi. Let's say he gives us a quarter, maybe a half, of his junk. We offer him all the pushers and junkies in our patch, plus a whole lot more he don't know about in the patches of our neighbors. Only there are no other junkies or pushers. And this time we don't give our pushers their heroin either.

"Instead, we set up another secret deal with another 'connection' some place different. Philadelphia, perhaps. We say we're part of a new business that's come over from Sicily. People will be expecting this after that meeting in Palermo last year. So, we sell all the junk we have to this other wholesale guy. We take his money and we get the next boat home. And the best part is we tell our new buyer that it is not for Don Genovese that we are working, but for Carmine Galante."

"You have it all worked out." Mario admired the ingenuity of his brother's plan. "How do we find these people, the men to give us the bigger share of the shipment and the other man to sell it to?"

Bernardo winked at him and grinned. "Leave that to me. I have made enquiries already—and there is much interest in the kind of trade I am proposing."

Chapter Twenty-Five

The smell of hot tarmac and aviation fuel, blending with the tang of oranges and lemons from nearby orchards, wafted into the aircraft as the door sprung open at the airport in Catania. The passengers filed down the steps, pushed into place by two swarthy men wearing oily overalls unbuttoned to the waist.

Jack's shirt was soaked with sweat by the time he had walked across the concourse and into the stifling atmosphere of the echoing airport building. He wasn't alone for long.

He had only just put down his bag to look around at the melee of passionate greetings and excited exchanges when he became aware of two men making straight for him. Thickset, a few years older than Jack, they were dressed in dark-colored pants, open-neck shirts, and jackets that would have benefited from a pressing from Jack's mom's iron.

They stopped in front of the new arrival, unsmiling and uncompromising.

"We have come to get you," one of them said. It was English, sure, but it took Jack a few moments for the words to make sense. He wondered if this would be a recurring theme on his trip and hoped that it wouldn't be. Talking to Lansky and Costello was an exercise in processing information as quickly as possible. He couldn't imagine having to do that through the haze of an unfamiliar accent.

Jack reached down for his bag, but the other man shot out a hand and had taken it before Jack's fingers reached the handle.

"My name is Marco Alliata. This is my brother Angelo." The

man who had greeted him nodded toward the entrance doors, beyond which cars and taxis were milling around. "This way."

"Jack Pagano," he replied, extending his hand.

Alliata ignored the gesture. "I know. The car is waiting."

He led the way through the crowd and out to a dusty Alfa-Romeo parked by itself in front of a sign clearly marked, "Polizia."

Angelo loaded Jack's bag into the trunk and then opened the front passenger door to let him inside before getting into the back. Marco Alliata got behind the steering wheel and started the engine. Jack noticed that he didn't take the ignition key from his pocket; it had been in the dashboard all along.

Marco drove with one hand on the steeringwheel and his elbow resting in the open window. He threw the Alfa into blind corners and accelerated out of them confident in his own quick reactions and disdainful of other road users. Neither he nor Angelo said much to Jack. They didn't appear to have any interest in him at all.

Jack couldn't relax in their presence. He was still sweating despite the breeze blowing through the car.

Mount Etna towered ahead of them. The volcano dominated the horizon and the landscape as an ever-menacing presence. Jack wondered what it must be like to live alongside something with a power so awesome and so random that it could lay waste to everything in its path and leave behind nothing but rock and devastation. Something Albert had written echoed in Jack's memory. "We Sicilians are a people formed by our land."

Seeing Etna looming over the city of Catania, Jack understood what he meant. To the Greeks who settled here in ancient times, the explanation was obvious: an angry monster that has been trapped beneath the mountain for thousands of years periodically loses his temper and spurts out fire from one of its hundred dragon heads. To Jack's way of thinking, that could account for the behavior of a lot of the monster's fellow Sicilians.

Marco Alliata skirted round the side of Catania, sticking to side streets and avoiding the city center. Jack sensed they were heading into the country again when the streets started to give way to larger houses set in their own verdant gardens and then groves of orange, lemon, and almond trees and vineyards fresh with ripening grapes. The fertility of the countryside surprised him. From descriptions he'd been given before taking off, he had expected a drier, arid land—stony, hard, unyielding. As he would discover, that description might have applied to the barren rocky areas of the island that lay to the west. But thanks to the ancient monster lurking deep below Etna, centuries of its outpourings had produced a land of unrivalled richness in which every available piece of ground had been cultivated in a heady mix of fruit fragrances and flowers. This was the first of several significant changes in perception Albert Anastasia's son would need to make in coming to understand his parents' homeland.

As the Alfa sped through sleepy villages, buildings of incalculable antiquity flashed past either side of the car. Houses that could have passed as villas only recently deserted by their ancient owners, churches that even now would have appeared little changed to the medieval worshippers who once congregated in them—Jack's sense of wonderment grew with every new vista. So, when the Alfa turned off the road to Nicolosi and entered an avenue of tall, stately trees, Jack was alive with curiosity.

The car slowed, passed through a towered gateway, and halted in a courtyard lined with buildings on all sides. A group of elderly women gathered at one doorway stopped their conversation and stared at the new arrival. A door opened in a handsome portico set at the top of a short flight of steps and an agile young man, with slicked-back dark hair and darker eyes, came down to the car and opened the door to let Jack out. He said something in Sicilian to the Alliata brothers that Jack couldn't catch. In a halting English, he then announced, "My name is Carlo Vizzini. The don will see you now."

Jack guessed that Vizzini was close to his own age. Shorter and more powerfully built than Jack, he had a lithe animal energy bred by Mediterranean sun and rough terrain. He led the way into a high-ceilinged hallway paved with echoing tiles. It was cool here after the heat of the car journey. Jack followed the clicking heels of Vizzini's shoes, which stopped at a pair of panelled doors at the end of the hallway. The young man knocked, heard a reply from inside, turned the brass knobs, and pushed open the doors to let Jack through before closing them behind him.

Facing him on the other side of a spacious room were tall French windows that opened onto a terrace. The other walls were dominated by large pieces of furniture, fitted with heavily decorated locked doors. One corner of the room was occupied by a large desk with a line of six or seven telephones. From behind the desk, a man close to Albert's build and age was making his way across the carpet to greet his visitor.

Without a word, the man placed his thick, heavy hands on Jack's shoulders and hugged and kissed him on both cheeks before uttering some dialect greeting that Jack didn't understand.

"You speak Sicilian," the man said in Italian this time, more as a statement than a question.

Jack replied that he spoke a little.

"Then today I will speak slowly and in Italian," said his host. "But you must learn to speak Sicilian better. You are here to learn many things. You understand?"

Jack nodded.

"Good. Because the first thing that you must learn is to follow what men like your father tell you to do."

Dominic Pagano was a powerful man, and not just physically. Jack got the impression that he did not raise his voice often, but when he did, that voice carried a message that was never to be forgotten. And Jack understood enough Italian and Sicilian to feel the force of the rebuke that followed. It was like having Albert and Costello and Lansky chastising him in unison. But now he'd had long airborne hours to prepare himself. This time he did not look away from the fierce eyes boring into him.

Jack stood erect and unflinching, breathing steadily. "I meant no dishonor to anyone, Signor. I did what I did because I believed it would help my father's friends. If what I did means I now have a price to pay, that is my burden—no one else's."

"And your mother? She has lost Umberto. Have you thought about her, if she lost her son as well?"

"My mother has told me all Sicilian women live with the fear of death. But she also sees my father living in me. She understands the things I must do and the chances I must take."

"Your mother is a wise woman." Jack detected a subtle change in Dominic Pagano's demeanor. The man placed his hands on Jack's shoulders and addressed him calmly, "You may have much to learn still, but I think you will make a good student."

Pagano held out his right hand and when Jack bent to kiss it, he patted his hair soothingly with his other hand. The subject was closed. They would not speak again about the circumstances that had brought Jack to Sicily. He dismissed Jack with the instruction to get settled in before dinner.

They gathered around the large table that sat in the center of the high-ceilinged dining room, above which the blades of a large electric fan swished steadily. It seemed incongruous to Jack that only he, Pagano, and Carlo Vizzini should be eating in such surroundings, waited on by two of the elderly women Jack recognized from his arrival in the courtyard outside. They spoke in a mixture of Italian and Sicilian, though Jack noticed Carlo's grasp of Italian was on par with his own; Sicilian was his native tongue and he used it whenever he could.

Two glasses of strong dark wine and a helping of spaghetti and veal he could barely manage relaxed Jack after the tiring journey from New York. Although Dominic Pagano clearly knew much about America, and probably a great deal more than he was careful not to disclose, it was clear that Carlo Vizzini was eager to discover all he could about the country he knew only from movies and brief encounters with American servicemen stationed throughout southern Italy. Football was something new to him and for a while their conversation was at cross-purposes until

Jack stumbled onto the distinction between soccer and the game at which he excelled.

Don Pagano smiled as the boys chatted away.

A plate of strong local cheese and a selection of grapes, figs, pomegranates, and peaches had been placed on the table with two more bottles of wine, when the dining room door opened and four imposing men entered. Jack took his cue from Carlo and respectfully got to his feet to greet them; Dominic Pagano remained seated.

One by one, the four men kissed his right hand and then walked round the table to greet his guest.

"Umberto Lanza," said the first, introducing himself before taking a seat at the table. The other three followed: Giuseppe Russo, Alessandro Gelso, and Michael Bellini.

Wine was poured for them, but the new arrivals did not eat. From what he understood of their conversation, these four men— all of them respected associates of Dominic Pagano—had been summoned solely to be introduced to Jack. No reference was made to where he came from or his connection with Pagano, but when he was addressed, it was with courtesy and a certain wariness. This encounter had been carefully orchestrated, and when the four visitors rose to leave at the end of the meal, they left Jack with the strong impression they would be meeting again.

After dinner, his host suggested that they should sit on the terrace to take a glass of Grappa del Etna, distilled from grapes born on the rich, fertile slopes of the volcano. Night was falling quickly and the air was perfumed with the evening scent of the villa's extensive garden, which blended with the powerful aroma of the spirit every time Jack took a sip from his glass.

The loud ringing of a telephone interrupted them.

For a man of his proportions, the don moved quickly, hurrying through the French windows to take the call. Jack was amazed to hear Pagano greet the caller in flawless English, "Heh, Max. How are you doing? Life treating you good in Chicago?"

He looked across at Carlo, as if to confirm what he was hearing. The young man raised his glass and said in his own limited English, "The don surprises you, no?"

Jack returned the toast. "You bet he does."

The telephone call lasted only a few minutes. Pagano rang off and rejoined them, bringing the Grappa bottle with him.

"My mom didn't tell me you speak such good English," Jack said with a knowing smile.

"Your mother has always been a very discreet woman." Pagano poured a shot of clear liquor into their glasses. "Bring that with you. Let me show you something."

He led the way back inside and sat behind his desk. "New York City," he said, indicating the telephone on the right of the row. Moving one by one, he identified the others: Chicago, Philadelphia, New Orleans, Naples, Rome, Zurich. The last in the line was introduced with a smile: Catania, Sicily.

"All of these are local numbers in each city," the don explained. "As you can see, American technology has brought many advantages to my country since the war ended. I can telephone anyone in any of these cities, but if someone should try to trace that call, or put a tap on it, they will go round and round in circles inside the city limits. I have friends at the NATO naval base in Naples who can do marvellous things. Wouldn't you agree?"

Jack raised his eyebrows in agreement.

Then another telephone rang, the New York City one. Pagano answered it, asked the caller to wait and then, with his hand over the mouthpiece, told Jack, "I'll wake you in the morning. We have many things to talk about."

He made sure the young man understood the Sicilian he was speaking this time.

Chapter Twenty-Six

For the next week, Jack woke early—at least by his own standards. Of course, it was the same early hour at which the Sicilian peasants had always risen for as long as they had worked the land. For breakfast, there was coffee and bread still hot from the oven and dripping with honey. Afterward, Jack would walk with Dominic Pagano until the heat of the day forced them to retreat to the cool of the villa.

In the early morning, the roads that ran around the perimeter of the Pagano estate and the tracks that crisscrossed it were dotted with men on their way to the vineyards, fields, and orchards. Some walked in little knots, chatting together. Others ambled along in carts pulled by patient donkeys or mules. Only occasionally did Jack see dust thrown up by the wheels of a car or truck.

For all his extensive business interests elsewhere, the bank of international telephones on his desk, and his easy command of English, at heart, the don was a man of the soil. Jack was touched by the pride he showed in the simple details of managing his eight hundred or so well-worked acres: a freshly greased latch, a spread of thoughtfully trained Morning Glory, a newly repaired wall, where only the clean faces of the carefully replaced stones betrayed that this work had not been carried out centuries earlier.

As they walked, Pagano spoke of the love he had for his Sicilian home. He knew its history in as much detail as that of his own family. Jack would later discover that several of the men he spoke of with intimate knowledge—owners of neighbouring estates, or merchants in Catania, Messina, or Siracusa—were in fact long since dead. It was as if their passing were a mere technicality. In a land where history could easily stand still, the passing of individuals counted for little. What mattered was the continuity they represented—a timeless link with those who had gone before, those who had shared the same passionate love of the land to which they gave their lives.

Century by century, his host ran through the roster of invasion and conquest that his ancestors had had to endure: from the Greek colonists who took root in Siracusa seven centuries before the birth of Jesus Christ to the field-gray battalions of the Wehrmacht, which had been driven from the island just fifteen years earlier. For most of their history, the people of Dominic Pagano's island had been ruled by foreigners, invaders who had taken their land, robbed them of their livelihood, and looked down on them with contempt.

"Who was there to help them?" Pagano asked. "Strangers governed them. Strangers made the laws. Strangers enforced those laws. And our people suffered. This is the way it has been for centuries. Maybe now you understand why we turned inwards to the family, to men of respect in the family."

Over the seven days Jack spent in his villa, the don gradually revealed the origins of the society in which he played so prominent a role—a society honoured for hundreds of years by those unable to help themselves, who had nowhere to turn when they sought justice or retribution. And who repaid the help they received with a fierce devotion and enduring sense of duty.

The name "Mafia" was never used. It never needed to be. The society Dominic Pagano described extended beyond the blue waters of Sicily. Its members were as familiar and as welcome across the Straits of Messina in Calabria and around the glorious bay beside which the city of Naples nestled. A century earlier, men of the same stamp had been sent to the New World to establish a similar society there, one to which the growing numbers of the poor and the powerless could turn in times of need. And in the centuries before that, men of this society had been sought out by the very powers that oppressed them, because they set a high value on the unflinching loyalty and steely ruthlessness with which these men of Sicily protected their own.

The evidence lay all around. Ancient ransacked structures stood proudly beside bomb-damaged bunkers or anti-aircraft batteries blown to pieces by Allied planes. And wandering past the ruins were Pagano's people, picking up their lives and carrying on just as their forebears had. Like those who had gone before, these present-day Sicilians maintained a deep, unspoken gratitude for benefactors, like their don, who had seen them through the worst of times and offered support as they faced an uncertain future.

That night, the evening conversation on the terrace turned to current events in Sicily, and the tone grew grave. Don Pagano explained that he had taken care to outline the island's history to Jack so that he would understand what was happening now. For over twenty years, he continued, heroin trafficking had been growing. He asked Jack what he knew of Vito Genovese. Jack's reply was guarded, but told Don Pagano enough to show that he was aware of the power base that Genovese was working to build in America.

"His strength comes from the west of Sicily: Palermo and Castellammare del Golfo," said the don. "Before he escaped to Italy twenty years ago, Genovese had moved a lot of money to Europe—and I mean a lot."

Pagano refilled their glasses with Grappa and carried on. He told Jack that Vito Genovese had used his money to set up the first of the heroin processing plants outside Palermo, buying off local police, law enforcement officials, and politicians. He had also had money to hire shifts of workers to produce heroin on an industrial scale.

No wonder he could supply Mussolini's son-in-law with as much heroin as he needed. Jack wondered what other services Genovese had performed for the fascist dictator. He remembered that Miller had alluded to making use of Genovese's right-wing associates after the war. Thanks to them, Miller and other masters of the dark arts of political manipulation made sure that Italy did not go the same way as neighboring Yugoslavia and end up the wrong side of the Iron Curtain.

Dominic Pagano began speaking quicker. His voice grew more earnest.

Around Palermo in particular, he continued, young men had been seduced by the easy money to be made from the drug business. In large cities like that, they mixed with American servicemen with fat wallets and an appetite for illicit kicks. From others, they got to hear about the fortunes to be made from China White and other concoctions produced from raw opium. Vito Genovese may have returned home to the US, but the production and distribution network he had set up was running as smooth as silk—and it was expanding.

"There was a sit-down last year in a big hotel," the don told Jack. "Some of the chief American operators were there, meeting with the families in Palermo. A dangerous man called Carmine Galante came from America. Have you heard of him?"

Sure, Jack had heard of him, and now he saw the connection.

Dominic Pagano acknowledged this with a nod of his head, before carrying on. The Palermo sit-down had been called to put in place a new distribution network for Genovese's Sicilian heroin, something on an altogether bigger scale than anything that had gone before.

"Can you tell me the street value of fifty kilos of heroin in the United States?" Pagano asked bluntly.

Jack had no idea and plucked five million dollars out of the air.

"I wish it was," Pagano answered. "Fifty kilos of heroin is worth more than four times that. Over twenty million dollars, Jack. The meeting in Palermo last year laid down the plan to make even bigger shipments to America. And that still leaves all of Europe, right here, to be supplied. This is what makes people greedy. This is what Albert saw happening."

"He said it would be the downfall of the families."

"And he was right," said Pagano. "Young men like Carlo, the sons of families with a proud history, are lining up to take these shipments to America. Not just to your big cities. They will smuggle this heroin across the country, till nowhere is left unpolluted. So, other young men will see how much money they can make and they will want to work this drug business as well."

It was a bleak analysis. Bleaker still because it confirmed everything that Jack had learned since Albert Anastasia had been killed.

Carlo Vizzini was the first to speak. "What is to be done, Don Pagano? If what you say is true, it cannot be allowed to happen. It must not."

His don reached over to pat his hand reassuringly. "The families in Palermo have been blinded by their lust for money. They don't see that a new invasion is coming to Sicily—new conquerors, new overlords who want to take control of all we have. These lords of the drug business think they can buy men's souls as well as their bodies with their narcotics. But the Palermo families and their friends in America are not the only ones who are making plans. Be patient, Carlo. Your time will come. And yours, Jack. Young men like you are our future. And that future is coming sooner than you may think."

Chapter Twenty-Seven

As the days passed, it was clear that Carlo had been designated as Jack's bodyguard. The next two weeks were spent mostly on the road in an effort to begin introducing the young man from America to other prominent associates of Don Pagano.

Had Francesco Barbino not been greeted so warmly by Carlo Vizzini, Jack would have been convinced they were about to be abducted. Barbino was the driver sent to collect the two young men from Don Pagano's house. Barbino was all muscle and brooding eyebrows. He carried a livid red scar on his left forearm, and when he picked up their bags, Jack saw the size of hands. They were like a prize fighter's.

Barbino had been assigned to drive Jack and Carlo wherever they needed to go. He didn't have a lot to say for himself and it was several days before Jack found out that his family had originated from across the straits, in Calabria. Indeed, one of the trips they took during that fortnight was to Reggio in Calabria, where they spent two days doing the rounds of local families who offered generous hospitality whenever the name of Don Pagano was mentioned.

Jack did little talking on these visits. Carlo had been instructed to take the lead. The young man with him was introduced simply as a relative of the don. That was enough. No further details were required. He was left politely to watch and listen, and what he saw and heard confirmed what Dominic Pagano had told him. His organization embraced far more than the Sicilian families close to home. His contacts and influence extended deep into the mainland of the Italian south, where families like his expressed to their young visitors the same concerns and anxieties about the build up of the narcotics business centered in Sicily. Wherever he sat down to be lavishly entertained with the best local food and wines set aside in deep cool cellars for special occasions such as this, Jack heard of the old order unravelling, of discipline within tightly structured organizations breaking down, of control over corrupt politicians, judges, and business leaders slipping away. He heard members of these Calabrian families asking Carlo Vizzini what, if anything, was to be done. He heard Carlo telling them to be patient.

Patient, but ready.

Soon into their travels together, Carlo told Jack that they were to start heading westward, in the direction of Palermo. "The don wants you to see for yourself what we have to stop." Barbino would drive them as far as Bolognetta, ten miles inland from Palermo. After that, Carlo would take over the driving to their destination.

Jack asked why they needed to switch drivers.

"Francesco will stay in Bolognetta. It's better he shouldn't be seen and better for us we shouldn't be seen with him," Carlo explained.

Jack still didn't follow.

"These people you will be visiting," Barbino said, "I ate them for breakfast when I was a kid."

Jack left it at that, but later, when Barbino was gone, Vizzini told him, "Francesco wasn't kidding you. Twenty years ago, when he was just twelve years old, his father was killed. This is a question of honor for any man, but for a twelve-year-old it's something special. Francesco is a true 'Ndranghetisti."

"A what?"

"This is the name for a man of honor in Calabria. He belongs to the 'Ndrangheta, the men of honor. Even though he was born in Messina, his blood is Calabrian. Imagine: A man of honor when he was twelve years old."

Vizzini's eyes seemed fixed at some point in the distance. As if the story were a physical thing, hanging in the air between them.

Jack remained silent.

"You've seen Francesco, so you can understand that he was big for his age and he was fearless. He hid the machine gun inside an old backpack and took the bus to Palermo like any other kid. The family who had killed his father lived near Monreale, on a farm by itself. So, Francesco hiked out to their place, knocked at the door to ask for a glass of water, and killed everyone inside when they brought it to him. He used two magazines to shoot them: four men, two women, and a kid about his own age—a girl. Then he drank his water, hiked back to Palermo, and caught the evening bus home. He still scares the shit out of people there. That's why he's staying in Bolognetta."

"Does that mean you and I have to go without being noticed?" Jack asked.

"The don wants you to see what he has been telling you—without being seen yourself. He believes you can do this, and so do I."

They left early in the morning and drove north to the coast road linking Messina with Palermo before heading west through Tindali, Cefalu, and Termini. There they turned into the hills until they hit the main road running from Palermo to the south of the island. A few miles farther on lay Bolognetta, where Francesco Barbino was left to settle into a good lunch inside a small trattoria off the main street.

An hour later, the heat of the early afternoon sun had driven most people to seek shade and a siesta. The air was buzzing with the hum of insects when Carlo switched off the engine and let the car roll a few more yards down the track he had turned onto. He raised a finger to his lips, indicating to Jack to remain silently in the car in case anyone was about.

They sat listening until Carlo felt confident that their arrival had not been noticed. He pointed toward the thick scrub that surrounded them. "Follow me. Don't make any noise."

Carlo led the way, pushing aside prickly branches and scrambling past clumps of thorny bushes. He stopped, motioned for Jack to crouch down by doing so himself. The sound of heavy footsteps crunching through stony dirt drew closer. Carlo kept his gaze fixed ahead, and as the footsteps grew louder, Jack saw a man pass by on the other side of the thicket with what looked like an old shotgun slung over one shoulder. The footsteps slowly disappeared, and after a minute or so, Carlo crept forward to check that he had gone before beckoning to Jack to join him.

"The guard looks like a shepherd." He winked at Jack. "But it is not sheep he is protecting."

They waited side by side for another five minutes before emerging onto a dusty track that led downhill into a secluded valley.

No one was around.

Carlo tapped Jack on the shoulder, pointed to a group of farm buildings, and started running toward them.

Jack followed, staying just behind.

Carlo stopped beside the nearest building and moved slowly along it to check round the corner.

If there were any guard dogs, they were taking a siesta too. The rough stone yard they slipped into was deserted. Open byres stood on three sides, with feeding mangers and partitions for stabling horses or mules. The fourth side of the yard was occupied by a large stone barn, with big double doors that could be swung open to admit farm carts. The doors were closed, and Carlo directed Jack's gaze to a square opening ten feet up in the nearest gable of the barn, situated just above the tiled roof on one of the byres. A drainpipe attached to the barn wall to collect rainwater from the gutter running the length of the byre helped them climb quietly onto the tiles, which rippled symmetrically in ochre-colored ridges along the roof. In the cleft formed between it and the barn wall, Carlo and Jack shimmied up to the opening and crouched beneath it, listening carefully before looking inside.

Carlo touched his nose, getting Jack to catch the smell. Wafting up to them was a sulfurous odor not unlike bad eggs.

Jack raised his eyebrows to enquire what it was. Carlo answered by miming a syringe being injected into his forearm. This was Jack's first encounter with raw opium.

At Carlo's indication, he thrust his head through the window to take a good look inside. As his eyes became accustomed to the darkened interior he made out two lines of workbenches running the full length of the barn. He saw large-scale pieces of equipment like the ones he'd used in chemistry class in high school, beside which a set of old-fashioned farm scales and iron weights made an incongruous contrast. At the end of one of the long workbenches was a stack of rectangular packets, which looked like loaves of bread wrapped in waxed paper. Carlo pointed his index finger around the interior of the barn for Jack to take in as much as he could. Then he crossed his hands to show it was time to go and began to edge his way down the roof to the drainpipe.

The noise of the tile dislodged by Carlo's shoe and its subsequent crashing to the stone surface of the courtyard below shattered the quiet that had settled over the afternoon. Both young men pushed themselves against the barn wall, listening for any reaction. Jack tugged at Carlo's shoulder and gestured at him to get as low as he could. Then he reached for one of the other tiles that had been loosened and lifted it free. The noise of crunching footsteps didn't take long to reach their ears, and as they grew louder they were joined by the sound of heavy breathing. Hidden from sight by the angle of the barn wall, Jack and Carlo listened to the scrape of footsteps on stone drawing closer.

Carlo seemed baffled as to what their next move would be.

Now it was Jack's turn to take control. He raised a finger to his lips. He'd been through exercises like this with Rip too many times to be fazed by a dozy peasant with a gun he probably hadn't fired in months. His pulse rose with a thrill he had not felt for a long time. He found himself breathing long and deep. All his time spent training in the Hole seemed to race before him in those brief seconds.

Albert Anastasia's son was ready.

While he waited for the footsteps to stop, Jack drew a handkerchief from his pocket. Then he swung his arm forward, sending a tile arcing around the corner of the barn.

It smashed to pieces on the hard surface.

At the same time, he stepped around Carlo, took three swift steps like a triple jumper along the byre roof to line up the guard below, and launched himself at the shoulders of the man, who had swung round in alarm when the tile crashed behind him.

Jack sent him sprawling to the ground and the weight of his landing winded him so completely that as he lifted his head to catch his breath, Jack shoved the handkerchief into his mouth and started to gag him.

Carlo had scrambled down by now and the two of them pulled the guard's jacket down from his shoulders, so that his arms were pinned helplessly by his side. With Jack forcing his face into the ground, the man had no chance to catch sight of his assailants. Jack's hand across his own eyes showed Carlo they needed a blindfold and he pulled free the scarf the guard was wearing around his neck and tied it firmly across his eyes.

No words had passed between them. They left no trace of whom they were or where they had come from. Nothing had been stolen. Nothing had been disturbed. If it wasn't for his state of shock and the fact that he was still bound and gagged when he was found, the guard's account of what had happened might have been dismissed as the ramblings of a man who'd had too much sun or too much wine. Both, perhaps.

As it was, the family who operated this out-of-the-way facility had been put on notice that it was no longer as inconspicuous as they thought.

More alarming was the knowledge that this was no chance discovery. Whoever had been sent on this reconnaissance mission had known where to look and how to melt away and vanish like cicadas in the scrub.

Chapter Twenty-Eight

When they returned to the Pagano villa, Jack was interested to see that Francesco stayed on. He parked the car beside an Alfa-Romeo that looked very like the one in which the Aliatta brothers had collected Jack from the airport. While Francesco disappeared into one of the other houses flanking the courtyard, Carlo and Jack went up the steps and into the don's house, where Dominic Pagano and Michael Bellini were waiting for them in the study.

This time, the greeting the don gave Jack was as warm as the first meeting had been stern. "Now you see what I have been talking about. And I see what they have told me from America." He added a comment in Sicilian to Carlo, which Jack only partially understood.

The smiles flashed by the other men made it clear that it was in fact a compliment.

Carlo Vizzini's account of how Jack had handled himself was reason enough for the don to break out his better wine and demand something special to grace his table to celebrate the successful return of the three young men.

Bellini double-checked the details as Carlo went on. The quantity of packets interested him particularly. Judging by his reaction, their account appeared to confirm what Bellini either knew or suspected.

Spread across the don's desk was a map showing Sicily and the area of sea separating it from the coast of North Africa, less than a hundred miles away at the nearest point. Don Pagano placed his finger near Palermo, gave the name of the city, and one by one named four other ports around the northwest coast of Sicily, touching them in turn.

"Each is owned by one of the families," Pagano explained. "They own their ports, so there is no need to be secretive once the cargo is unloaded. Where they have to be careful is on the way to the port."

He moved his hand eastward off the map. "The opium is shipped from Turkey and ports in the eastern Mediterranean, like it has been for hundreds and hundreds of years.

"To bring it here." Pagano slapped the palm of his heavy hand on the western tip of Sicily. "Genovese and his friends have been very clever. A ship at sea is always in danger. It used to be a danger from pirates. Now governments with strong navies are a danger too. So they take their precious opium this way instead." His finger traced a loop along the North African coast until it stopped in Tunisia.

"You see these islands," Pagano said, indicating Lampedusa, Linosa, and Pantelleria, evenly spaced between Sicily and the Tunisian coast. "They bring their opium this way, in short voyages, in small ships, keeping it from sight, keeping their enemies guessing. And when they reach Sicily they hide here until it's safe to sail to their own port."

Jack studied where Pagano's thick finger was pointing. It was an island lying off the west coast of Sicily.

The name on the map read Favignano.

Pagano jabbed the map with his finger. "This is where we will surprise them: in their own back yard."

Don Pagano outlined the plan for a raid that had been pieced together since Jack's arrival in Sicily. Jack and Carlo were to be driven by Francesco on another tour of Don Pagano's associates, going toward Siracusa this time and on around the southern coast. Along the way they would stay with certain close friends and would be joined by members of their families. They would end up at the opposite end of Sicily, in Erice, high in the hills above the port of Trapani and the island of Favignano.

The timing was important, the don told them. A large shipment of opium was due to arrive off Favignano in two weeks time, hidden aboard a small freighter. It was common practice for smuggling vessels to hold to in the lee of the island before being given word to proceed around the coast to their port of destination, half a day's voyage in the case of Palermo itself.

"It is while the ship is there, we will strike," Don Pagano explained.

The six men who would be joining Carlo and Jack would make their way out to the anchored coaster under the cover of darkness. They would board her and remove the opium—an estimated thirty to forty kilos.

Jack did the math quickly in his head. That would make 100–120 kilos of China White, with a street value of more than a hundred million dollars.

"What about the crew?" asked Carlo. "Won't they try to stop our guys taking the stuff?"

"The crew won't know anyone was ever on board," the don answered with a smile. "The captain will give it to them. He may carry this cargo, but he does that only to see and hear things we need to know. He comes from Calabria, not from Palermo. He sees what is happening with this narcotics business. He takes a big risk doing what he does. But he is a brave man."

"An 'Ndranghetisti," Jack said quietly—half question, half conclusion.

Don Pagano looked surprised, but there was pleasure in his expression, too. "Yes—a man of honor—that is what he is."

Carlo looked perplexed. "How can he give it to them, Don Pagano? So much opium? So much money?"

"When the crew find him, the captain will be tied up. The crew will have been locked in their quarters. It will look as if pirates have come aboard, overpowered the watch, and stolen their precious cargo. It will be dangerous for the captain, but he is not afraid of danger. He knows how it will hit the Palermo families and their friends in America."

"It will be like a bomb exploding among them," Carlo said.

"A bomb," the don agreed. "Now, Jack, you have listened to me, but you have said nothing."

Jack wasn't entirely sure whether Don Pagano was seeking his honest opinion or the same wide-eyed endorsement that Carlo had shown. "I think the impact back home will be enormous. If this much opium goes missing, Genovese, Galante, and the others will lose tens of millions of dollars. Someone will have to answer for that, for sure."

"Believe me, I would not ask you if I did not want to hear all that you think. You have other thoughts. I can tell. Please, share them with me."

There was something missing. Jack kept thinking back on Albert's notes. How would he plan this? What would he do to make Carlo's bomb send a shockwave way beyond America?

And then he remembered the name John Bazzano.

Albert Anastasia's son began to run through the scheme that had crystallized in his mind. When he was finished, the don smiled and wished them luck on their trip, which would begin the next morning.

Chapter Twenty-Nine

Vito Genovese had never really trusted Carmine Galante, even after Genovese had gone into hiding in Italy during the thirties and Galante had been taking care of business for him. However, he had to accept that Galante was good at what he did, and a man with no ambition was not a true man in Genovese's eyes.

Galante had always coveted the power and prestige wielded and enjoyed by the heads of the five families in New York. In the aftermath of Apalachin, Genovese had been looking for a way to reassert his authority. The way to do it, he had decided, was to promote the cause of Carmine Galante.

Everyone knew Galante had abandoned him to join forces with the Bonanno family. However, it was also generally acknowledged that Genovese had maintained a "professional" relationship with his former lieutenant, even after the defection. There were certain assignments that called for Galante's expertise and cold-hearted ruthlessness. If Genovese were to offer Galante his support in taking over the Bonanno family and installing himself as its capo, it would send a powerful message that Don Genovese was still very much in business and was not to be messed with. It would also put the heads of the other families on their guard and divert their unwelcome attention from Genovese himself. Boosting Galante's ego would be a small price to pay.

As it happened, Genovese needed Galante at this time. A little local difficulty had arisen in the Bronx. Any of Genovese's enforcers could have been entrusted to deal with the situation, but given the circumstances, it presented a perfect opportunity for Galante to appear to be supplying his services to his former boss. Besides, Galante had a talent for settling business like this in a way that people remembered.

"Two of the connections from Sicily, new in the city, seem to want to do things their own way," Genovese explained to his former lieutenant. "They seem to have forgotten the importance of the loyalty they learned back in Sicily, and they ain't learned the meaning of loyalty here yet."

"So, you want them to learn this lesson?" Galante asked.

"No. I want them to be the lesson. I want these fuckheads to show every slippery dick in this city that if anyone tries to be clever with me, he stops being clever—period."

Galante knew the pair Genovese was talking about, though he was careful not to let on. His own sources had already informed him that two brothers, the Sapienzas, had been putting out feelers. Word had it that they were in the market for more than the regular shipments of heroin they received through Genovese's operation.

At the same time, Galante had heard the Sapienzas were sounding out buyers in Philadelphia. By all accounts, they had been putting it about that they were new dealers with a significant quantity of merchandise to bring to the market.

What caught Galante's interest was that the Sapienza brothers were letting it be known they were part of Galante's own outfit. Even more fascinating was the way the news was being greeted. Established dealers in Philadelphia, apparently loyal to Vito Genovese, had sent word secretly that they would be prepared to transfer their business to Galante's new operation, once Genovese was removed from the scene.

For Carmine Galante, the idea was intriguing. Like senior mob bosses across the country, he had speculated what might become of the would-be *capo do tutti capi* after the catastrophic events set in motion by the Apalachin bust. Galante had run several scenarios through his mind. Once or twice he had indulged in the idea of taking over from Genovese himself.

Even Carmine Galante had dismissed this as fantasy—until now.

"Will you do this thing for me?"

"Of course," Galante answered. "Send me what I need to know and it will be done."

"Thank you, my dear friend. This, I will not forget."

Trust me, you won't, Carmine Galante thought.

Chapter Thirty

Jack wished he could have spent longer than three days with Umberto Lanza in Siracusa. The mild maritime climate and the luxurious spread of southern vegetation made the city a delight to stroll around. But it was its casual antiquity that enthralled him most. The remains of its ancient glory, still impressive in their ruin, made him feel like he was walking through the set of an epic movie: *Quo Vadis,* or *The Last Days of Pompeii.*

The Greek colony that had brought this hub of the ancient Mediterranean into being fascinated Jack. Here were people sailing from their home for a new life in a new land, and this is what they had created—a society and culture that had given birth to Archimedes, one the greatest mathematicians the world had ever seen. Archimedes, the man who had defied the power of Rome with the power of his mind and spirit. It was thanks to Archimedes, Jack recalled from his history classes, that Siracusa had resisted the Roman onslaught for so long. In the fierce defense of his people and everything they represented, this man of science and theoretical math had designed weapons no enemy had ever encountered. Inspired by him, his fellow citizens had stood firm against their greatest foe, defending to the death what they held dearest. When he himself was killed, struck down in his study by a Roman soldier's sword, Archimedes had chosen to remain fixed on the one thing that had sustained him all of his adult life rather than abandon it to save himself.

In Siracusa, Jack felt closer than ever before to his Sicilian origins. It was also there that he and Carlo collected the first of their crew: Umberto Lanza's son, Salvatore.

Jack's historical interest in Gela, their next stopping point, came from the more recent past. He was too young to remember the Allied invasion of Sicily fifteen years earlier, but Miller had mentioned in passing that the beaches around the long shallow bay had provided the chief landing places for the US Seventh Army in July, 1943. "I watched our boys come ashore from behind the German lines," he'd told Jack. "I gave Patton a box of cigars I'd liberated from the Kraut officers' mess in Ragusa." On the high ground, just outside the town Miller had mentioned, Francesco halted the car to let them take in the magnificent view of the Golfo di Gela running westward as far as their third port of call, Licata.

After three days in Gela they were joined by Angelo Cavatajo and Gaspare Navarra, who followed behind them as they left through the cotton fields on the road to Licata driving in a beat-up Fiat truck, seemingly without a care in the world. Though, as Carlo confided to Jack, both men had made their bones while they were still teenagers.

In Agrigento, the Ferro brothers, Simone and Leonardo, fell in with Don Pagano's growing team of determined young men. And the last member of the assault crew, Cesare Albano, was gathered when they stopped for several days at his father's prosperous farmhouse in the vine-clad plain across the Mazaro River from the fishing port of Mazara del Vallo.

The day after their arrival at the Albano estate, a man on a motorcycle drew up in the courtyard and spoke to the gatekeeper. The man was directed toward the main entrance, where he asked to speak to Cesare's father. It was he who went in search of Jack and escorted him to a room off the main entrance where the motorcyclist was waiting bareheaded to speak to him.

The man nodded to Jack respectfully and waited for the door to be closed, to ensure their privacy, before telling him in carefully enunciated Sicilian, "I have a message for you from Catania. Don Pagano sends you his greetings."

"Please return with mine," Jack answered, feeling gratified that the man had no difficulty understanding what he had said.

"My don wishes you to know that the voyage began yesterday. He says you should expect it to end in three days. That is what he asked me to tell you,"

Jack smiled in appreciation. "Thank you. If Don Pagano sent you so far to give me this message, you must know how important it is. Signor Albano is a hospitable man; he would not want you to leave without taking some refreshment. Please go to the kitchen, his cook will look after you, I'm sure."

Don Pagano's messenger returned a toothy grin, nodded his head again in parting, and let himself out into the courtyard. Jack went to find Carlo to pass on the news. Don Pagano's trap was set. The next morning, they would leave for Erice, where, if the gods that had long watched over Sicily were with them, the trap would be sprung.

Chapter Thirty-One

The Bontade family had been on edge ever since the mysterious daytime attack on one of their watchmen two weeks earlier. Extra guards had been posted, tough young men well known around Palermo. They would make it clear that the Bontades would not tolerate any further interference in their business. Throughout the region, those who needed to know were put on notice that the Bontade family were serious about protecting their assets and their interests. Instead of the trusty lupara, the traditional weapon of choice for shepherds all over Sicily, the guards now carried automatics.

Trip wires with rattling cans ran along the fringes of the scrub close to the isolated farmstead where Jack and Carlo Vizzini had gone. Now there were guards at the doors of the barn and the entrance to the farmyard, as well as the ones patrolling the perimeter. For two weeks there had been no further disturbances and nothing in the neighborhood had reached the ears of the Bontade elders to suggest there would be.

For Tommasso Manzella, however, the shiny automatic shoved into his belt was little substitution for the bars and girls of Palermo he was usually enjoying at this time of night. Outside the old stone barn, it was so dark you could see every star in the sky, or so it seemed. And for every star there had to be a cicada or some other creature of the night straining his nerves with each sudden burst of noise.

Tommasso was leaning against the barn wall, taking a long drag from his Lucky Strike, when the bright beam of the military lamp appropriated from a US supply depot and carried by his partner Roberto came swinging round into farmyard and caught him full in the face.

Tommasso shielded his eyes with his right hand. "You want to blind me?"

The beam came closer and grew more intense. Irritated and disoriented, Tommasso threw away his cigarette and lunged toward the dazzling light to knock Roberto's hand away and maybe land one on him to teach him a lesson.

But it wasn't Roberto Liggio on the other side of the blinding light. From where Francesco Barbino's cousin, Paolo, was standing on the other side of the lamp, what happened was almost comical. Manzella lurched toward him blinking, his hands reaching for the lamp. The automatic flashed bright in his waistband. Paolo had learned his craft as a pickpocket, and relieving Manzella of his gun was a cakewalk. In the same swift motion, Paolo brought the butt of the automatic thudding into the back of Manzella's head and sent him to the ground unconscious.

Paolo let out a low whistle, which brought his brother Massimo out of the shadows. Together, they rolled Manzella onto this front, tied his hands tightly behind his back and gagged him with a scarf. They dragged him out of the farmyard and dumped him beside the inert body of Roberto Liggio, who had been disarmed and bound moments earlier.

Paolo gave three quick flashes of the lamp up the stony track, which were answered by the sound of an engine starting and a vehicle reversing quickly down toward them. It was a small delivery truck. Leaving the engine running, the driver opened the rear doors so that the two unconscious men could be heaved inside. Paolo and Massimo got in after them. They slammed the doors shut and the truck crunched and skidded up the track, disappearing into the night.

In Erice, the teenager Pagano had sent to deliver his next message could not have been north of sixteen, but he impressed Jack with his serious demeanor and earnest desire to deliver his message correctly.

"Don Pagano wishes you to know that the packages are secure," he told Jack confidentially.

"Did he tell you when they will arrive?"

"Tomorrow night, like you expect. That is right—yes?"

"It is," Jack answered. "Thank you for your trouble, my friend."

The young man astride the murmuring scooter was still looking at him eagerly. "Please, tell me your name," Jack added. "So I can be sure to commend you to Don Pagano."

"They call me Vurpi," the young man answered with pleasure.

"Vurpi? Like Volpe in Italian?"

"Yes, it's the same word. Vurpi is Sicilian."

"Vurpi—the Fox. I'll remember that," he said. "I don't suppose I need to tell you to be careful on your way back."

"No, Signor, but thank you."

Jack watched him slip the Lambretta into gear, turn carefully in front of the house, and then pop his way down the hill. His eyes followed the scooter as far as the first sharp corner, where it disappeared from sight, a thin cloud of dust in its wake. From his vantage point close to the massive walls, which still showed signs of Roman repair work, Jack looked out over the matchless panorama. Far below lay the port of Trapani, nine miles down the twisting road finished five years earlier. Beyond was Favignano. Turning to his left, Jack squinted toward the southern horizon, back along the road they had taken from Cesare Albano's home, over the bay where the waters of the Mazaro flowed into the sea and out to a distant shape rising from the blue of the Mediterranean. This was the conical peak of Pantelleria, the third of the island stepping stones from North Africa. Somewhere out there, a hundred million dollars lay hidden in the fetid hold of a tramp steamer. Don Pagano was right; it really was a dirty business.

Chapter Thirty-Two

Whoever had given the *Vesuvia* her name clearly had a sense of humor. In her youth, when her paint was fresh and her engines young, she could have sailed under a different name—the *Venus*, perhaps. But now she was old and blistered, with a smokestack billowing an oily cloud behind her. *Vesuvia* suited her well.

From Gibraltar to Beirut, the Mediterranean was littered with down-at-heel freighters like her, anonymous crafts carrying goods along the coast or hopping from island to island, picking up what trade they could find. For Captain Vincenzo and his crew of six, it was a good enough living—particularly when their inconspicuous little ship carried the kind of illicit cargo that was now directing them toward the western tip of Sicily.

His special clients were cautious men, so cautious that Vincenzo had never met them face to face. They worked through intermediaries. The first time, he had been drinking in a waterfront bar in Algiers when a man smelling of Pastis and speaking with a French accent, or rather Corsican, as Vincenzo later discovered, struck up a conversation with him. The man seemed to know that he was sailing for Marseilles the following day, and after an appropriate fee had been agreed, some extra cargo had been stowed in the *Vesuvia*'s hold. Vincenzo never asked what it was, though he had his suspicions when he saw the men who came to retrieve it from the wharf where his ship was berthed in a line with the other beaten-up, nondescript coasters.

A later run-in with members of a significant family in Taranto had brought Vincenzo to the attention of the 'Ndrangheta, and through them, to Don Pagano. The don had seen that the captain was just a seafarer making a living from whatever needed carrying from one port to the next. The master of the *Vesuvia* was encouraged to spend time around the seedy bars and clubs, where the pitiful masses washed up by the narcotics trade sold themselves, their dignity, and their children for whatever they could make to satisfy their cravings.

He was a decent man at heart and it didn't take him long to understand the consequences of carrying these shipments. When Don Pagano's associates offered to double his fee from the traffickers in return for details of what he was carrying and where, Captain Vincenzo had been happy to help out. For the safety of his crew, he was careful to keep these dealings to himself. So when he had set course for Favignano that morning, he told them that they would hove there briefly, awaiting orders before proceeding to their next port of call.

His ship had been designed with work in mind; little concession had been made to grace or speed. Most of her length was occupied by the main deck, through which two hatches gave access to the hold. There was a small area of raised deck in the bows and a small bridge in the stern, from which a companionway led down to Vincenzo's cabin and the cramped quarters occupied by his crew.

A stout mast fitted with a derrick for moving cargo in and out of the hold gave the *Vesuvia* her only elevation. There had been a time when Captain Vincenzo speculated about realizing the money he was saving and maybe buying a younger ship. These ideas had melted away when his friends in Calabria pointed out that his grimy little freighter disappeared among all the others when she was in port and attracted no attention at all while she was at sea. And, as she ploughed her way through the smooth surface toward the coast of Sicily, he was content to let his money steadily grow in the Swiss bank account Don Pagano had thoughtfully supplied. It allowed him to be generous when he wanted to be, and for this voyage he had taken aboard enough good wine to ensure his crew would be sound asleep that night as the *Vesuvia* wallowed in the bay on the western side of the island, well out of sight of the Sicilian coast.

Jack Pagano, on the other hand, discouraged his companions from drinking more than an acceptable amount of wine with their evening meal. There was a high enough sense of excitement around the table. He needed them to be sharp and quick.

Jack had been careful not to push himself forward among the group of other young men Don Pagano selected for this job. He noticed the admiring way Carlo Vizzini had described their exploits at the processing barn and the knowing glances in his direction from Carlo's listeners. That, he believed, and his close connection to the don, gave him the authority he needed to direct the night's proceedings. After all, Jack reminded himself with mounting satisfaction, Don Pagano's plan would have been very different without his inspiration.

When the meal was over and the plates cleared away, he ran through the details a final time. Don Pagano had insisted Jack was not to go out to the *Vesuvia* himself. There had been no discussion and no dissent. Carlo understood what needed to be done and the others were to take their orders from him. There was a practical consideration as well. Jack's command of Sicilian was making good progress, but it still could not be risked among native speakers. In the heat of the moment, communication was everything. Perhaps it was a face-saving move by Don Pagano, Jack reflected. Either way, he would be staying at their hideaway in Erice.

A fishing boat had been provided to take the raiding party out to Favignano. To avoid attracting attention, they would sail from Trapani with the rest of the nighttime fishermen and return with them a little before dawn. Captain Vincenzo would be looking for the signal. When he saw it, he would lock the door to the crew's quarters in case any of the boozed-up sailors came to and needed the john or a breath of fresh air. By the time the fishing boat inched quietly alongside five minutes later, everything would be ready aboard the *Vesuvia*.

Chapter Thirty-Three

Carlo and the others left for Trapani at a little after eight o'clock in the evening. Francesco drove the Fiat truck Angelo and Gaspare had brought along from Gela. With the others crammed in the back, he would drop them in town and then return to keep watch with Jack. The group was told to disperse in Trapani and make their way one by one to the fishing boat. This way they could slip aboard without attracting attention.

As Carlo and his crew drifted from the boulevards skirting the harbor, another truck pulled up beside their fishing boat. Two men dressed as fishermen unloaded two bundles of nets, carried them down the gangway into the stern of the boat, and stowed them below decks in the spacious fish locker. Then they sauntered back to their van and drove off, passing groups of other fishermen who had converged on the waterfront to prepare their gear and get their boats ready for the night at sea.

Over the next half hour, Carlo and the others ambled down to their boat and went aboard. They all had some experience of working small craft like this and busied themselves convincingly until everyone was aboard and it was time to leave. Carlo took command in the tiny wheelhouse, sending two of them to cast off. Salvatore went forward to untie the bow line attached to the buoy and chain anchored in the harbor. In the stern, Simone and Leonardo stowed away the gangplank while Cesare untied the mooring rope secured through an iron ring in the quay. With her navigation lights glowing against the starlit sky, the fishing boat chugged away from the brightly lit waterfront and blended into the flotilla heading out of the landlocked harbor toward the barely discernible horizon.

When they were clear of land, Carlo posted lookouts. He wanted to be well clear of the other boats before making the rendezvous with the *Vesuvia*. In a straight line, the crossing to Favignano would take less than an hour, but he was prepared to spend time heading in a different direction to shake off any company before cutting his lights and making for the bay where Captain Vincenzo was waiting for them.

The air was still warm. In the boat's wake, a steady line of white water flecked with phosphorescence cut through the darkened surface. Carlo had told them not to smoke and to keep their conversation to a minimum; on a still night at sea, sounds were audible a half mile away.

The engine chugged on. The other fishing boats gradually disappeared into the night, pinpointed here and there by their large lamps shining down into the water to draw unsuspecting fish to their nets.

Carlo had originally planned to set course through the channel separating Favignano and the smaller island of Lavanzo that lay to the north, but when he saw the majority of the other boats moving westward, he swung the wheel and turned the bows south so that they would pass around the eastern tip of Favignano. Once he was south of the wedge-shaped island, he turned west, keeping the shoreline starboard. Half an hour later he switched off the navigation lights and cut the engine revs. A few dots of light were visible in the interior of the island, but there were no signs of life close to the shore.

Carlo edged the boat forward, whispering to the others to look for the dark outline of the *Vesuvia* against the shore. Ten minutes later, Angelo tapped him on the shoulder and pointed twenty degrees off the starboard bow.

"Try the light," Carlo told him. "Three flashes. If it's the *Vesuvia*, she will answer by flashing on her navigation lights three times as well."

Angelo moved deftly to the side of the boat. Two of the others helped him swing the boom holding the big light and its reflecting shade over the starboard side so that it was poised above the dark surface. Seconds later, the sea beside them was illuminated by a bright light that came and went three times.

Sticking his head out of the wheelhouse, Carlo peered across the dark expanse of water, searching for an answer. When it came—a faint misshapen triangle of red, white, and green lights—it was farther off than he had expected. Whoever had spotted the *Vesuvia* had better eyes than he did. Still, there was no mistaking the signal. Carlo increased the engine revs slightly and turned the wheel toward the lights.

Salvatore was already in the bows with a boathook when the outline of the freighter loomed out of the darkness twenty yards ahead. Carlo slowed the engine, shifted the drive astern to slow them, and then cut the engine completely to let the boat make her final approach in silence.

As they slid alongside, a boat hook reached down from the side of the *Vesuvia*. Leandro and Gaspare were waiting with ropes, and as soon as they were alongside, the two of them jumped nimbly onto the freighter's deck and made her fast.

Carlo followed them next, pulling himself up and landing lightly on the deck. A man holding a boathook came toward him. "Captain Vincenzo?" asked Carlo quietly.

"Who wants to know?" asked the voice in the darkness.

"Carlo Vizzini. Don Pagano has sent me to meet you, with my friends."

"Good. But be quick and be quiet. My crew are locked down below. They can't get out, but if they wake, they may hear things, and it will not be the fighting that is supposed to be taking place."

He directed Carlo to a hatch in the deck, which had been moved to one side to reveal a square black hole into the hold. "What you're looking for is hidden under those sacks of grain toward the bows. There are fifty packets. Each one weighs a kilo.

I suggest we line up in a chain to pass them down to your boat. That will be the quickest way."

Carlo picked up the urgency in his voice.

"Don Pagano is a bold man to steal this much," Vincenzo added. "I hope he knows what he is doing."

"He is not stealing," Carlo answered. "He is only redirecting. And we only need five packets, not fifty."

The captain's silence conveyed his surprise.

"There's been a change of plan. This way is much better. More effective for Don Pagano." Carlo added, "And much safer for you."

Vincenzo took up position over the hatch and directed the Ferro brothers in the hold below, where the gentle thud of sacks being manhandled soon filled the darkness.

While this was in progress, Carlo got Angelo and Salvatore to remove the hatch in the deck of the fishing boat and told them to heave the two bundles of nets out of the fish locker. The nets were heavier than they expected and they hissed to Gaspare and Angelo to give them a hand.

"Put them over here," Carlo whispered from the gunwhale close to the *Vesuvia*. The four men stumbled over with their awkward bundles and dumped them on the wooden deck, which reverberated with two hollow thuds.

Carlo knelt beside the first bundle and started unravelling the net. "Open that one up too," he whispered. With five pairs of hands pulling the nets apart, it didn't take long to see what was inside. Even in the starlight, it was clear they contained an unexpected catch.

"Mary, Mother of God," exclaimed Salvatore.

The four young men stared silently at what they had revealed.

Side by side beneath the stars lay the Bontade family guards: Tommasso Manzella and Roberto Liggio.

"Leave the nets behind," Carlo ordered. "Just get these two onto the *Vesuvia*."

The four men beside him hoisted the two lifeless bodies unceremoniously over the side of the freighter and onto the deck, where Vincenzo and Carlo were waiting to drag them to the opening into the hold.

"Are you ready to pass up the five packets?"

Carlo was answered by the first oblong-shaped bundle.

"Are they dead?" asked Salvatore.

"No," Carlo told him brusquely. "Forget about them. They're staying here. We're not."

In less than five minutes, five packets had been retrieved from the hold, and Simone and Leonardo Ferro had been hauled out as well.

"Did you put everything back like it was?" Carlo asked.

"Yes," Leonardo answered. "No one will know those sacks have been moved."

"Okay. Put the hatch back, and then get on the boat." Carlo then ordered Salvatore to start the engine and got two more to stand by the ropes to cast off as soon as he was on board. "I'll tell you what is happening when we're under way." He turned to Vincenzo. "Have you got the cord?"

The captain handed over a length of strong line.

Carlo knotted the rope into a loop and then wrapped it around the captain's wrists until he heard him flinch. "Sorry, but it's got to look real."

As Vincenzo settled against the gunwhale, the way he thought attackers might bind and leave him, Carlo bent over the two unconscious guards and removed something from each of his jacket pockets. Vincenzo saw a flash of metal and then heard a click followed by a second one. "Good luck, Captain. We must be on our way."

"Aren't you forgetting something?"

Carlo looked at the captain blankly. "What?"

"I don't need to be unconscious like those two, but I need to look as if I have been."

Carlo hesitated.

"Come on, man," Vincenzo told him. "For what the don is paying me, I can take a little discomfort. The mouth. It makes more blood—more of a show."

"If you're sure," Carlo answered.

"It's for my good too."

Carlo silenced him with a stunning blow that split the captain's bottom lip and sent his head crashing against the gunwhale. There would be an impressive bump by the time he was found.

"Two for the price of one," Carlo beamed, giving the captain a friendly poke with his boot and rubbing his bruised knuckle.

Chapter Thirty-Four

Despite the glow of success that had flooded over him after Carlo and the crew from the fishing boat had returned, Jack's plan allowed no time for self-congratulation. News of what happened in the fallout from their visit to Erice would reach them in the security of Don Pagano's villa. There were hasty farewells to the men from the south of the island coupled with respectful expressions of future success to the young man from America. Jack sent them on their way home wondering how many he would meet again and deflated in the knowledge that this assignment, successful as it had been, was over.

Francesco took the road south from Trapani, following the coast as far as Agrigento, and then cut inland to cross the center of the island to Catania. They arrived at the Pagano villa late in the evening two days later, but the don himself greeted them at the top of the steps and showed them to the dining room, where the table was set and food was brought. This time Francesco was invited to join Jack and Carlo while the don took his seat at the head of the table and shared a glass of wine with his young men.

He was guarded in what he told them, though Jack understood him well enough by now to see that his plan and the way he had carried it out had met with approval. Don Pagano invited Carlo and Francesco to describe the events of the past few days, leaving Jack to listen to their account and weigh up the details that clearly impressed them the greatest. What pleased him most were their references to him as Giovanni. Until they had set out for Erice he had always been Jack; after Erice they would always remember him by the name his father had given him.

When the meal was finished, Don Pagano asked Carlo and Francesco to excuse them, so that he and Jack could talk in private. Both men rose from the table when the don gestured to Jack to follow him to his study and then settled down over a fresh bottle of wine to savor their success.

"Word has come from America already," Don Pagano told Jack when the two of them were alone. "They say that Vito Genovese is like a mad animal. They say he trusts no one. After that sit-down the police broke up last fall, some people were asking serious questions about him. Now, those people see that he cannot even control his own supply lines. The crack has opened and Vito Genovese has fallen to the bottom of it."

"You mean Costello and Lansky have moved already?"

"Yes," answered the don. "Genovese and twenty-four of his men have been arrested for narcotics violations."

Don Pagano delivered this news with such little emotion that it took Jack a moment to register what he had said. "Genovese has been arrested? I can't believe it happened so quickly."

"All they needed was for the crack to be pushed wide open. You and Carlo and the others did that in Erice. Everything else was in place. You got Genovese looking one way, and then they snuck in and knocked him cold with a sucker punch."

Jack let out a sigh of astonishment. "Wow…"

"Indeed. But now it is time for you to return home."

The plans for Jack's return to America had never been specified because they had remained fluid. The weeks spent in Sicily had pushed Haddonfield, even sultry, sweet-scented Miami, to the recesses of Jack's thoughts. Detroit had faded further.

Jack remained a guest in Don Pagano's villa for a week after his return from Erice, during which time accounts of the in-fighting between the Grecos and Bontades filtered through to him. On the day before Jack left, Don Pagano called him to his study and handed him a copy of the paper from Catania.

"You can understand this newspaper?" he asked.

Jack nodded.

"Turn to page four." Don Pagano told him.

Jack did as he was asked and scanned the columns to find something familiar. He thought maybe he was looking in the wrong place until he saw the word *Vesuvia*. It was set under a small headline: "LOST AT SEA: NO SURVIVORS."

Jack read the stark announcement that wreckage had been found off the coast of Sardinia from a freighter: the *SS Vesuvia*, out of Palermo bound for Genoa. Jack checked the date. The article had been filed three days earlier in the Sardinian capital, Cagliari.

A lump began building in Jack's throat. "What does this mean?"

"It means our new friends do not like to be messed with," the don answered. "It means they have powerful friends in the government."

"Do you know what happened?

"They say a coastguard cutter challenged Captain Vincenzo off Capo Teulada, in the south of Sardinia. They say the captain refused to stop his ship. So the cutter opened fire on her. It wouldn't take much to send her to the bottom."

"What about the men on board? Surely some of them must have got away?"

"They did. Six men went into the water and swam toward the cutter, where the crew had a scrambling net waiting for them. Only, when they were real close, the captain of the cutter ordered his men to open up on them with the forward machine gun." Pagano held his stubby fingers apart in front of his face. "Bullets this big, Giovanni. Captain Vincenzo and his men were in little pieces when the fishes started feeding on them. They say the sea was still red half an hour after the cutter steamed away."

Jack felt hollow inside.

The sense of triumph he had privately enjoyed since returning from Erice deserted him. He had never met the master of the *Vesuvia*, though Carlo had spoken well of the quiet, earnest man.

"It was a good plan, Jack. You must not hold yourself responsible for this. Even the best plans cannot account for what men like this will do when they are threatened." Dominic Pagano studied the look of shock and surprise on the young American's face. "You must always remember this."

Francesco and Carlo said goodbye ten days later. The parting with Carlo was not something Jack had been looking forward to. The two young men had grown close in their weeks together. Though raised in such different worlds, it had taken little time to establish the bonds that united them. Both had placed trust in the other and seen that trust rewarded.

Don Pagano had arranged for Jack's return trip. He had told the boys to deliver him to the airport. From there Carlo did not know what would be in store for Jack on the other side of the Atlantic, though he knew better than to ask.

For that matter, neither did Jack. At least not exactly.

"Go safely, my friend," Carlo said, hugging him warmly.

"You too, Carlo."

Francesco, strong and silent, held out a mighty hand, and squeezed Jack's with feeling. "*Arrivederci, Signor,*" he said solemnly in Italian.

"Giovanni, Francesco," Jack corrected him in Sicilian. "*Pi tu, Francesco—lu me nomu e Giovanni, sempri Giovanni.*"

The big man smiled with appreciation. "*Grazie, Signor Giovanni.*"

Chapter Thirty-Five

"Business like this has to be done in secret," Bernardo Sapienza tried to impress upon his brother. "How do you expect someone like this to behave, Mario? Is this man going to walk to our door in the middle of the day? Is he going to call out 'Mario, Bernardo—I want to buy your narcotics'?"

"Don't be stupid," Mario answered. "But is this the right way to do business, Bernardo? We go some place we have never been before. We meet a man we have never met before. And he takes us to another place we don't know."

"If you have a better way of finding a buyer for this much heroin, you tell me."

"Would we do this if we were at home?" Mario grumbled.

"If we were at home, we wouldn't be able to do this!"

"Just because we don't know the place we are going doesn't mean it isn't safe. The owner comes from Palermo. I know this because I have checked it out. Thank God I am not as stupid as you, when you choose to be."

"Since when has it been stupid to be cautious? What do you know of this man we are supposed to meet? Tell me who he is. Who does *he* belong to?"

Bernardo didn't find this as easy to answer. The truth was that he didn't know for certain whom their contact was. He'd received a message from his potential buyer, who wanted to use an intermediary to bring the Sapienzas to the meeting place.

"The owner is a good friend of mine," the message explained. "His place is quiet. We won't be disturbed and he is very discreet.

"Anyway, there'll be two of us," Bernardo insisted. "If we don't like the way things are going, we can clear out. There will always be another buyer."

Mario still wasn't convinced. "How can we be sure to keep this secret from Genovese's people?"

"In the same way as the man who wants to trade with us, of course," his brother answered with frustration. "Do you think this man wants to be caught by any of Genovese's soldiers? He needs to be sure about his safety even more than we do. We belong round here—or have you forgotten that too?"

Their conversation had broken up after that and they were barely speaking to each other as they waited at the rendezvous for their escort to appear. However, their spirits lifted when he showed up.

The man addressed them jovially in Sicilian, asked if they were hungry, because the place they were going served the best linguini he had ever tasted, and led them to an old Chevrolet parked in a back street.

Bernardo got in beside the driver, Mario took the back seat. The driver seemed totally at ease and kept up a constant flow of talk all the way to Hoboken, across the Hudson River in New Jersey.

They drew to a halt outside a dress shop. "We'll leave the car here. The place we're going is around the block. Five minutes, if that."

Once more he didn't seem concerned to be alone with Bernardo and Mario, but led the way to a glass door beside a window on which was painted the name San Lorenzo.

Their escort opened the door. "My favorite place in New Jersey. Sit anywhere you want." He turned the sign on the door so that it read CLOSED from the sidewalk outside. "The owner is a good friend; we have the place to ourselves tonight."

The restaurant was long and narrow. Along one wall was a painting of the Bay of Naples. Dusty fishing nets with round glass floats decorated the back corners, beside the doors to the restrooms and the yard behind. There were prints of Etna and

Palermo as well. The place embodied the worn-out, poverty-ridden lands of southern Italy.

A diminutive man with a drooping moustache appeared through the swinging door from the kitchen. "Good evening, Signor. I am working in here. If you need anything, please call. The other gentleman will be here soon, I think."

"We'll get what we want, then," replied the escort, waving the owner back to his chopping board and cooker.

The three men sat at the table laid for four while the clock above the kitchen door ticked away. A bowl of fresh crusty bread sat between them, and Mario was breaking a piece, showering the paper tablecloth with bread crumbs, when the kitchen door swung open again.

Bernardo turned to greet the man he had come to see and found himself looking at two men, not one. And one of them had a face that made Bernardo feel sick and weak at the knees.

Standing next to him was Carmine Galante.

Mario dropped his piece of bread. The barrel of a snub-nosed pistol pressed against his temple. Beside him, their escort had the same cheerful grin as he clicked back the hammer of the handgun and raised the index finger of his other hand to his lips, to tell Mario to keep quiet.

Any chance Bernardo had of crying out was stifled by the man standing next to Galante, who slipped a kitchen towel over Bernardo's mouth and jerked his head backward.

Carmine Galante took a long-bladed knife from his pocket. He picked up one corner of the paper tablecloth, placed the blade against the edge of the paper and cut steadily through it with a regular sawing motion.

There would be no further trading for the Sapienza brothers that night, or any other. After their butchered bodies were found in the street, Bruno Pafundi lost no time in claiming them as his boys. The word was passed to track down the killers and, although they were never identified, the trail somehow led right to Vito Genovese's heavily guarded door.

Chapter Thirty-Six

MEMORANDUM

To:	**Ambassador Kennedy**
From:	**James Lovall**
Date:	**November 6, 1958**
Subject:	**Election Strategy**

I know that complacency is not in your nature, sir. So I hope you will allow me to look beyond Tuesday's success, while acknowledging Jack's outstanding achievement in securing a record 73.6 percent of the vote in his Senate race.

In turning our attention to the bigger "ballgame" in two years time, we need to consider who we must get to bat for us. Their work on the McClellan committee has already introduced JFK and RFK to a section of the American TV audience; but the challenge we face is in getting JFK better known across the nation as a whole. May I suggest the time is now right to encourage your press associates, such as Hearst, Luce, and Krock, to begin spreading the word? Perhaps something along the lines of "The Amazing Kennedys" would capture the positive atmosphere we must develop. Features on Mrs. Jacqueline Kennedy are sure to go down well. I would also advocate targeting publications such as: Life, Redbook, *the* Ladies' Home Journal, Coronet, *and the* Reader's Digest.

Over the next twelve months, the American people need to understand why JFK is the greatest attraction in the country today. I think we can rely on these gentlemen and titles to deliver that.

May I propose that we pencil January 2, 1960, into our calendars? Coming right after New Year, Saturday, January 2, 1960, would be an eye-catching date for JFK to declare his candidacy for the Democratic nomination for the presidency. It would make excellent copy in the following day's papers and, as you need no reminding, more people read the papers on Sunday than on any other day of the week. His declaration would attract even greater attention if JFK were to announce it in the same hearing room where TV audiences have seen him and RFK grilling senior organized crime figures for the McClellan hearings.

Chapter Thirty-Seven

Rip saw the glow of the newly lit fire burning inside Jack the moment he laid eyes on the young man at Idlewild Airport. Carmella felt it in the warm embrace Jack gave her when Rip returned him to Spruce Street. Word had reached her that her son had lived up to expectation, and the enthusiasm and detail in which Jack related his time with her family satisfied her deepest hopes. He had needed no fanfare from his mother upon his arrival in her homeland. What he had achieved, he had accomplished by himself.

For Meyer Lansky and Frank Costello, the cloud of what had happened in Detroit had been dispersed in the maelstrom into which the Palermo cartels and their associates had been sucked.

"Vito Genovese don't know which way to turn," Lansky told Jack when they met beside the ocean, on the sands at Long Beach a week after he got home. "The son of a bitch ain't got no idea what hit him. Three months ago he thought his organization was running like a well-greased machine. Now— it's like a bearing has seized and the whole thing is cooking up real quick. Genovese goes before a grand jury next spring," he concluded. "He won't never come out of prison. You can take my word for that."

They continued along the beach. Sand kicked up in the autumn breeze. Lansky got Jack to take him through his time in Sicily stage by stage. He got him to repeat what Don Pagano and the heads of the other families had told him about the grip the narcotics operations had on business right across the island.

He showed little surprise when Jack told him of the growth of drugs—heroin in particular—throughout southern Italy.

"Give them the money, they'll go for the biggest kick," Lansky told him.

"Did Don Pagano tell you what happened to the crew of the ship?" Jack asked.

"Sure he did," Lansky answered. "In business, you get casualties like you do in war. When the stakes are high, Jack, a man has to weigh his chances and make his choice. Risk and return—that's what it's about. If things had worked out different, the fellas on that ship wouldn't be complaining. Don't beat yourself up about it. You got other things to concentrate on now that you're home."

Their conversation turned toward the fall and college. The University of Miami had awarded Coach Sullivan's star end a football scholarship, though Lansky noted that Jack showed less immediate enthusiasm at the prospect of playing for the Hurricanes than he might have a year earlier. Sicily had given him a chance to put Rip Collins's careful tutelage to the test. It didn't take a genius to see the self-assurance it had given him.

The fall semester had left him strangely detached from his expectations of life as a college freshman. His scholarship had landed him one of the best rooms on campus, with a stunning view across verdant gardens to the ocean, and he had returned the Hurricanes' faith in him with some impressive displays on the football field. In class, he was pleased to find that his studies stimulated him, and the faculty were pleasantly encouraged by the start he had made. Meyer Lansky would have approved of the diligence with which Jack applied himself to his business studies; Frank Costello would not have been disappointed by the way he approached his political science program. But it was in acknowledging their interest and approval that Jack registered the source of his unease. College life was too bland, too structured, and too predictable. He had his summer in Sicily to thank for that.

Out running or training with the football team, he caught himself wondering what Carlo Vizzini was doing at that moment. There had been times he was reading in the library when flashes of Don Pagano's study came to him and he felt the older man silently scrutinizing his work. And down at the beach, Jack had found himself more than once lost in thought as he stood gazing at the ocean, imagining a red stain spreading across its dappled surface beneath which fish gorged themselves as the SS *Vesuvia* settled forever into the seabed.

Carmella had sensed the source of Jack's distraction right away. Her questions about campus life and Miami in general had drawn little reaction. In Sicily, his eyes had been opened; back home it was like he had been fitted with blinders.

However, Frank Costello had been adamant on this point. "You've got to learn to pace yourself," he told Jack. "You did a great job this summer. But that's over now. Period. And until the next time, you've got to melt into the background—disappear like a chameleon."

Jack wanted to know when they would need him again.

Costello refused to commit himself. "You'll get word soon enough."

This left Jack to pursue his studies feeling more than a tad frustrated. In high school, football had given him a release when he needed it, and now football had been supplanted by something wholly different.

Rebel action down in Cuba had been gathering momentum in recent months, and on January 1, 1959, offered sanctuary by the equally repressive dictator, Rafael Trujillo, Fulgencio Batista fled to the Dominican Republic. His flight left Fidel Castro free to enter Havana as its victorious liberator.

In America's progressive circles, the thirty-two-year-old revolutionary was touted as the "George Washington of Cuba," and the *New York Times* editorial paying tribute to his assumption of power had trumpeted, "The American people wish him good fortune."

Jack was mystified.

The city was swelling with Cuban exiles. Each day, the numbers of desperate, anxious people grew. Jack would go to the harbor to watch them arrive, walking down the companionway with little more than a bag and a dwindling hope that they might see home again some day.

Jack had neither seen nor heard anything from Miller for more than six months, but when his call came toward the end of February, Jack was not surprised. In various ways, Miller had been circulating in his mind. Detroit, Sicily, and now the news from Cuba; Miller's reappearance was not unexpected.

The rendezvous was set in Lummus Park, facing the river in Downtown Miami.

They walked on in silence, eventually halting beside a group of tables where people were absorbed in games of checkers and chess.

Miller nodded toward two elderly men steeped in concentration over a sparsely populated chessboard. "Do you play?"

"I like to play, but I wouldn't say I was much good," Jack answered.

"It fascinates me. It's not just the strategy," Miller said. "It's the deception, the bluff, which gives me a kick."

They watched three moves in as many minutes before one of the players gathered a bishop in his gnarled fingers and tapped it against his opponent's king.

Checkmate.

They continued walking toward the river, bristling with boat docks.

"I hear things worked out this summer," Miller said. "Better than Detroit, at least."

"Better than Detroit," Jack agreed.

"There's a shit storm stirring. Like I knew there would be. I know Cuba. Havana was my first assignment. There are people here who think they've covered all the bases because they've been sending guns to Fidel and his friends. But I'm not so sure. I've seen it before, Jack. A country finds itself in a vacuum, like they did in Europe after Hitler and Mussolini, and you've got no control over what gets sucked in. We had to work our asses off in Greece and Italy, and even France for Christ's sake, breaking the unions in Marseilles. I don't know for sure what is going to happen or when, but it won't be long."

He left it at that and switched the conversation to Jack's life as a student. Miller joked that his own college days were too far off to recall in detail. Somewhere in New England was the closest he came to disclosing the whereabouts of his alma mater.

"How do you get on with the faculty?"

Jack was friendly with his teachers to a certain extent, but he was careful not to grow too close to them.

"You know what they say about teachers," Miller started, "that you can only judge how good they are by how their students perform?"

Jack understood what Miller was getting at.

"Well, I could do with a little help down here right now, Jack. And I thought maybe you'd like to get involved."

"Like in Detroit?" Jack asked warily.

"No, Jack. You don't make mistakes like that twice."

"What exactly do you have in mind?" Jack asked.

"You won't have heard," Miller began, "but Castro has opened the casinos again. All of them, Jack—only six weeks after shutting them down when he took over. I need to know what deals have been done, who's done them, and what everyone is getting out of it."

"And you expect me to be able to come up with answers like that?" Jack answered, almost laughing at the idea.

"So long as you follow the leads I give you. There are two men down here with big stakes in Cuba: Santo Trafficante in Tampa, and Carlos Marcello in New Orleans. They're not as big as Meyer in the casinos, but Meyer works only the casinos. Trafficante and Marcello do a lot of other business, in and out of Cuba."

"Narcotics?" Jack asked.

"Narcotics and arms. Everything's in place," Miller said. "It won't take much to build up what's already there. The question is, where are the arms going out and the junk coming in, when everyone steps up a gear?"

"This is what you want me to find out?'

"I'm going to give you three names and I want you to give me all you can find out about them, most importantly how they connect to Trafficante and Marcello."

"And they're here in Miami, all three of them?"

"Two are in New Orleans: David Ferrie and Guy Banister. Ferrie's a hotshot pilot. I guess Banister's a hotshot in his own right. FBI man. He did intelligence work in the war."

Jack waited to hear the third man's name, but Miller didn't seem like he was going to mention it. "And the third man?"

"He's originally from Chicago as well, but he's been in Dallas since 1947, taking care of business for the Chicago mob." Miller leafed through the pages of his book. "He operates a sleazy joint called the Vegas Club. You can find that for yourself, though. The most recent home address I have is 4727 Homer. That's from six weeks ago. Rubenstein, Jacob Rubenstein."

While Miller was speaking into one ear, Jack could hear Meyer Lansky in the other. He was reminding him that for what Miller had done, there would be restitution. This trip to New Orleans, these men he was to follow, would settle the debt. He had no choice.

However, he did have one condition.

"All right, Miller. It sounds like a plan. But this time, I bring my own partner along. I don't mean to offend you—and I know Joe Gordon was a loyal friend of my father's—"

"There's no need to apologize." Miller didn't seem at all surprised. In fact, if anything, he seemed impressed with the young man. Whereas Jack had been content to let Miller call the action last time, his months in Sicily had made him a man of action and resolve. Not only that, but it seemed they had already fallen into sync. "Rip Collins is on the next flight out."

Chapter Thirty-Eight

The second the phone began to ring, Husky sensed who was on the line.

"Yes?" he said expectantly.

"Good work," said the familiar voice. "Very good work."

"Pleased to be able to help."

"No really. What you gave us has made a valuable contribution. Our fat friend from New Orleans can't dodge these bullets." The speaker paused. "Is he ready? Does he understand the situation?"

"Perfectly," said Husky.

"So he's going to take the fifth?"

"He can't afford to do anything else."

"Good."

"That way we win both ways. We ask the incriminating questions and when he refuses to answer, we get to give the answers we want people to hear. That's smart."

"Kind of you to say so," said the caller. "And what about the other gentleman—the one from Tampa? Is he ready too?"

"That's another smart move," Husky acknowledged. "With his passport, he knows he can get back into this country when the heat's off, not like his friend who has to sit tight and sweat."

"I expect he's looking forward to spending his summer in Havana. He must be feeling more optimistic than he was at New Year."

"Well, Castro can't survive on fresh air and promises."

"Nor can the people he made the promises to."

"Opening the casinos again—it still beats me. It's a perfect blind. Just when everyone expects a new kind of action, suddenly it's business as usual."

"That's what we hope."

"Do we have a date yet for our fat friend's appearance before the cameras?" Husky asked.

"March 24th."

"It's going to be quite a show"

The caller chuckled. "You deserve something appropriate for your pains. I'm only sorry that what they roll in Havana isn't to your taste."

"I guess it's my loss," agreed Husky. "But I can wait."

"I'm sure you can."

Chapter Thirty-Nine

Jack and Rip spent the first two nights quietly getting the lay of the land in New Orleans. On the third morning, the car they had hired cruised through the central business district west of the French Quarter. Jack had telephoned Guy Banister's secretary two days earlier, telling her he was interested in interviewing her boss for a college newspaper article he was writing on the history of law enforcement.

Banister was away, she'd told him, but he could try again two days later. "Telephone in the afternoon," she said. "He's meeting a client in the morning."

They found Lafayette Street adjacent to Lafayette Square. The address Miller had given Jack was a shabby, mousy grey building on the corner of Lafayette and Camp Street. The sign on number 531 read, GUY BANISTER ASSOCIATES, INC. INVESTIGATORS. Around the corner, on the ground floor of the same building, was Mancuso's restaurant, where they decided to wait.

They took their time over coffee, two buddies passing the morning chatting about nothing in particular and giving away no clue that each was keeping careful watch on the street outside for anyone visiting the office above.

Restaurant customers came and went—regulars for the most part, it seemed. Around an hour after Rip and Jack had arrived, a heavily built man in his early sixties took a seat at a table and was joined a few minutes later by a dapper-looking man, who seemed out of place in the seedy surroundings.

"What can I get you, Mr. Banister?"

"My usual," the older man answered. "What do you want, John?" he asked his companion.

"Coffee," replied the other man. "Espresso, if you have it."

"One black coffee coming up."

It took Jack a moment to register the change in Rip's demeanor. He'd shifted his position and was now sitting so that his face was turned away from the two new arrivals, though he could still catch what they were saying.

Jack had a good view of the two men. Guy Banister had a ruddy complexion and blue eyes that stared right at you—unnervingly like Albert Anastasia's. He wore a small rosebud in his lapel. Jack speculated what Banister's relationship might be with the other man—the one Banister had called John. He was a few years younger, more finely built, and in better physical shape. He was well-dressed, too, but his clothes were more expensive, more fashionable than Banister's regulation business suit. He looked like the kind of man Jack had seen in show business magazines. Or a big shot in the movies, maybe, with a blonde on each arm. What he was doing hanging out with Banister in a dump like Mancuso's, Jack had no idea.

Rip ordered another coffee while they listened to the two men talk. They had a common interest in Chicago, that much was clear—and in Cuba. For the older man, Castro's takeover sounded like the most recent in a chain of setbacks, which he took as almost personal in their intensity. He must have assumed he was in likeminded company because he spared nothing in expressing his loathing of "niggers," "Jews," and "commies." He hated "commies" worse than anyone, Jack concluded.

"The mayor himself invited me to this city to be deputy chief of police," Bannister announced bitterly. "Then two years ago they push me out of the force and into retirement, and all because I showed some cocksucker waiter that this is still a country where the right to bear arms means something."

From what Jack could glean from their discussion, Banister's private detection business was struggling. Jack wasn't surprised;

the man was already into his third large martini.

"Carlos is seeing you though, right?" asked the man with him.

"Steady there." Banister glanced nervously round the restaurant. He lowered his voice so Jack could barely hear. "Marcello takes up the slack, sure he does. But no one ain't never seen us together. You understand what I'm telling you? He puts business my way and I make sure he knows what the Bureau and the other agencies are doing. It works good that way."

His companion patted his arm reassuringly and said he understood.

Banister continued, "When I was in the bureau at the beginning, it was the FBI that took care of all US intelligence in Latin America, and we were damn good. They gave us a job, we found the right people and we got it done—period. None of the fuck-ups they have now." Banister swallowed another swig of Martini. "If the Bureau was still running the show in Cuba, this Castro bum would be six feet under."

"I'll drink to that." The man sipped his coffee, and then told Banister quietly, "See here, Guy. A man with your experience, your contacts, shouldn't be tied to one organization. You're used to spreading your wings. That's what we want you to think about. You know that. Give it some serious thought. What we're proposing is the same, in reverse—just on a bigger scale. Way bigger."

Jack would have liked to have listened for longer, but he caught Rip's eye and noticed that most of the other tables were emptying. They called for the check, paid, and left in conversation without even a second glance at the two men.

Only when they had driven off along Camp Street did Rip mention the conversation they had been listening to. "No prizes for guessing which is Banister."

"Do you know the other man?"

"It's a good few years since we saw each other and I've changed more than he has. His name is John Rosselli. He used to be the outfit's man in Hollywood."

Jack was gratified that his hunch had been right.

"Rosselli's moved on to even bigger things now," Rip continued. "He takes care of business in Las Vegas for the Chicago boys."

"He looks the perfect front man for that kind of glitz."

"Don't let yourself be taken in by what he looks like," Rip cautioned. "There's another side to Johnny Rosselli. He's a killer, Jack. A stone killer. Miller will be very interested to know that Johnny Rosselli has come all this way to visit Special Agent in Charge Banister."

David Ferrie proved to be more elusive. There was no sign of him for nearly a week at the address Miller had given Jack, though when he did show up, his absence was explained. Ferrie was dressed in a pressed uniform and peaked cap bearing the insignia of Eastern Airlines.

Rip and Jack watched the apartment until well into the evening, when Ferrie reappeared in pale pants and a jacket, got into his car, and drove off. Rip tailed him as far as Bourbon Street and stopped a few cars down from where Ferrie had parked. They watched him exchange gags with a group of young men hanging around the door of the club and then he went inside. Jack and Rip waited five minutes, and when it was clear that Ferrie was staying there, they left their car and followed him into the jazz-throbbing interior of Dixie's Bar of Music.

The club was packed with men. Some were dressed like bikers, head to toe in leather. Most were casually turned out in sports shirts and pants. Some of the younger ones paraded in tight-fitting denims as opposed to several of the older clientele who were decked out in business suits, collars, and ties. Miss Dixie had a reputation for looking after her clients and the atmosphere was relaxed, or as relaxed as any bar could be where singles entered hoping to leave as one half of a couple.

Rip fetched two beers from the bar and ambled through the crowd with Jack in tow as they looked for a free table. They spotted David Ferrie talking with three young men. The table two along was vacant and Rip took Jack's arm and guided him to it.

The dim lighting of the club made David Ferrie's appearance even more bizarre. To Jack, he looked like he was still wearing a Mardi Gras mask. Above his eyes, Ferrie sported two arched eyebrows, absurdly etched in thick greasepaint. And above these a tatty red wig rested at an uneasy angle on his bald head.

Ferrie did most of the talking. He seemed to have some position in the Civil Air Patrol. It soon became clear that this was the link with the young men. Ferrie was a commercial pilot, but he took pride in describing some of his moonlighting, flying all kinds of aircraft into remote locations around the Caribbean. Guatemala, Honduras, Haiti, the Dominican Republic, Cuba—Ferrie had flown to them all, though he was coy when one of his young listeners asked what he had been doing on these flights.

"Let's just say I wasn't flying in charity workers," he joked.

"You mean these were secret?" asked another. "Covert operations, like in the movies?"

"Give me a break. I'd like to see any of those movie airmen drop a Dakota packed full of guns and high explosives into some of the jungle airstrips I've landed at, in the dark, and then take off again with a full load of seriously valuable merchandise."

The young men looked suitably impressed. "Was that for the military, Dave?"

"Everyone with a gun is somebody's military," Ferrie answered. "Who the fuck cares anyway, so long as it keeps the wheels of commerce turning." He drained his glass. "Now which of you boys is going to get your captain another drink?"

The young man who volunteered was on his way back from the bar when Jack felt Rip's arm slip round his shoulders. Rip leaned his head close, so his lips were almost touching Jack's ear. "Don't look up," he whispered. "Johnny Rosselli is coming toward us. We're going to go slowly to the door and get the hell out of here."

"Hey, how you doing," they heard Ferrie say when he saw Rosselli approaching. He stood up to shake hands enthusiastically."Boys, let me introduce…"

But Rosselli stopped him there, raising his hands in mock embarrassment. "That won't be necessary, David. It's you I've come to see."

There was an awkward silence before Jack heard Ferrie say, "Okay, fellas, I'll catch you later. This gentleman and I have some business to discuss."

Chairs were pushed back, farewells were made, and Jack felt Rip squeeze his hand and lead him away. He tried to look calm, but sweat was forming in his palms and the walk to the door was like slow motion.

Chapter Forty

Twenty-four hours later, they were in Dallas, outside Jack Ruby's Vegas Club at 3508 Oak Lawn Avenue.

On the drive to Texas from New Orleans, they had talked through what they had unearthed. Johnny Rosselli's visits to both Banister and Ferrie didn't look like a coincidence. Ferrie had been out of town, and Rosselli had probably arranged to meet when he got back. Jack and Rip guessed he'd fixed to see Banister on the same visit to New Orleans. But did either Banister or Ferrie know Rosselli was seeing the other? That was something they couldn't answer, though the link between the two men made fascinating speculation.

"What do you reckon the chances were of us catching Rosselli with both Banister and Ferrie?" Jack asked Rip.

"Pretty long, I guess," he answered. "So long, in fact, you have to wonder if it was chance at all."

Jack wasn't sure he understood. "What are you getting at, Rip?"

"Only that Miller knows a lot about other people's movements. Isn't it possible he knew Johnny Rosselli was going to be in the South around now and he sent us to see if the pieces of the jigsaw fitted together?"

Jack Ruby's twelve years in Dallas had been spent trying to scrape together a living from a series of sleazy nightspots and failing for the most part; the owner of the Vegas Club was no stranger to debt.

He'd been more successful in establishing good relations with the Dallas Police Department, which was just as well given his reputation for pistol-whipping and sapping people—customers, for the most part, that he had taken a disliking to. Although he had been arrested several times for carrying a concealed gun, breaking state licensing laws, assault, and breach of the peace—not to mention over a dozen traffic violations—the only penalty he had received was for a traffic summons. Years of bringing sandwiches to police officers on duty, slipping them drinks on the house, and introducing them to easy women had kept Jack Ruby out of harm's way.

Word had it that Ruby used this "good old boy" reputation to cover his more sinister activities—the ones Miller was interested in, Jack guessed. Since the mid-1950s, Ruby's permission was needed to cash in on the major narcotics trafficking network growing in ports around the Gulf of Mexico. Rip heard that the Ruby family had been involved in the drug business for decades, though Ruby himself was now playing in an altogether bigger league.

Which accounts for Miller's interest, Jack reflected.

Narcotics weren't Jack Ruby's only trafficking venture. He dabbled in gunrunning, shipping weapons stolen from the Department of Defense and National Guard arsenals to renegade bands throughout the Caribbean and Latin America. Rip reckoned he didn't make much money from that either, even though the illegal arms market had opened wide since the US government's embargo on arms sales to Cuba in 1958.

"He sounds like a nice guy," Jack commented when Rip had concluded his character sketch.

They'd found Ruby's home address and the Vegas Club on their first day in Dallas, but there was no sign of the man himself. On their first visit to the club, the proprietor wasn't around and they were told to try back the next evening.

Now they were outside, on the point of encountering the man who had his particular way of making people feel unwelcome, Jack was starting to feel nervous.

"Come on," Rip encouraged him. "We go in here just like we did at the joint in New Orleans. It's like the exercises we used to do, Jack: over and over and over again, until it's second nature. If these are the places our targets hang out, we have to hang out in them as well. So long as we spend money and don't start a fight, Ruby won't give us another look."

"It may be second nature to you," Jack told Rip. "You've had years of doing this kind of thing. But I had a bad experience my first time, remember? This place is different from where we were in New Orleans."

Rip opened the car door and stepped out into the street. "That's why I'm on the case too."

The Vegas Club was well patronized by powerfully built men dressed in open-neck shirts and sports jackets. The club was throbbing to the sound of a five-piece rhythm and blues band led by a saxophonist parading along the bar top blasting out a solo as Jack and Rip arrived.

It didn't take long to identify the man they were seeking. Paunchy, balding, and dressed in a dark suit, pale shirt, and tie, Jack Ruby was glad-handing among his regulars and scarcely noticed the two newcomers. A quick glance must have told him they weren't high-rollers. Taking a seat by one wall, Rip scanned the room for familiar faces, but he didn't recognize anyone.

When the band took a break, Jack saw Ruby collecting two drinks on a tray from the bar and making his way across the dance floor to a door at the back of the club.

Rip watched as Ruby carefully closed the door. "Back office is my guess."

"Why two drinks?" Jack hadn't seen Ruby touch a drop all the time they had been watching him.

"We'll have to wait and see."

They got their answer twenty minutes later. The door at the back of the club opened and Ruby appeared, followed by two men.

"Dave Yaras," Rip said under his breath. "Well I'll be damned."

"And the other one?" He was small and wiry, with dark eyes, crinkly hair, and olive skin. It didn't take much to guess he was Latin.

Rip did not recognize the man.

Ruby escorted the two men to the club entrance, shook both their hands, and saw them out.

"Drink up," Rip said, "and let's get something to eat. I want to start heading back tonight. We've found plenty to satisfy your friend Miller. Though it wouldn't surprise me if he didn't already have a hunch that Yaras would be down here like Rosselli."

Chapter Forty-One

Miller was impressed when Jack took him through what he and Rip had come across on their trip, although he gave nothing away to suggest that he might have known in advance that Jack and Rip were likely to run into the two men from the Chicago outfit. In fact, he gave every impression of being particularly interested in them.

"You're right about Rosselli being a high-roller," Miller confirmed. "I guess you know that he takes care of the casino business in Las Vegas for Giancana and the Chicago outfit."

"We thought it would need someone like him, someone important, to set things in place when the trafficking in Cuba builds up," Jack explained. "Does that make sense?"

"It seems logical to me."

"If I heard them right," Jack continued, "Banister has plenty of experience in undercover gunrunning. It sounded to us like Rosselli wants him to use that experience—use those contacts—to bring narcotics back into this country."

"It would make sense," Miller agreed.

"And Ferrie's a pilot, the kind of pilot you'd need to run secret missions like that. If Ferrie and Banister don't know each other already, we reckon it won't be long before they do."

Miller was quiet for a moment, thinking through what Jack had told him.

"Okay," he said. "Tell me about Dave Yaras."

"You know how he comes from Chicago, like Ruby? Maybe they know each other from there; if so, they go back a long way. Rip says Yaras worked as a hit man for Sam Giancana.

"What's interesting about Yaras is where he connects with people in the South. He knows Jack Ruby. But apparently Yaras has an office in Miami that Santo Trafficante uses when he's in town.

"And, the way Rip puts it, just so he doesn't feel left out, Carlos Marcello also knows Dave Yaras. Twelve years ago, Yaras was arrested for killing a man who was causing Marcello trouble. After one witness was murdered and another disappeared, Yaras was released and the police never brought any charges against him. "So he has useful contacts in the South as well as back home in the Windy City."

"Johnny Rosselli included?" Miller suggested.

"Almost certainly, we think."

"Why do you think he was with Ruby and that other guy?"

"Rip and I reckon it's to do with Cuba. The man we saw with Yaras and Ruby looked like he could come from Cuba, and, until two months ago, Yaras ran several gambling operations on the island."

Miller started putting the pieces of information together, checking with Jack that he had heard him right. "So we got Ruby with Yaras and this Cuban type. Yaras who knows Marcello and Trafficante…"

"And who's connected to Chicago," Jack reminded him.

"And who also has connections to Cuba."

"That's the people for you," Jack said. "Now, here's the geography. Meyer Lansky talked about the shipping routes from the production plants in Europe. Miami, Tampa, New Orleans, Galveston: There are your ports of entry and the people to run the narcotics distribution. What we couldn't figure out at first was how they move drugs around the country.

"The volume involved would need an army of couriers. But seeing Dave Yaras gave Rip an idea. That office in Miami I told you about, the one Trafficante uses: It belongs to the Teamsters. Dave Yaras helped organize Teamster Local 320 there. And he's also closely involved with the Teamsters' president, Jimmy Hoffa."

Miller was looking at him quizzically.

"It seems so simple, so obvious," Jack continued, undeterred. "They go everywhere and nobody gives them a second thought. It has to be the perfect distribution network. Forget couriers or secret flights. Rip and I think that they're using trucks to ship narcotics all over the country, just like any other commodity. And they're using Hoffa and the Teamsters to do it for them."

Miller weighed everything Jack had told him. Then his face broke into a wide grin. "Well, you certainly connected some dots on this trip. It sounds like an unusually profitable spring break. This is good, Jack, very good. Make sure you tell that to Rip."

Jack grinned with relief. This was something to be pleased about, and it felt good to have shown Miller—and Rip—that he could be useful.

"You get back to your studies, Jack. I hope I won't need to distract you from them for a while. Enjoy your summer."

Miller was as good as his word; Jack had graduated from college before Miller called on his services again.

Part III

Chapter Forty-Two

Late in the summer of 1959, rumors started picking up that Santo Trafficante had been imprisoned in Cuba. Jack's information implied that Trafficante was one of a number of underworld figures Castro was parading in front of the Cuban people as an example of how he was already taking steps to root out "gringo gangsters." Jack was amused by this. The prospect of Trafficante in jail would be a perfect distraction from the timely addition to Fidel's coffers of his share of the skim from the casinos.

The upcoming US presidential election was the only national event in which Jack and his fellow students shared a common interest. There was a thrill of expectancy around the campus when Jack Kennedy won the Democratic nomination in July 1960. Young, handsome, and charismatic, Kennedy promised to blow away the smog of the leaden Eisenhower years and lead the nation into a golden era. Set against him, in the eyes of Jack's fellow students, Vice President Richard Nixon was not an appealing choice.

However, Jack could not forget the reason he had come to Florida. On one of his visits to Miami Beach, Meyer Lansky had directed him toward a New York career development and placement firm that had recently opened for business in the Coral Gables business district, not far from the university. Lansky was suspicious and asked Jack to find out why the recently installed company was showing such a keen interest in offering its services to the Cubans exiled in southern Florida.

A few days later, Jack went to the address Lansky had given him. His mentor had been right about the Cuban connection. In the hour that Jack watched, a steady flow of people came and went from the suite of offices; most had been young men with Latin features and coloring.

Jack returned the following day, an hour before the office was scheduled to close. This time he was taking careful note of anyone staying late after work: the janitor doing his rounds, the cleaning staff—a group of a dozen women who finished their work by eight in the evening. Around the back of the building, Jack investigated the fire escape and other likely ways into the offices. From the design of the windows, he knew they wouldn't present a problem to someone schooled by Rip Collins.

A little over twenty-four hours later, he was back, hiding in the shadows of the alley behind the office building. He waited until after ten o'clock, then he shinnied quietly up the wall using a service pipe to pull him as far as the fire escape. Two floors up, he checked for lights in the company's offices.

They were dark.

Reaching from the fire escape, he felt round the nearest window frame for a security sensor and located one at the point where the window opened. It was a design Rip had showed him, and a strip of metallic foil held in place with chewing gum short-circuited the alarm. Slipping a knife blade into the gap between the panes, Jack eased back the catch and then pulled steadily downward to slide the window open wide enough to climb inside.

After checking that no one was in the alley, Jack clicked on his flashlight and searched the office. A large map of Cuba hung on one wall with a series of handwritten notes identifying a number of locations, marked with a series of symbols. Most of the markings were around the Cuban coastline. Landing sites for the traffickers, Jack reckoned. What he couldn't work out was why several inland sites, particularly in the western half of the island, had also been highlighted. A ring had been drawn around the old colonial city of Trinidad, more or less centered on the south coast of Cuba.

As he knelt to examine the desk drawers, Jack heard a noise in the hallway outside. Light footsteps approached the door, passed by, and moved steadily down the hallway. Jack listened to the sound of the door opening in the office on the other side of the wall, waited a minute, and then slipped silently into the hallway to see what was happening.

Whoever entered ahead of him had left the door open, though they hadn't switched on the light. From the shadows, Jack saw a hooded figure silhouetted against the window on the far side of the office. The figure drew open the top drawer of a filing cabinet and switched on a flashlight. Jack pulled back, but the beam from the flashlight remained fixed on the drawer. There was a steady click of files being drawn back on each other. Whoever was in the office had no idea they had company. Keeping his breath steady, Jack readied himself, looked inside once again, and crept around the door to hide behind it

One after the other, the files clicked on. The intruder reached the back of the top drawer, slid it shut, drew out the one below, and began click, click, clicking through the files that one contained.

A loud bang like a car backfiring made Jack jump. Light flooded in through the open door with the sound of footsteps pounding down the hallway toward the office. An image of Reggio's apartment in Detroit leapt before his eyes.

"Second on the right!" yelled a voice.

"I've got it," another voice shouted back, almost in Jack's ear.

The bright neon light spilling into the office from the hallway abruptly darkened into the extended outline of a man's body. A burly form rushed past Jack and shone a flashlight on the figure by the window. Two dark brown oval eyes, wide and frightened, and the full lips and sensuous mouth of a girl Jack's own age.

The hallway light was blocked out almost entirely by a second man, who came panting into the office, holding an automatic up beside his head.

"We've got you now, you little runt," shouted the first man, pushing aside a chair as he advanced roughly toward the girl.

He raised his handgun and brought it crashing down toward the hooded head, but the girl was too quick for him. Her silhouette buckled in the middle and then disappeared behind her attacker. There was a heavy thud and a groan, followed by the sound of bodies falling to the ground and something metallic spilling across the carpet.

The second man was only a pace away from Jack, who sent him slumping against a desk and left him sprawled across the floor with a chop to the back of his neck.

By the time Jack reached the two grappling on the floor, the man had rolled over and pinned the girl down with his left hand around her throat and his right fist clenched to strike her. Jack checked his balance and slammed his foot into the attacker's right shoulder. The force of the blow sent the man sprawling sideways, cursing and clutching at his arm as it flopped at his side.

The girl sat up gasping for air. The hood of her sweatshirt had fallen back and her face and slim neck were framed by hair as dark as her eyes, cut in a loose fringe and swept down, thick and soft, over her ears to just above her shoulders.

Jack grabbed the loose folds of her top and yanked the girl to her feet. "We've got to get out of here."

She pushed him away and backed toward the door.

She was no match for Jack. He grabbed her wrist and dragged her out of the room.

The man with the dislocated shoulder had lurched to his feet and was fumbling in agony for his automatic. Outside the building was the sound of tires screeching to a stop and doors opening and slamming.

"Trust me," Jack whispered as he pulled the girl into the office he had entered from the fire escape. "I'm your only way out of here. It's one of me or Christ knows how many of them."

"Which way?" Her soft Spanish accent caught Jack by surprise.

He pushed her toward the window. "Up the fire escape."

"Up?"

"Yes, up the steps—quickly."

While the girl climbed onto the sill and through the window, Jack closed the door, grabbed a chair, and wedged the top rail under the door handle. Out in the hallway, men were shouting and ripping open doors room by room.

On his way to the window, Jack shoved a desk stapler into his pocket and tucked a bulky Dade County telephone directory under his arm.

The girl was already one flight up the fire escape when Jack got through the window and began racing up after her. Below them, heavy thumps on the barred door were followed by the sound of cracking wood and a loud bang as the catch and hinges gave way.

In the shadow of the wall two flights up, Jack heard one of the men shout, "The fire escape." He gestured to the girl to stay quiet. Then, holding the phonebook like a discus, he sent it arcing across the Miami night, down through the darkness to thump into the dust and dirt of the alley floor. Next he drew the stapler from his pocket and, taking a more precise aim, threw it banging and rattling across the alley ten yards further on.

"They got out the back way," a man's voice shouted from the office window.

"Fuck it," said another. "Who's covering this side of the building?"

"I thought you were."

"Screw you."

"Reynolds will have our balls on a skewer."

"So let's get after them."

The window slammed shut. A few moments later the light from the hallway was switched off and around the other side of the building he heard voices being raised and the sound of three car engines starting and wheels spinning as they sped away in different directions.

Jack caught himself breathing deeply to steady his nerves. Beside him, the girl was braced against the wall, her fists clenched.

"It's okay," Jack whispered. "They're gone."

The girl sighed and touched his sleeve. "What do we do now?"

"We can't stay here. "

The girl nodded

"Follow me," Jack whispered.

He led the way, tiptoeing down the metal treads, keeping to the shadows, and listening carefully for any sound in the alley below. It was too risky to lower the final flight of the fire escape. Instead, Jack pointed to the service pipe and mimed climbing down to the ground.

The girl nodded again and Jack swung his leg over the safety rail, took hold of the cast-iron pipe, and lowered himself swiftly downward. His companion needed no urging and followed without hesitation.

Jack got her to wait in the dark beneath the fire escape while he went to check the street at the front of the building. The men who had come after them had disappeared. The offices were dark and silent.

"Got a car?" Jack asked the girl.

"No."

"Then how did you get here?"

"I walked."

"Do you live near here?"

"Yes."

"Me too," Jack told her. "Let's get you back where you'll be safe."

"Why were you in there?"

"Why were you?"

"I was looking for something...looking for someone."

Jack weighed the risk she had taken and the danger she now faced.

He took the girl's hand. "It will look better if we leave like this."

"Better how?"

Her hand was soft and warm. It felt good to hold. "More convincing if anyone from there sees us."

She squeezed his fingers tightly.

Out of the alley and in the brightness of the street, it was tempting to hurry across to the other side, but Jack deliberately walked down a block before crossing at the next intersection. Neither of them spoke. Jack felt the girl's body brace as a car approached and relax as it passed by. Another block on he felt he should let go her hand.

"We could be heading for any place in Coral Gables by now," he told her. "Those men have no idea who we are. They'll never catch up with us. So why don't you let me take you home?"

The girl looked wary. "It's not far. I'm all right from here. Don't you worry."

"I'm not worried…" he began. "I mean…well, you know… you look like you can take care of yourself and all. What I mean is, I'd like to walk you home—if that's all right with you."

The evening breeze blew her hair across her finely arched eyebrows, beneath which her large brown eyes gazed steadily at him. Her lips parted in a smile showing a row of even white teeth. "That would be nice," she said. "But could we go somewhere first? Get a coffee, something to eat? I feel all shook up."

Jack Pagano felt all shook up too, but for a different reason. "Sure. Where do you want to go?"

"There's a diner near here. The kids on the campus go to it. It stays open late."

"The one close to the medical school?"

"Yes," answered the girl with surprise. "Are you a medical student?"

"No. Business, with political science."

"Okay," she said. "So you know the way."

"Are you studying at the university too?" Jack enquired.

The girl paused before she answered, "Since last fall. Hispanic studies."

"If I'm taking you to dinner, maybe I should know your name," Jack hinted cautiously.

"You're not taking me to dinner. I pay for myself," she told him. "But my name is Olivia. Olivia Hernandez."

He held his hand out stiffly. "I'm Jack Pagano."

"Well, Mr. Pagano, I'm pleased to meet you."

They didn't say much on the way to the diner. The sense of shock at what had happened in the office building caught up with them both and when Olivia took hold of Jack's arm, after a car slowed beside them momentarily, words didn't seem to matter.

Jack had been in the diner on and off, but he didn't count himself a regular and no one recognized him when they entered and found a booth in a corner. They ordered coffee and hotdogs and slumped back in their seats.

"Do you want to tell me about what you were looking for?" Jack asked.

"You wouldn't be interested," Olivia answered.

"I might be.

"So what were you looking for?"

He told her he didn't know. It was the truth.

The girl sitting opposite raised a questioning eyebrow. "You know how to fight very well for a business student."

"And political science," Jack reminded her.

But Olivia Hernandez would not be diverted. "Did the same person teach you how to do what you did to those men?"

"No. Another man, a friend of my father's, taught me how to take care of myself."

"You're lucky," Olivia answered, and Jack saw her face grow sad and anxious. "My father didn't have friends like that."

Jack picked up on the use of the past tense. "Your dad's not around anymore?"

The girl turned her head toward the window and answered, "No. He's dead." Then she looked back, facing him as she added, "My father was killed, Jack. He was shot dead by men he thought he could trust."

Albert Anastasia's son reached for her right hand and squeezed it soothingly. "So was mine, Olivia. So was mine."

Chapter Forty-Three

It took a couple more meetings for Olivia to feel completely at ease with Jack and for him to be less guarded in what he divulged to her.

He liked the girl; he needed no reassurance about that. He normally kept his emotions on a tight leash. He had enough going on in his life, he reasoned. Getting tied up with a girl like Olivia, any kind of girl for that matter, would only complicate things further. Still, there was something more than the line of her nose, her compelling eyes, her lithe figure, or the way she sometimes held her head that attracted Jack to Olivia Hernandez. It wasn't just their two dead dads, either. There was a sense of endeavor about her, a drive to achieve a goal, which Jack recognized and respected. And there was the knowledge that the situations they found themselves in were not so different.

Like it or not, Jack knew there were people looking out for him wherever he went. Olivia had none of that backup. All alone in a country that wasn't her own, and still she was pushing hard for what she wanted to find. She told Jack her story piece by piece, and not always in the right sequence. But he was patient, and when he had the account of what had happened to her in full, his understanding, his feelings deepened.

Olivia was the daughter of a Cuban intelligence officer during Batista's time in office. She told Jack that her father had been secretly recruited by a US counterpart working undercover in Havana, in what appeared to be an operation to crack down on narcotics trafficking and gunrunning.

Olivia's father was good at his job and supplied a lot of high-level intelligence to his US contact, for which he was well paid, she admitted. What he could not have known, however, was that the US agent was deeply involved in illicit trafficking himself. The information supplied by Hernandez was used to inform senior personnel in the trafficking syndicate of what their opponents in law enforcement agencies knew of their activities.

In time, Hernandez uncovered details of a significant arms-for-drugs deal that was scheduled to take place on an isolated stretch of coast. This information was passed to his American contact and a joint operation was planned to intercept the smugglers, for which Hernandez assembled a crack team of top agents.

The traffickers' boat had landed precisely as expected. But when Hernandez and his men moved forward to arrest the crew and their accomplices, their American partners turned their guns on them and killed them in cold blood. The only Cuban survivor was a radio operator secretly left behind to guard their vehicles. It was he who passed word of what had happened to Hernandez's family before being found dead in his apartment.

Olivia and her mother fled to Florida after the revolution fearing reprisals by Castro supporters against members of Batista's security forces and their families. The shock of her husband's death, followed soon after by the Cuban revolution and escape from her homeland, had been too much for Olivia's mother, who suffered a severe stroke from which she had recently died.

Alone and filled with vengeance, she told Jack, she had set out to track down the American agent who destroyed her family.

"Is that what you were doing in the office when I found you?"

"Yes," she said, with an air of resignation. "I look everywhere I can, Jack. But who am I looking for? Where do I go to find him? Sometimes I wonder if I will spend all my life searching for this man."

They had gone to the movies to see *Psycho*, which had been released a few weeks earlier. The suspense and terror of Alfred Hitchcock's masterpiece had gotten to Olivia, who was more forthcoming afterward as she and Jack sat on a campus bench enjoying the warm Florida night and the view across the lake to the fountain.

Jack was anxious not to spoil the evening, but he sensed Olivia had opened a door to her deepest feelings and was waiting for him to follow her through it. "It must have been pretty scary for you, going into those offices on your own like that," he said.

"After that scene in the movie, taking a shower will be a lot scarier," Olivia joked.

"What made you choose those offices?"

"A friend of mine told me about them. He said this company was recruiting men who had come here from Cuba to do secret work back home."

"Sure," Jack answered, trying to keep things straight in his mind. "This friend. Is he your boyfriend?"

"No. I don't have a boyfriend. He's just a friend. He helped me when my mother died. His niece was my friend at school, but this man does not have a family of his own."

Jack felt annoyed with himself at the sense of relief that flooded through him when Olivia said this, but he couldn't deny the lift in his spirit.

"And did your friend join this firm?"

"No—but he said there are many Cuban men like him going there."

The details interested Jack, who was matching what Olivia was telling him with the map of Cuba he had studied. "But you think this company is some kind of front."

"I'm sorry. What is 'front'? I don't understand."

Olivia's English was so good Jack had forgotten that it wasn't her first language. "A front? It's like a cover, a disguise. It hides what's really happening."

"Yes—a front. I think that is what it is."

"I think so too," Jack said, and went on to describe what he had found marked on the map. "My guess is this company is a front for smuggling narcotics."

"That was why you were in the offices?" she asked.

"Yes. The man who gave me the lead thinks this is what's happening and it looks like he's right. But why did you want to go there?"

"My friend talked to me about the secret things the people in this office do in Cuba. It sounds like the things my father was investigating. The American men who killed him had come from here, from Florida. I thought, perhaps, I might find something about my father, or the secret service men he worked with. If I found that information it could be—how you do say it?—the lead I am looking for."

"But you didn't find it?"

"No," she sighed. "How could I? There were so many names, Jack. I didn't know any of them, so which ones should I look at?"

Jack thought of the help he had gotten from Miller and Rip and Costello and Lansky. Olivia was groping in the dark.

"How did you get in there, anyhow?" he asked.

"With the women who clean the offices," she answered. "I wore denims and that baggy top and talked in Spanish. No one noticed me, and when the other women were leaving the building I hid in a washroom until it was dark."

Jack was impressed. "It was just bad luck those men found you. I guess they saw the flashlight through the window."

"You wouldn't have made that mistake."

"No—but I've been trained, remember? For years and years I've been trained, Olivia. Rip would skin me alive if I did that."

"Rip? Who is Rip?" she asked, snuggling closer to him.

"Rip is my father's friend. The man I told you about."

"The man who taught you how to fight like you do?"

"That's the one. I've known him since I was a kid."

"And the other man? The one who sends you to do dangerous things. Have you also known him since you were a kid?"

Jack reached his arm around her shoulders and drew her closer to him. "No. I only met him after my dad was killed. They worked together. My dad asked this man to help me when he was dead."

Olivia raised her head from Jack's shoulder and asked, "Why did he do that?"

"My dad knew he was going to die. He knew someone would kill him. So he planned for these men to help me and my mom when he was dead. He planned everything, Olivia, everything that's happened to me, right down to coming to school here."

"He must love you very much," she said.

Jack felt confused. "I've never thought of him in that way," he answered, running his fingers through her hair.

"But he is your father," she exclaimed.

"He was. But I only saw him once. For seventeen years I didn't know I had a father. Then the week before they killed him, he came to see my mom and me. Just the one time. Then he was gone forever."

The girl placed a hand on Jack's cheek and kissed him gently for the first time. "I'm so sorry for you. For seventeen years I did have a father, and then he was gone forever. I know how much it hurts."

A lump was rising in Jack's throat.

Then he felt his lips brush against Olivia's and the lump in his throat dissolved in the smell of her hair and the touch of her firm, smooth skin.

This is for real, he assured himself. This is no front.

Chapter Forty-Four

MEMORANDUM

To:	**Ambassador Kennedy**
From:	**James Lovall**
Date:	**September 5, 1960**
Subject:	**Voting Strategy**

With the presidential election now sixty-five days away, Labor Day seems an appropriate date to finalize our strategy.

While acknowledging our gratitude to the faithful in Boston and their inspired leader, CC, our friends in Chicago also demonstrated their ability to "get out the vote." You will agree, sir, that their combined efforts ensured JFK's unprecedented success in the West Virginia primary.

I believe, therefore, that we should draw on the services of close friends in Chicago to get out the vote nationwide in the presidential election. I have in mind SG, JR, and, of course, MH. Polling analysis indicates that their ability to martial the union vote will be most needed in the following states: Nevada, Missouri, Michigan, and Illinois. The latter is crucial to JFK's success, as we have discussed, and, as I know, you have made clear to SG and his associates. Without Illinois, victory cannot be guaranteed. There are sldo concerns in Texas, but I trust that LBJ and his team will be able to use their expertise to ensure victory there.

Can I confirm that MH will be undertaking the same intensive campaigning that proved to be so effective in securing JFK the Democratic nomination in July?

Turning to the candidate himself, our friends in the press should be commended for their diligence in enhancing positive public awareness of JFK, while tactfully ignoring his habitual peccadilloes (about which we have already spoken). RN is not to be underestimated, however, and in my opinion we must exploit the television advantage JFK undoubtedly has over his Republican rival. There are to be four TV debates, the last of which will inevitably be the most significant in winning floating voters. I propose that we use this debate to call RN's bluff as follows:

• *RN's base is his arch-anticommunist stance.*
• *As we know, RN has been working on the secret invasion plan for Cuba, Operation Pluto.*
• *In order for this operation to retain any chance of success, it cannot be acknowledged publicly. Furthermore, any hint of it requires vehement denial.*
• *Two days before the final TV debate (October 19), JFK will issue a statement to the press [key wording to follow] which will force RN to deny the existence of Operation Pluto.*
• *Such a denial will show RN to be both soft on Communism and a hypocrite.*
• *The statement will show JFK to be a purposeful champion of democratic principles—able to make tough decisions in the interests of liberty and the defeat of Communism.*

I believe this approach will secure a significant win for JFK in the TV debates, less than three weeks before viewers go to the polls.

Chapter Forty-Five

Olivia had never seen snow and, despite the bitter cold—which in the end sent her running with happy shrieks for the warmth of the house—she basked in the new white wonderland of Haddonfield at Christmas.

Carmella had been intrigued when Jack telephoned a week before the winter recess, asking if he could bring a friend home for the holidays.

"Of course your friend can come," she told him. "What's her name, Giovanni?"

"Olivia," his mother heard him answer with relief. "Olivia Hernandez—and thanks, Mom. Thanks so much." Then he remembered something. "You'll find her real helpful I'm sure, with cooking and all, you know?"

Carmella smiled. This was a side to her son she had not known before. "It sounds like we'll get along fine. Tell Olivia I'm looking forward to meeting her. Tell her she's very welcome to join us."

The girl waited nervously on the doorstep beside Jack when Carmella opened the door. The snow filtering gently down on the cold December night contrasted with her dark features and golden complexion. For an instant, Carmella saw something of herself as a young woman and smiled at her son, who was looking at her eagerly for silent approval.

"Come inside, my dear." Carmella kissed Olivia on both cheeks. "You must be freezing."

Olivia brushed the snow from her hair. "Thank you for letting me come to stay with you, Mrs. Pagano."

"It's our pleasure," Jack's mother answered, drawing her into the warmth of the house, where a fire crackled brightly in the parlor beside the Christmas tree. Jack and Olivia had taken a little time to unpack and unwind before she demanded they go enjoy the snow. Accustomed to such cold winters, Jack wasn't sure how much joy there was to experience, but he wasn't going to argue with the girl.

They took a brief walk around the neighborhood and over to the park. As they passed the boarded-up sign and the entrance to the Hole, Olivia caught Jack eyeballing it ever so slightly.

"That is where you train with Rip, yes?" she'd asked.

Jack eyed the opening, trying to see it as if for the very first time. "Is it that obvious?"

"No. Not really. If you hadn't mentioned it before and I hadn't been thinking about it, I can't imagine I would have ever noticed it."

She wrapped herself in the crook of Jack's arm. Jack could feel the cold slipping in through his parka. They made their way back to the house, the snow flurrying and their breath suspended in front of them.

Back at the house, they slipped into some dry clothes, hanging the damp ones to dry in the bathroom. There were still decorations to hang and Olivia had insisted on helping Carmella prepare the evening's meal.

"Jack," Carmella called from the kitchen. "Keep that fire banked up. This poor girl still hasn't thawed out yet from the cold."

She could hear Jack place the decorations he'd been handling back down in their box and pace across the living room to tend to the flame.

Olivia smiled. She removed one tray from the oven and carefully placed it up on the stove top. Behind her, Carmella lowered another tray into the oven.

"Oh, he's always loved the Christmas holiday," Carmella told Olivia. "This must be so different than Christmases back home."

"It is," she answered. Olivia spoke little of her parents; only occasional references to her childhood and home life ever slipped out in unguarded moments. "Jack showed me where he trains with his friend, Rip." Unsure whether Carmella had any interest in the subject, she added, "I'm glad he does that and not me."

On the contrary, Carmella was interested that her son had confided so much in this girl. There was a slight feeling of surprise, though it was not unpleasant. "I don't think Rip would mind training someone as pretty as you."

The two women smiled. "I don't have the same discipline as Jack, Mrs. Pagano. He trains hard, his grades are good—he's different from other boys."

"He always has been," she answered. "I expect there are a lot of other boys who think the same of you."

Olivia gathered eggs and arranged them next to the large mixing bowl she had placed on the counter. "I think so. But I'm also sure that many men must have liked you too. Before you met Jack's father, I mean."

"Umberto was different." Carmella took a few of the plates down from the cupboard. Olivia closed it behind her.

"That's how I feel about Jack."

"Yes. I can see you do." Carmella watched as the young woman cracked the last of the eggs on the side of the bowl. The yoke slimed its way to the bottom and Olivia tossed the broken shell in the trash. "You must find it very hard without your parents. Where I come from, the famiglia is our world." Carmella hesitated. "Of course, without a father, it was different for Jack. But Umberto looked after us well, even if he wasn't here himself."

"Jack told me how his father was shot dead. The same as mine. That was a short while before my mother passed away." Olivia stopped beating the eggs and placed the whisk on the countertop. "Sometimes it is like an ache inside me. It feels like they are with me, but I can't see them. Do you know what I mean?"

Carmella placed her hand on top of Olivia's. "I know exactly what you mean."

"We were so happy together. When I was old enough, my mom and I used to travel with my dad. We didn't like to be apart, and we never thought we would be." She felt herself drawn into Carmella's arms. She began to sob, the heat of breath bouncing back against her face. "I'm sorry. I don't mean to do this at your Christmas. I try to be strong for my parents. I know what I have to do for them, and now I am the only one left. The man who killed my father took more than his life, and he will pay for what he has done. But it used to make me feel so alone, and then I met Jack, and now I feel so guilty for being happy. I just—" The sound of her voice gave way to more tears.

"You shouldn't, my dear. Your parents would only want you to be happy. And I can see that you are. So is Jack." Carmella held her close, her face nested in Olivia's thick hair. "Believe me: You will never be alone again. Now you are a part of this family."

After a few moments, Olivia slipped out of the kitchen and to the bathroom. As she made her way past the living room, Jack had already shuffled from the doorway and back to the decorations. He didn't suppose she'd noticed him listening in.

Carmella finished placing the rest of the meal in the oven. Olivia was resourceful and independent, she had concluded. Resilient as well. That much was clear from the way she had overcome the loss of both parents. But there was a gentleness about her, a warmth and tenderness that reassured her. Jack was safe with this girl. Olivia would not hurt him.

As the three of them finally sat down to dinner that evening, Carmella was filled not only with the constant mixture of sadness and pride that her son would be going back out into the dangerous world his father had left behind, but with a deep and abiding sense of great hope for her son and the approaching new year.

Chapter Forty-Six

James Lovall also regarded the turn of the year optimistically.

The presidential election hadn't been easy, as the margin of the victory for the Ambassador's boy had shown. Jack Kennedy had slithered under the White House door in November by the thinnest of majorities: one tenth of one percent of almost seventy million votes cast nationwide. Lovall took pride in that. His stage management had worked to perfection. Ambassador Kennedy glowed with triumph when the decisive result had come in from Illinois. He was convinced that his understanding with the Chicago outfit had secured the state for his son. James Lovall knew otherwise; a little appropriate persuasion from him had tipped the scales Jack Kennedy's way.

The Republican stronghold in the farming belt of southern Illinois was the danger area, where Republican polls would be counting thousands of uncast votes. A brief conversation with Chicago's mayor, Richard Daley, had ensured that he would hold back announcing his county's vote totals until the final tally was published in the rural south of the state. After it was clear that Cook County needed to deliver a 450,000 majority to Kennedy in order to carry Illinois, Mayor Daley finally announced the results and the Ambassador's son took his county by 456,312 votes.

Lovall also prided himself in guaranteeing there would be no cries of foul play from the Republican party after the election. Richard Nixon may not have had a fortune the size of the Ambassador's to spray around and buy votes, but there had been dark deals and questionable donations in his campaign as well.

These, Lovall knew, would prevent Nixon and his supporters from pushing too hard for an investigation of the huge sums of money given to and spent by either side. The Republicans could only lick their wounds, privately curse the Ambassador and their ill luck, and wait to try again in 1964.

Meanwhile, Lovall had been busy. Most of the cabinet posts had been decided well in advance, but the appointment he had kept in reserve as a Christmas teaser was the Attorney General. He had treated himself to two glasses of his best port the evening it was announced that Bobby Kennedy, the president's younger brother and former campaign manager, would assume responsibility for that portfolio. Lovall speculated what kind of Christmas the Ambassador's associates in Chicago, or the other men who had already been harangued by his younger son during the McClellan Committee hearings, would be enjoying with the prospect of their nemesis directing the Justice Department for the next four years.

Chapter Forty-Seven

The first of the tableaux woven into the Camelot tapestry grabbed the front pages twelve weeks after the Ambassador's son was inaugurated as the thirty-fifth president on a bracing January day in Washington, D.C.

Reports of the air raids on military targets in Cuba began circulating among Olivia's exile friends on the morning of April 15th. Two days later, the first troops stormed from their landing craft onto a beach on the south coast of the island: the liberation of Cuba had begun.

"It's happening at last!" she told Jack. "Just like the president said on the television last year."

Jack had to think for a moment before remembering the final debate between the two candidates in the run-up to the presidential election, the one in which President Kennedy had said something about supporting Cuban freedom fighters in exile. Through her contacts, Olivia had picked up rumors of an exile force training in Nicaragua and possibly elsewhere in Central America for an invasion, but she hadn't dared to hope that it could happen so soon.

"Think about it, Jack. I'll be able to go home whenever I want, and you can come with me. You'll love Havana. We're going to have such a good time there this summer."

Jack's visit to Cuba was put on hold indefinitely in the days that followed. First came reports that Cuban resistance was better organized and more robust than exile propaganda had implied. Then the widely expected uprising in the country to support the invading force failed to materialize. However, the *coup de grâce* had come when the US inexplicably failed to send vital air support that would have guaranteed the success of the invasion. As it was, the Cuban Brigade that had come ashore full of expectation remained largely pinned down in the swamps and beaches where they had landed, until they ran out of ammunition and willpower. After five days, the final shots were fired and the remnants of the invasion force were rounded up and marched off to prison, leaving behind the bodies of their dead comrades and the broken hopes of tens of thousands of their fellow countrymen eager to return home on the marshy shoreline.

"Bay of Pigs!" Olivia exclaimed bitterly when the full disaster had been shone in the light. "That is the right name, Jack, the right name. The ships were there, waiting. So were the planes. All Kennedy had to do was give the order and those brave men would have been saved."

Jack didn't know what to say. "Do you know anyone involved?" he asked.

"I don't know," Olivia answered. "I don't know. Maybe. None of my friends from Miami were there. But there are others from home, perhaps. People I know, who were fighting, people who could have died because no one gave them help when they asked for it—help they had been promised, Jack."

Over the weeks that followed, Olivia's bitterness was eclipsed by the raw anger Jack saw among more militant members of the Cuban community in Florida. They vowed to carry on the struggle, but this time on their own terms, not as puppets of the gringos in Washington who talked big but did nothing when the shooting started.

Jack saw that Olivia, who had personal experience with treachery at American hands, carried resentment about the Bay of Pigs deep in her heart. He didn't interfere with these feelings— didn't try to ease her anguish. Handled correctly, it would give an edge to her determination to succeed in her quest. Jack realized that they were following parallel tracks, heading toward the same goal. If he could help Olivia find the double-crossing US agent who had killed her father, chances were it would lead Jack to the men close to the Cuban end of the trafficking cartel that he and Rip had seen being put in place.

That was the reasoning of Jack the pragmatist. The Jack who had walked through Cooper Park on snowy afternoons arm in arm with Olivia Hernandez, or the Jack who had sat with her head resting in his lap watching patterns made by the flames in the parlor fire, saw things differently.

Chapter Forty-Eight

MEMORANDUM

To:	**Ambassador Kennedy**
From:	**James Lovall**
Date:	**May 1, 1961**
Subject:	**Cuba**

The events of the last two weeks bring to mind the words of Thomas Jefferson: "The tree of liberty must be refreshed from time to time with the blood of patriots and tyrants. It is its natural manure." The patriots' blood has been shed in Cuba; press and television coverage has left us in no doubt about that. However, the tyrant still reigns in Havana, gloating over our misfortune. Now is the time, I would suggest, to work the situation to our advantage.

At the same time, RFK will be occupied with pursuing the underworld and criminal elements targeted during his time with Senator McClellan and his committee. This initiative will gradually disengage us from those who have served their purpose and are now no longer of use to us. At the same time, it will open a schism within the wider national syndicate that can only work to our advantage. Divide and rule will be the order of the day, Sir.

We should actively pursue these objectives in the wake of the Bay of Pigs:

1. Ensure that heads roll in the CIA.

2. As a result, take a controlling interest in all covert operations overseas. (Divide and rule once again.)

3. Establish the value of using assets supplied by JR and other associates in Chicago, Miami, and New Orleans.

4. Arrange the permanent removal of FC.

5. In association with item 4, plan and successfully execute an invasion and permanent "liberation" of Cuba.

I propose that we use the investigation into the recent debacle, headed by General Maxwell Taylor, to initiate items 1 and 2. For item 3, removing RT in DR would lay down a suitable marker. JR has been working with the agency on this and has assets in place to execute such an assignment successfully. They can move in four weeks.

Items 4 and 5 must, of necessity, take longer to prepare. It is unfortunate that security at the Miami station was compromised by intruders last year. However, what needs to be done will require a far larger operational area while remaining close to the source of appropriate personnel.

Our aim should be to achieve items 4 and 5 by the fall of next year. That will leave two years to build toward the next presidential election, by which time ties with former (discarded) associates will have been cut by RFK. JFK will also be riding high in the polls as the liberator of Cuba, thereby fulfilling the pre-election pronouncement that helped secure floating voters after the last round of TV debates with RN.

Chapter Forty-Nine

Meyer Lansky had taken to spending the Memorial Day holiday at the Fontainebleau Hotel in Miami Beach. This year he was staying a few weeks longer. Jack didn't ask the reason; Lansky would tell him if he needed to know.

Jack didn't want there to be any barriers between him and Olivia, but what he did with and for his mentors had to remain secret—for his safety and for hers, there could be no compromise over that. So when Lansky called him for a meeting in his penthouse, Jack went without telling her. He didn't feel good about it, but he had little choice.

Crossing Biscayne Bay in the hot midday sunshine, Jack remembered the first time he had come to Miami Beach. The lush tropical gardens, the brightly colored buildings, the open-topped cars and exquisitely tanned flesh wherever he looked—Meyer Lansky's playground was quite intoxicating.

The taxi stopped outside the towering arc of the Fontainebleau, and a purple-uniformed bellhop hurried to open the door to let Jack out. He gazed upwards to the blue sky and the white railings where Miller had been leaning and looking out at the ocean when he'd first been summoned here.

He didn't feel any better about keeping the meeting secret from Olivia when Lansky asked him, "What's all this I'm hearing about you and a pretty lady?" as they walked across the deep-pile carpet out onto the terrace. The view was even more spectacular than Jack had remembered, but right now, he was too preoccupied to enjoy it.

There was no sense denying what Lansky presumably had on good authority.

"We like hanging out," Jack answered lightly. "You know."

"Of course you do," answered the little man with a twinkle in his eye. "And you should at your age. Why else go to college? You can learn all you need to get on in this world on the street, like I did."

Jack grinned in reply.

Lansky's eyes narrowed. "So, are you going to tell me about her, or do I have to send someone to find out for me?"

Jack tried not to sound as defensive as he felt. He sketched Olivia's brief biography, hoping that would suffice.

"That's the history lesson, but what's she like, Jack? You know what I mean. What's this kid like who's got you steamed up?"

Jack felt himself blushing. "Like you say…I guess she's pretty. And she's smart. She speaks English almost as good as Spanish. I like to be with her. That's all there is, really. We get on well together. And my mom likes her."

"That's important," said the little man. "If the mom don't like you, it's going to end in tears."

He told Jack to pull up a steamer chair, and when they were both settled in the shade of a parasol, Lansky poured them glasses of iced water and asked, "Are you going to tell me how you met her as well? I don't recall you showing this kind of interest in other chicks."

Jack had been hoping he could have skirted round that particular subject, only because he didn't want Lansky to view Olivia as some kind of rival or distraction to the assignments he undertook for him, and Costello and Miller. However, there was no point in trying to disguise how he had met Olivia; Lansky might have had some idea and Jack didn't want to get caught trying to mislead him.

"She was in that office building you got me to check out last year. The career development and placement firm from New York. The one where I found the map of Cuba."

"Ah, yes, the map of Cuba," Lansky answered. "I don't remember you mentioning that you ran into a beautiful spy at the same time you were playing James Bond."

Jack stood his ground. "At that time, it wasn't important. It—she—only became important later."

Meyer Lansky sat patiently, waiting for Jack to continue.

"I've told you she's important to me, Meyer—I'm not going to deny that. But I think she could be important in what's happening in this whole Cuban set up."

Lansky smiled. "Carry on. I'm listening."

"Like I said, Olivia's father knew a lot about the trafficking that took place when Batista was in power. Before he was killed he got close—real close, I believe—to the people pulling the strings. After Castro took over, thousands of people escaped here, right? A lot of them are people like Olivia's dad: intelligence people, people working undercover for the old regime. But I suspect that there are also plenty who had to get out because they had been working for traffickers, shipping in arms for Batista maybe and shipping out narcotics to come over here."

"So, what are you getting at?" Lansky asked, sounding more interested.

"Olivia has contacts with all kinds of people in the exile community. I think she could be our way into discovering which of them are tied up in the rackets, who their associates are, and maybe even how they connect to what Rip and I saw last year in New Orleans and Dallas."

"And you'd be prepared to use this girl to get that kind of information—maybe put her life on the line?" Lansky's voice was cold, all business—just as Jack had come to expect it would be.

"She's already putting her life on the line," he answered. "You can see the kind of risks she's prepared to take, sneaking round those offices on her own. This way she'll be safer, because she'll be with me."

"But what does she get out of helping you get under the skin of the Cubans holed up here?"

"The chance of finding the man who killed her dad."

"Is that so?"

Jack detected an air of skepticism.

He was stung by this. He sat upright; his voice rose. "She has a far better chance that way than trying to do it all by herself and maybe getting killed in the process. And don't think she wouldn't go that far, Meyer, because she would. Olivia has got nothing to lose in this world. Nothing at all—you hear me?"

"Nothing but you, it would seem," he concluded quietly.

"I don't know about that."

"Let me be the judge," Lansky answered. "Though, from what you tell me, I think you're right about this girl. But don't let her get too close to what you have to do, Jack. It will be better for both of you. I think you understand why."

Jack said that he did. "You can trust me on that, Meyer. She knows nothing about Albert or what I do for you and Frank."

"Keep it that way."

Chapter Fifty

A week before Christmas, 1961, Husky had taken a telephone call late at night.

Instead of the familiar pause before their conversation started, the voice on the other end of the line began speaking as soon as the receiver was lifted. Husky listened to what he was told in astonishment.

"Let me get this straight," Husky said. "You're telling me that J. Edgar Hoover, head of the FBI, has sent several memoranda to Attorney General Robert Kennedy informing him that Giancana and the Chicago outfit gave money to his brother's presidential campaign last year—right?"

The caller confirmed that.

"And these memoranda also say that Giancana and the other bosses are starting to get angry, because they don't think they are getting what they paid for—what they had been promised by Joe Kennedy?"

"That's what I'm telling you," said the caller.

"And now Joe Kennedy has had a serious stroke in Palm Beach?"

"That's right," said the caller. "Interesting isn't it?"

"A cynical person might call it convenient," said Husky. "I suppose this means that the president's father won't be appearing in public anymore?"

"You have to understand, this is a very debilitating stroke. Kennedy Sr. can barely speak, or so I'm told. It looks as if he will be confined to a wheelchair."

"It couldn't happen to a nicer fellow," Husky replied. "So, it seems that Hoover has got an arm lock on the White House. It puzzled me how he clung onto his job. He seems so out of place in Camelot."

"But it's understandable now, isn't it?"

"It certainly is. Thank you for letting me know."

"My pleasure," the caller signed off. "Happy holidays."

Chapter Fifty-One

Lansky invited Jack to the Fontainebleau for lunch. Even over the phone, Jack had been acutely aware that something was off.

Sure enough, things were not good.

Lansky chewed his lobster without enthusiasm. Jack had seen him nervous at the time of the Cuban Revolution, but this was something deeper. For the first time in their acquaintance, his father's friend was worried, seriously worried. For the first time, he didn't have the answers before the questions were even asked.

They sat around the table outside, shaded by a bright canvas awning.

Jack poked uneasily at his lobster and salad.

"Where is all this heat coming from?" Lansky asked rhetorically. "I'll tell you where. From that Bobby prick in Justice. That's where. Last year there were nineteen convictions for what they call racketeering. The way things are going there will be pushing a hundred this year. Wherever you look there's an IRS audit. On top of that, you got the Feds tailing Giancana and some of the other fellas, mocking them in public. That ain't right. That ain't right at all." Lansky pushed his plate away, seemingly too disgusted to eat. "You hear what happened to Marcello?"

"I heard he got taken out of the country back at the beginning of April."

"Bobby Kennedy had Carlos in his sights because Carlos had been fighting the immigration authorities for years," Lansky told him sourly. "So he and his attorney go down to the Immigration and Naturalization Service office in New Orleans—like they do every three months—only this time Carlos is told he's being deported to Guatemala of all places. They rush him to the airport in handcuffs. He can't even telephone his wife. When they get to the airport, the engines on the plane are running and a small army of police march him onto the plane and it's 'Bye-bye, Carlos and his attorney.' Bobby takes the public credit and tells everyone he is 'very happy Carlos Marcello is no longer with us.'"

"That's what I heard," Jack said.

"Yeah, well, what you didn't hear was that less than six days later the IRS files taxed liens for more than $835,000 against Carlos and his wife," he continued. "It's not just insulting, Jack. It's hypocritical. Carlos Marcello had been giving money to Johnson's run at the presidency, and the vice presidency after that. He'd been backing Kennedy's running mate for years."

"What happened in Guatemala?"

"That faggot pilot you saw Rosselli with in New Orleans fetched him back last week," Lansky concluded.

"David Ferrie?"

"That's the one—Ferrie. He flew Carlos back in secret. But it won't be long before Bobby and the boys from Justice are after him again. Take that from me."

Carlos Marcello wasn't the only one to be suffering at the hands of the president's younger brother, he continued. Jimmy Hoffa, the Teamsters' leader, was being targeted as well.

"Hypocrisy again," exclaimed Lansky. "Look at the money Hoffa has thrown LBJ's way. Is this any way to repay the people who help you? I don't think so. But getting mixed up with backing Kennedy was never my idea—or Frank's."

Jack asked why.

"Because we had Nixon in the bag; we have for years. This last election should have been a cakewalk. Nixon should be in the Oval Office now. He's always shown respect to the people who've seen him all right. There'd be no trouble for Carlos or Hoffa if Richard Nixon had gotten elected."

"So what went wrong?"

"Joseph Fucking Kennedy—that's what went wrong," Lansky replied.

Jack had never heard him curse this way before. Lansky had seemed like a different person the entire day.

"I didn't trust Joe Kennedy in his bootlegging days. I didn't trust him after the Crash of '29. I sure as hell didn't trust him after he backed Hitler and the Nazis. So why should I trust him when he promises Sam that we could do things the way we want, without every federal agency and bureau breathing down our necks, just so long as we gave his boy the keys to the White House?"

"Sam?" Jack needed clarification. "You mean Sam Giancana from Chicago?"

"Sure I do." Lansky got up from the table. He walked to the rail and gazed out across the lawns and gardens to the golden sands and the wide blue ocean. Jack joined him, resting his forearms on the rail and breathing in the warm sea breeze scented with fresh cut grass and tropical blooms. "Joe promised Giancana he could do things the way we want just so long as we gave his boys the keys to the White House."

Jack nodded in agreement, unsure what his reactions was supposed to be.

"Sam and the boys had busted themselves to get out the union vote. Joe Kennedy controlled the White House, like they both agreed, and then Joe stabs Sam in the back. Five weeks after Jack Kennedy gets elected, his old man makes Bobby Kennedy Attorney General. From then on the shit starts flying—like I always thought it would. And just to make Sam look real dumb, Joe rubs his nose in it by getting the Feds to shadow him every place he goes. Sam Giancana can't go to the john without a G-man peering over the stall to check what he's doing."

Lansky slapped his hand on the white-painted railing in frustration. "It's going to hit business bad all over. And while Bobby is turning up the heat, it leaves the door wide open for other people to push in and start setting up their own businesses."

This, Jack realized, was the core of Meyer Lansky's concern. Eighteen months of disruption in Cuba had shown what could happen to even the best-run business. The casinos were open again, sure they were, but the money they were taking was a fraction of what it had been when Batista was in power.

Jack wanted to know if there had been any developments since he and Rip had travelled to New Orleans and Dallas. He saw an opportunity to get back in the action again. "Do you think I should be checking things out?"

"Not at the moment," Lansky answered. "Frank and me are watching this real close, Jack. We're getting hit from every angle and we don't think it's a coincidence. It seems to us like someone is pulling the strings to cause trouble everywhere, so that they can break up what we got going and move in themselves."

"Who would have the power to do something like this?" Jack asked in genuine bewilderment. "Who could organize an attack on such a big scale? You're talking about a structure that reaches into every corner of the country, Meyer."

The little man smiled in amusement. "You're telling me this?"

Jack smiled too, realizing the absurdity of what he had said.

"There's a new kid on the block, Jack, and we ain't got a goddamn idea who he is or what he's going to do next."

Chapter Fifty-Two

By New Year 1962, Jack was ratcheting up his studies in anticipation of graduating that summer.

The weeks passed in an accelerating blur of revision, cramming, and examinations that suddenly came to an end in the small hours of a summer morning, when he woke up and realized that, apart from graduation and its attendant razzmatazz, his college days were over.

As if by reflex at that thought, his fingers reached out and found the long curve of Olivia's naked back as she slept beside him.

Someone like Olivia Hernandez had been the last thing on Jack's mind when he had enrolled as a freshman. His thoughts had still been full of his Sicilian summer, he remembered—of nights beneath the canopy of Mediterranean stars, heady with Grappa del Etna and the fragrance of Don Pagano's moonlit garden.

Jack ran the nail of his index finger softly along the gentle arc of her spine to the nape of her neck, where her hair spread loose on the pillow. Four years ago, Olivia had been the one factor he had not taken into account, and yet, as she lay beside him breathing peacefully, he felt that if he left the University of Miami with nothing more than the love of this girl, his transition to adult life would be complete.

Once she overcame her initial wariness, Olivia had been totally open with Jack. From sharing family reminiscences, to more recent intimacies, she held back nothing. She trusted Jack, and in that trust lay the key to her innermost secrets: the fierce passion with which she would hunt down her father's killer, the uninhibited passion she showed for Albert Anastasia's son.

Jack drew his eyes from the golden skin and dark brown hair, and rolled away to face the curtains, through which the first light of dawn was beginning to show.

Albert Anastasia's son.

The name itself would mean little, if anything, to Olivia at first. But it would only be a matter of time before that name began to gather a history and a reputation. This was what Jack feared. He'd had many nights like this, spread over nearly five years, to work through the conflicting emotions. How could he expect Olivia to take it on board, no matter how delicately Jack might have presented his situation?

And why should she?

Jack had seen the looks this girl drew from other guys when they were together. He thought sometimes that only his status in the football team had prevented someone else from making a move on her. This was the reason he had avoided specific details about his father, and as time moved on and they drew closer, the risk of destroying what they shared grew greater.

His dad had been a businessman, he reasoned. And he *had* done undercover work for the government. None of that was untrue. It was just that it told only part of the story and it was the other part Jack dreaded Olivia discovering.

The shrill light of early dawn was the time to see things clearly, whether Jack wanted to or not. His college years had given him a framework, a matrix to operate within. Those boundaries would be removed soon and, beyond the general thrust of his father's directive, he had no firm idea of where he would be sent, or what he would be doing.

Ever since Sicily, he'd had little fear of personal danger. His concerns were for Olivia, what they had now, and what he longed for them to have in years to come.

He rolled back and nestled close to her, gliding a hand over her slim waist to rest his fingers against the smooth, flat skin.

Olivia responded sleepily, moving her hand to stroke Jack's hair.

He closed his eyes. Somehow he had to guard this girl from what the future held for Enrique Hernandez's daughter and what the past held for Albert Anastasia's son.

Chapter Fifty-Three

"Would it have gone all the way?" Husky asked.

The man on the telephone paused before answering. "I doubt it. Armageddon will have to wait a while, I think; the old world order still has much to offer investors."

"Truman pushed the button," Husky reminded his caller.

"That's because Truman was told to. Besides, Hiroshima and Nagasaki are a long way from Houston and New Orleans."

The presence of Russian missiles in Cuba had threatened to change the face of the world forever.

"All the same, this business was a close-run thing."

"It was meant to be," the caller said. "It scared the shit out of everyone, just as it was supposed to do. The rumor mill has started already, claiming that Kennedy has cut some kind of secret deal with Khrushchev not to invade Cuba, provided the Soviets pull out their missiles. As far as John Doe is concerned, Cuba is off the agenda. No one is going to be foolish enough to risk blowing us all to kingdom come just for a box of his favorite cigars—that's the way they're going to look at it. Anyway, they've got space—the new frontier—to keep them busy, now we're going to put a man on the moon in the next eight years."

"And in the meantime?" asked Husky.

"Business as usual, my friend. Business as usual. When the shouting dies down, nothing has really changed."

"So we continue as planned?"

"Everything is planned," said the caller. "Nothing happens by chance. You have your instructions; I have mine."

"And we're still on schedule?" Husky checked.

"Like clockwork, my friend. As I said, nothing happens by chance."

Chapter Fifty-Four

Olivia's spirits continued to rise in the weeks following those seven chilling days in October. The naval blockade of Cuba was lifted. Against all expectation she started picking up hints that, in spite of what had happened, Castro might be prepared to cut a deal with the Bay of Pigs prisoners.

This sounded too good to be true, but as November gave way to December it became clear that something concrete was scheduled to take place. On December 22nd Olivia received the news she had been longing to hear for twenty months: that almost all the 1,100 or so fighters captured at the Bay of Pigs had been released and were being returned to the US. In return, the American government would be handing over $53 million worth of pharmaceuticals, baby food, farm equipment, and other goods banned by the U.S. trade boycott, which had been put in place after the revolution.

A lot of people called this payment a ransom. The Cuban leader referred to it as an "indemnification;" though, as Jack later heard from Frank Costello, Castro held back the release of the three invasion force leaders by eight hours until the last $1.5 million had been paid into his personal bank account.

But these were small stitches in the blanket of goodwill and happiness that enveloped Miami that December. A week after their safe return, the Cuban Brigade were formally welcomed back by a crowd of 40,000 friends and well-wishers, gathered to give them a heroes' reception. Leading the celebrations were the president and first lady, who walked to the podium on the fifty-yard line between ranks of cheering onlookers.

On the face of it, it had been a bold move on Jack Kennedy's part to accept the invitation to address the men whom many had accused him of betraying; behind the scenes, his good reception had been squared in advance. The moment the three brigade leaders stepped onto the tarmac at Homestead Air Force base in Florida, Attorney General Robert Kennedy had called them to the telephone and, in the days that followed, convinced them that secret plans to topple Castro and liberate Cuba were pushing ahead despite any perceived assurances to the contrary. The brigade leaders had agreed to put their resentment behind them. They would be a key part of this secret invasion force, the president's brother had promised, and so the President and Mrs. Kennedy were given a rousing reception that sunny afternoon in the Orange Bowl.

Squeezing Jack Pagano's hand, Olivia watched Jack Kennedy unfold the sand-colored flag bearing the silhouette of a soldier charging into battle, rifle leveled, bayonet fixed. The president paused a few seconds and then declared in a voice rising with emotion, "Commander, I can assure you that this flag will be returned to this Brigade in a free Havana."

That sealed it; the American president's redemption was complete. Olivia let go of Jack's hand and joined thousands of her fellow countrymen as they applauded the man who had dared to show his face among so many who so recently had wished him ill.

She beamed at Jack happily, squeezing his arm and kissing him affectionately. "It's going to be a wonderful New Year."

Jack did his best to respond in kind, but he could not share Olivia's optimism. The previous day he had answered the telephone and heard Miller's voice telling him, "There's work to do. I'll see you in Miami, January 2nd."

Chapter Fifty-Five

Miller looked older, Jack thought. He had the same energy and his wits were still sharp. It was his demeanor that had changed. His hair showed more light than dark and his eyes carried shadows beneath them that Jack did not remember from the last time they had seen each other.

Olivia was enjoying the most recent of a series of "yellow-ribbon" parties for returning fighters that had turned the holidays into an extended fiesta. She understood that Jack could not be with her at all of these, so his meeting with Miller had come about without the need for explanation or excuse.

He'd rented a boat, eight feet at the most, Jack had estimated. They whipped around the Atlantic, the January air a little colder than Jack would have preferred. Though he had to admit there was no chance of anyone overhearing what Miller might have to say. Judging by his demeanor, he had not flown down to discuss trivial matters.

Sure enough, Miller wasted little time on pleasantries. "Let me ask you this. How much have you heard about racketeering and trafficking since the missile crisis? Since the president told us that an American would be walking on the moon by the end of the decade?"

Jack had to acknowledge the campaign against organized crime had been overtaken by more recent events.

"But you and I both know that business doesn't stop because it doesn't make the headlines. It's building, Jack. It has to be. All this attention to plots against Castro, secret invasion plans, secret navies, phony businesses, economic warfare, hit-and-run raids back and forth to Cuba—you live here, you don't need me to tell you what the word is on the street. Everyone has been getting so worked up about military action against Castro, they don't see the obvious things."

If he were honest, Jack probably had to count himself among the band of the blind. All through the previous year, Olivia had spoken guardedly of secret raids on the Cuban coast carried out by small bands of exiles in fast motorboats. She told Jack about secret camps in the Louisiana swamps where Cuban men, and a few Americans, were being trained to use all kinds of weapons. There were hundreds of them, she had been told—enough to equip a small army. But it was Miller's reference to the phony companies that had triggered Jack's interest. Olivia had friends who she said were registered as employees of companies like this.

"Companies that are not companies, Jack," she had explained.

"You mean they only exist on paper? False companies, which don't have real offices, or business premises, or real people working for them?"

"That's right. It doesn't make sense. But my friends get their money. Every week they get paid like in a regular job."

It made sense to Jack. Meyer Lansky had given him an erudite course in the finer details of money laundering through the very kind of phony companies Miller was talking about.

"Everything they need is in place," Jack told Miller.

"And all courtesy of Uncle Sam," Miller said gravely. "My information is that there are dozens of shadow companies. Over fifty million dollars passed through those accounts last year. And who's to say whose money it is. No one is entering it in a ledger. The CIA can't claim it's theirs because they're not supposed to be conducting economic warfare and military sabotage against Cuba. The Department of Defense can't run an audit on it because no one in the Pentagon is supposed to know what's going on. Meanwhile our friends can slip their narcotics business right alongside and no one can tell which is which.

"These fellas are smart, Jack. This is the major league. Whoever is running this show is into some serious business."

Miller cut the boat's engine. They sat bobbing in the water, though Jack wasn't sure why. He could, however, see where the conversation was leading. "You want me to check it out? Is that what this is about?"

"It's what your old man would want," Miller answered. "What you found with Rip was the business end being put in place. Now I need confirmation that the operational side is up and running."

Jack felt a distant excitement building inside. "Where do I go to find this confirmation?"

"There's an old navy base that your school now uses as its south campus: 1,600 acres of wooded land they used for blimps during the war. Don't ask me what the University of Miami wants it for, but it's being leased at the moment to an outfit called Zenith Technological Enterprises. I don't know what they do. All I know is they have guards in gray uniforms patrolling the place. You can draw your own conclusions." Miller reached behind the seat and came up with a small portfolio. He opened it and handed Jack a sheet of paper. "This was taken five years ago, but it can't have changed too much."

The photograph's heading read: "1958 AERIAL SURVEY. RICHMOND NAVAL AIR STATION. U.S. GOVERNMENT INSTALLATION."

Jack glanced at it. A road wound diagonally across the picture from the top right-hand corner to the bottom left. Groups of buildings stood along it in clusters on either side. In the bottom half of the picture, a grid pattern of smaller roads had been laid down among the trees, which dotted all but the top segment of the photograph like pockmarks. Miller seemed to know a lot about the place already. What was stopping him investigating it further himself?

He chuckled when Jack asked this. "Too many of my old buddies are on the payroll. It wouldn't be good for me, or them, if we happened to run into each other."

Miller tucked the photos back where he'd produced them from.

The engine kicked back to life. Miller let the boat run forward before circling back to the shore. Jack wasn't sure this would be quite so easy.

"I'll be back here in a couple of weeks. See what you can find for me." Miller added, "You can get that chick of yours to fill you in on the background to Zapata. She sounds like a smart lady."

Chapter Fifty-Six

Jack had no intention of getting Olivia involved. He also questioned his ability to bluff his way into ZTE pretending to be a disgruntled agency man. However, Miller's description of the place matched what Lansky had been talking about. Jack had a pretty good idea what he was going to find out for Miller; it was what he might find to help Olivia that spurred him on.

In an operation of this size, he thought he might find some reference to her dad. As if maybe that would help explain his secretiveness. Olivia had taken to studying in the library weekday evenings. She was in her senior year, and as graduation approached, Jack noticed a growing determination in her to get high grades.

Jack was reconciled to enjoying less of her company until the summer. It was only for a few more months, he reasoned. It also gave him time to look into the matters he and Miller had discussed.

The buildings were standard defense fare: unimpressive wooden offices furnished with drab government-issued desks and chairs, and monolithic warehouses. Despite the round-the-clock guard, breaking into them was easy. Jack worked his way methodically through one after the other, night after night. It was nearly as easy as Miller had promised. He waited until the guards switched around midnight to break in. Depending where he was looking that night, he had roughly an hour or so before the guard conducting his rounds forced Jack into hiding.

As his investigation started, it quickly became clear that the sales charts and business license hung on the wall of the reception office were as phony as the company name.

On this night, climbing down a rope through the skylight of one warehouse, Jack found himself surrounded by cases of small arms ammunition, mortar shells, heavy machine gun belts, and an assortment of rifles and submachine guns—enough to arm a sizeable force.

He forced the lock of a door designated Transportation, through which he found immaculately kept records of over one hundred cars under lease, details of several airplanes, along with supply ships, speedboats, and small inflatable landing craft.

In one building, he disabled an alarm like the one in the offices where he had met Olivia, and slipped through a window into a room that looked like a realtor's show room. Around the walls were photographs of houses, a motel, and transportation-company warehouses. There wooden huts that looked like they were in some kind of lumber camp, a publishing company, shipping companies, and air freight agencies.

One set of pictures caught Jack's attention. They were photographs of a luxurious mansion. There were pictures taken from the street outside, from the back, and looking down the manicured lawns to the water's edge where a crowd of inflatable dinghies and sleek motorboats were moored like a marina.

In one of the offices, he found filing cabinets containing file after file of names—all neatly typed and arranged in alphabetical order. At the head of a hallway was one room containing files with American-looking names. Jack checked the other rooms and found that they were filled with files of names as well— exclusively Spanish names. At a rough guess Jack reckoned there were five Spanish names to every American name.

A sound in the hallway. At first it was so faint that Jack had to convince himself he wasn't just imaging it. It grew louder, clearer. It was the night guard, slightly ahead of the schedule Jack had worked out over the last few months.

Whereas in the past this might have conjured imagines of Louis Reggio's apartment and jackbooted law enforcement officers busting the door from its hinges, Jack remained calm.

He ducked beneath a desk. His pulse never rose.

The steps were slow and measured. If the guard had heard someone, he would have stepped a little more lively. Better yet, he might have called for backup. This was only one guard, and he was taking his time as he paced from one end of the corridor to the other.

This was just the guard making his routine rounds of the facility, Jack assured himself.

He waited until the last footstep had time to echo and fade, and then he gave it another two minutes. His haste would only give him away. If nothing else, Jack's experience was making him patient.

By the time he headed back to his room, it was quite late. The prospect of a good night's sleep was making Jack more tired by the minute. As he turned the corner and made his way to his room, he saw his front door was open. It was just a crack, enough to keep the cylinder from catching.

He approached slowly, placed his ear as close to the door as he could without letting the squeaking hinge give him away. Jack was always careful not only to close his door but to lock it as well.

There was silence on the other side of the door. Slowly, he pushed it open.

The harsh moment of anticipation gave way to the warm feeling of relief that washed over him.

"This is a nice surprise," he said, the door clicking shut behind him.

Olivia backed away. "It is a surprise. But not so nice as you think." Her voice was different: cold, almost angry.

"Is something the matter?" Jack asked. "I don't understand what you mean."

"You tell me," she answered. "You are the one who disappears without telling me where you go."

Jack felt a lump forming in his throat. "Look, Olivia, it's not what you think."

"You don't know what I think, Jack. If you were so smart, you'd know that I come here sometimes to see you when I'm tired, when I can't read my books any more. I come here, Jack. I knock on the door. But you don't answer because you're not here. And I go crazy thinking where you might be."

Jack felt himself blushing, but his mouth seemed full of sawdust and he couldn't make his tongue work.

"Then I see you the next day. We have a good time. We are happy together. And you say nothing about where you have been the night before. Nothing, Jack. Not a word. The first time, I think maybe you have gone for a run. The second time I try to think of another reason. But after that, when you still say nothing to me, I start to think the worst."

She paused for Jack to say something, but he was lost.

Olivia stepped closer to him. "Who is it, Jack? Who is this girl that makes you so excited you go to her night after night while I am in the library with my books?"

At last, Jack's tongue freed itself and he blustered, "Girl? What girl are you talking about, Olivia? There's no girl. How could there be?"

"Exactly," she answered, raising her voice. "That's what I said to myself, so many times, Jack. 'How could there be another girl?' But still you disappear in secret until I couldn't take it anymore."

Jack could see she was trying to hold back her tears, but in the end they got the better of her. "I can't take it anymore," she sobbed, pushing him aside and rushing to let herself out of the room.

Jack felt like he had been nailed to the floor. Olivia's outburst came out of left field, and for a moment he was powerless to respond.

Olivia was out the door and hurrying down the hallway.

"No!" Jack shouted, freeing his feet and his reactions. "No! Olivia," he yelled. He chased after her and grabbed her shoulder. "You don't understand."

Jack had pulled her around roughly and was shouting in her face. She was alarmed and tried to draw back, but Jack held her firmly and yelled again, "You don't understand."

"Anything the matter?" asked an elderly man who was looking round the stairs. It was the janitor of the lodging house.

"No nothing, Mr. Randolph," Jack answered. "Senior year pressure, that's all. You know how it is. Sorry if we disturbed you."

The janitor shuffled back toward his room. "You'll know about senior year pressure when you get arthritis and don't move so good anymore."

Olivia was standing stiffly in front of Jack, wiping her eyes with a handkerchief.

"We've got to talk," he told her. The girl started to move away. "Please, Olivia?"

Jack had no script prepared for what he told her. In a way, that probably made his explanation more believable. He started with the south campus and what he had been doing there. Then he moved back to Miller. After that his pathway through Lansky and Costello was straightforward. So was Sicily, his time with Rip, training, the Hole, everything. Olivia sat listening without trying to interrupt. She looked patient at first, but as Jack delved deeper into his life, patience gave way to interest; resentment to reassurance. Jack reached the point where he had covered pretty much everything that Albert Anastasia had laid down for him. Ahead lay his greatest obstacle: explaining Anastasia himself.

"You remember that I told you I only met him that one time?"

Olivia nodded, not wanting to break his flow.

"There was a reason for that," Jack continued. "A good reason. My dad made all these plans for me, asked his friends to look after me like they have, so I could do what I have been telling you about: investigating places and people, collecting information—all of that stuff. He wanted me to discover all this for myself. He wanted me to see inside what he called a mosaic, Olivia. To understand early on what it took him his whole life to figure out and what in the end got him killed.

"What I'm trying to say is, my dad did this for me because he didn't want me to end up like him. He had to do some hard things in his life. He killed people and sent other men to kill people. But he did this to protect what he believed to be important: people he cared for, a way of doing business, a way of life. He wanted me to learn all that he could teach me, but he wanted me to use that knowledge in my own way, not to have it abused by other people. Not to have it distorted. And when he saw the way things were going, and he saw he couldn't do anything about it, he got ready to die because living any other way would have been to cheat on the principles that had guided his life.

"That's why he stayed away from my mom and me—to keep us safe. But, when he knew his end was coming, he found he couldn't go without seeing her one more time—and seeing me for the only time."

Jack fell silent. He rested his head on the back of the sofa. There was a rustle from Olivia's chair. She uncurled her legs and moved to kneel on the sofa.

"The first time you told me about your father, I said that he must love you very much," she said. "Now I understand why."

"Do you also understand why I wasn't allowed to speak about any of this?"

Olivia put a finger to his lips. "I think your father's friends would not want me to know any of this. Isn't that so?"

Jack knew she was right, but he felt less guilty than he thought he might have. He drew her close beside him and felt the warmth of her breath on his cheek.

Jack made two further visits to the south campus. He did tell Olivia about these, and she in turn gave him the names of Cuban intelligence officers who had served with her father. Jack worked his way through the carefully indexed names, but nothing on file at Zenith Technological Enterprises matched Olivia's list.

He could tell she was disappointed, but she tried to make light of it, teasing him: "Even the great Jack Pagano cannot find this man."

Miller was not disappointed, though. He took careful note of what Jack told him. They had two sessions of debriefing in Miller's hotel room close to the airport. Miller was keen to go over in detail the weapon stocks Jack had found and the different types of boats he had seen.

It was a sizable operation, Miller concluded.

"When will you have enough to move against them?"

"This business isn't an exact science," Miller said. "My guess would be by the end of the year. I'll keep you posted, though. You've done a great job here, Jack. I'll make a point of telling Frank and Meyer."

Jack felt a pang of disappointment. Working his way stealthily about the former naval station had given him the buzz he had first experienced in Sicily. "When will I hear from you again?"

Miller sensed his eagerness. "Be patient. Things are building. I'll be back at you just as soon as we're ready to go."

Chapter Fifty-Seven

Since flying Carlos Marcello back from his temporary exile in Guatemala in secret, David Ferrie had become a regular visitor to Churchill Farms. Marcello saw that Ferrie had a good mind and, once he fixed on an objective, he was tenacious—like a mongoose clinging to the flayed snake dying between its jaws.

Marcello needed tenacious minds. His long-running feud with the Department of Justice looked likely to be landing him in court in the fall. David Ferrie had been hired as an investigator and seemed to enjoy the world of intrigue. Marcello had him tracking down evidence to support his case fighting deportation. He was also a useful go-between with associates in Texas, notably Joe Civello, who took care of business for Marcello in Dallas.

During the last twelve months, he had gotten involved with a former FBI man in New Orleans, a man whose political viewpoint and extreme right-wing orientation mirrored that of Marcello himself. Guy Banister was no stranger to the bottle, which Marcello also found kind of endearing. The man was basically finished, but Marcello had thrown him a lifeline of sorts. Banister had made sure to grab it. Since then, he hadn't looked back. As New Orleans swelled with bands of renegade Cubans and detritus discarded in the aftermath of the Bay of Pigs, Banister had taken a more central role in a number of anti-Castro groups, notably the Cuban Revolutionary Council and the Anti-Communist League of the Caribbean.

These groups had training camps in out-of-the-way locations north of Lake Pontchartrain and deep in the bayou. Banister kept up a regular supply of weapons and ammunition, all of it clearly identified as US military hardware. David Ferrie wasn't going to turn down the chance to get involved with camps filled with virile Latin men; he'd used his time with the Civil Air Patrol to get taken on as an instructor.

Ferrie fidgeted with the bank of telephones and telex machines in the office suite of Marcello's ramshackle barn.

Marcello sat slumped in one of the leather sofas. "For fuck's sake, will you come and sit down and leave those alone?"

"This is power, real power," Ferrie said, apparently unaware of what Marcello had just told him. "Shit, man. You can speak to anyone in the world from here. I bet you could pick up any one of these and get right to the Pope. Think of it, a hot line to the Vatican. That's awesome. Or the White House. You could call up that son of a bitch in the Oval Office and show him who runs things around here. You could do that, Carlos. You really could."

"For Christ's sake, will you shut up!" Marcello yelled. "Have a drink and quiet down—or, when he gets here, John and me are going to have our few words in private. Understand?"

Ferrie lit a cigarette and paced about the room, trying to stay silent. Marcello helped himself to a whisky and checked the time. The man from Chicago was due any time now.

Five minutes later the alabaster telephone rang. "Your guest has arrived."

"Bring him right over." Marcello replaced the receiver and growled at Ferrie. "Remember what I told you: No playacting."

The man with the absurdly arched eyebrows stubbed out his cigarette and immediately lit another.

Johnny Rosselli had no objection to dropping into Churchill Farms. Carlos Marcello understood how to make guests feel exclusive, how to keep their presence away from prying eyes. It was a policy that Rosselli had perfected in his own dealings with important visitors and clients in Las Vegas. He liked the way Marcello's "barn" had been decorated. The Italian influence appealed to Rosselli, even if it was slightly old fashioned. The heavy chandeliers and deep leather chairs reminded him of a hotel he liked in Palermo. Marcello was vulgar in many ways, but his appreciation of style and elegance registered with his visitor—it made Marcello tolerable.

"It's good to see you, John." He levered himself out of his seat to greet the debonair man who had just landed in the jet his casino, the Tropicana, made available to VIPs.

"And you, Carlos. You look well, despite this nonsense with Justice."

Marcello dismissed the subject with an angry wave of his hand, like he was knocking away an irritating insect. "You know Dave Ferrie?"

"Who could forget?" Rosselli said smoothly. "How are you, David?"

"Fine, Mr. Rosselli, I'm just fine."

Marcello took the seat at the head of the boardroom table and gestured to the other men to sit either side of him.

"Sam and I want to be clear about things down here," Rosselli began.

Marcello bridled at this. "You think we can't handle something big like this?"

"You've got a lot going on. You and we have a partnership. So we just want to be sure our friends here are in complete agreement with what is being laid down. That's all."

Marcello tried to look conciliatory.

"And we don't have a bad record," Rosselli added, driving his point home.

"Yeah, that hit on Trujillo last year was classy," Ferrie blurted out. "Murder, Incorporated couldn't have done any better."

"I'm glad you appreciated it," Rosselli told him. "Our friends in Washington had no complaints. Makes this business so much easier. Don't you agree?"

"Dumb fuckers," said Marcello. "It's like they want us to play along with them. First they get the Cubans all worked up, give them guns, promise them every hair in Castro's beard. Then they pull the plug and expect them to disappear down the drain and out of sight."

David Ferrie couldn't resist speaking out. "Carlos is right. Two weeks ago those motherfuckers turned off the faucet to the Cuban Revolutionary Council—the outfit that works out of Guy's office. The agency set them up, for fuck's sake, then they cut off the money." He drew a finger across his throat for emphasis.

"Most unfortunate," Rosselli told him. "But the matter is in hand. I'm telling you this in confidence, so it mustn't leave this room."

Ferrie saw the look Marcello was giving him and held up his hand to show he understood the consequences of disobeying Rosselli.

"Like I said, this is in confidence. But in two months' time the Cuban Revolutionary Council will receive two hundred large from us. Sam and I have it in hand. That should make them feel favorably inclined to do what needs to be done."

"That's very generous." Ferrie tried to sound respectful.

Marcello gave him a grudging smile.

"Our Cuban friends have no need to be concerned about money," Rosselli continued. "I've just come from Texas. Clint Murchison is backing this all the way down the street—and he's not alone. Some serious players are joining our team. You can tell your Cubans that."

"Hell, maybe we should ask the IRS to make our donation tax deductible...seeing as how Uncle Sam is asking us to make it."

Marcello laughed politely. "What about the timing, John? It's kind of hard keeping a lid on some of these guys. You know what they're like: hothead, dago types."

"The timing hasn't changed. Everything will be in place in the fall. Our man will be primed and ready to go. But we can't be rushed. The hit on Castro failed last November because of poor intelligence: the shooters got the wrong man."

"You mean someone actually got to pull the trigger on that fucker?" exclaimed Ferrie.

Johnny Rosselli smiled. "The CIA had snipers hidden in trees and bushes lining the road. They had machine guns and rifles and they still didn't kill him. They hit the driver of the second jeep and the man sitting next to him. Through a telescopic sight it was Fidel, no mistaking. Except they found out afterward it was Castro's lookalike bodyguard they killed. The great liberator of the Cuban people was in another jeep."

Ferrie and Marcello looked at him in silent amazement.

Marcello spoke first. "Wait a minute. Did you say November last year? But that was right after—"

"The crisis over the Russian missiles," Rosselli interrupted. "Can you imagine what the White House said when they found out? There's the president making all kinds of secret deals with the Ruskies, promising no harm will come to Fidel. Meanwhile his Central Intelligence Agency is sending assassins to Cuba by the boatload."

"Well, I'll be damned," Ferrie said.

"But nothing is going to go wrong this time. What I can tell you—and you can tell the Cuban leaders who need to know so they can keep their fighters in line—is that the invasion is scheduled for early December. It hasn't yet been fixed exactly where the hit will be, but the assassination will take place a few days before that. Tell your friends that Thanksgiving is going to have a special significance this year."

Chapter Fifty-Eight

After Olivia's graduation, she and Jack made up for lost time with visits to the Everglades and lazy days at the beach, while meals that lasted for an hour or longer replaced hasty sandwiches and guzzled hamburgers. Their life through the early summer evolved into a pattern of languid ease—the calm before the storm, as Jack would look back on it.

They sprawled out on the beach, let the warm sun wash over them. Jack lay relaxed, his eyes closed. In a beach chair next to him, Olivia lay on her stomach and browsed the newspaper.

It was here she spotted a name that made her heart skip a beat.

Jack saw her grow pale and her hand was trembling as she reached for her coffee. "What is it?"

"Someone from the past."

"Who?"

"Me." Olivia passed him the paper and pointed to the personal column. "You see that name? It's my name, Jack. The name I had in Cuba before my father was killed."

In the cramped box of newsprint Jack read, "Maria Sanchez, Olivia Sanchez, wife and daughter of Enrique Sanchez of El Vedado, Havana, believed to be living in the Miami area, please contact below for information to your advantage."

"So your real name is Sanchez?"

"You are not the only one with secrets from the past. We changed it after my father was killed."

Giovanni made no comment about Olivia's name change. "Do you know who this is? It's a New Orleans telephone number."

"I don't know. I don't know that number. It must be someone who only knows me from home." Olivia looked again at the advertisement. "But why make contact now? My mom and I came here four years ago.

In her confusion, Jack was a step or two ahead of her. "Whoever it is knows you are living here, but doesn't know that your mom is dead. Maybe it's someone who has just got out of Cuba trying to find you."

Olivia wasn't convinced. "All the people we knew left Cuba when we did. They had to, Jack. It wasn't safe to stay. Some people would have blamed us for the bad things that Batista had done."

"The only way to find out is to call the number."

The man who answered the telephone when Olivia dialed the number in the newspaper spoke with a Cuban accent. He didn't give his name and he didn't check Olivia's identity in detail; that would wait until they met in New Orleans.

"Next Friday, August 9th," the man told Olivia. "Telephone this number at nine o'clock that morning, we'll arrange to meet."

Jack was uneasy about the arrangement. He didn't want to frighten her, but Rip would have been cautious. "How do you know this isn't some kind of crank? You know, the kind of guy who gets obsessed with a woman."

"In that case, he's been waiting a long time. I should be flattered." She flicked his nose playfully.

"I'm serious, Olivia. You have no idea who this man is. At least let me shadow you. Arrange to meet him somewhere public, where there are a plenty of people. Tell him you'll feel safe that way. Unless he tries something, he won't know I'm there."

She looked dubious.

Jack tried a different approach. "I got you out of trouble once and I didn't even know you then. Please let me do this for you. You do kind of owe me, don't you?"

"This could be my only chance, remember. If you do anything to scare this man away, I'll never speak to you again."

Jack had his warning.

New Orleans in August was steamy and bustling with people on vacation. On Thursday evening, the night before Olivia's meeting, she and Jack checked into a small hotel on Carondelet Street, where the streetcars rattled by outside their window. The next morning she telephoned at nine and the meeting was set for midday.

Somewhere public? No problem, her contact told her. He suggested Jackson Square.

"The French Quarter," Jack said. "That will be an education for you, Miss Hernandez."

"Who's the man about town?" she scoffed. "Just you stay out of sight, Jack Pagano."

They left the hotel at eleven-thirty. Jack let Olivia go first and tailed her at a sensible distance. She didn't appear to be in a hurry and Jack had to slow down when she stopped to look in a shop window on Canal Street.

"Hands off Cuba! Hands off Cuba!" a man with hooded, narrow eyes was shouting as people passed by, taking little notice of him. It didn't seem as if he could have been much older than Jack.

"Hands off Cuba!" the man shouted, thrusting a piece of paper toward Jack, who took it absentmindedly.

"Thank you, sir," said the young protester. "It's nice to meet a man of principle."

Jack shoved the piece of paper into his pocket.

Olivia's contact had told her to go to the coffee and doughnut stall on the side of Jackson Square leading to the French Market. "You'll love the doughnuts," he said. "They're hot, fluffy, and square-shaped. You get three for ten cents. When I hear you make some comment about that, I'll come introduce myself."

Jack followed Olivia into the Quarter along the dark side of Decatur Street. It felt good to be in the shade, and he could see her looking up to admire the delicate cast-iron grill work of the balconies on either side of the street.

When they reached Jackson Square, he watched her cross to the opposite side to the coffee stand. Jack stayed in the shade and joined a group of tourists while their guide showed them points of interest before they moved over to St. Louis Cathedral, which stood at the top of the square.

The man who Jack saw get into conversation with Olivia didn't look sinister. He guessed the guy was in his early forties, though twenty months in a Cuban jail couldn't have done much for his health. He watched them walk over to a bench where they ate the doughnuts Olivia had in the paper bag; the guy ate two, Jack noticed, while Olivia had the third.

They talked for fifteen minutes and then stood up to say goodbye. Jack saw them shake hands. Olivia appeared friendly, but not ecstatic.

Part of the story, but not all, he decided. She still doesn't know who killed her old man.

They had arranged not to meet until they were back in their hotel room. Although Jack could see that the man made no attempt to follow Olivia, he maintained his cover and tailed her back to Carondelet Street, keeping half a block behind her all the way. She didn't look for him once. She didn't look in any shop windows either.

Jack knew the signs.

Olivia was focused. The man had given her a start and she was pulling it apart in her mind, looking for clues.

Chapter Fifty-Nine

"Jack," she said lightly, when he tapped at the door to be let into their room.

He was right about her being preoccupied. The room was close and hot. He felt like lying flat on the bed to cool off, but he took a seat in the corner and let Olivia take the floor.

"Well, he didn't tell me his name, which I kind of expected. And he didn't really need to, because he wasn't one of the guys who worked with my dad. He's one of the fighters captured after the Bay of Pigs; we were right about that. When he was in jail, he got to know someone who did know my dad. These two men got to know each other pretty well. He'd told the man he wouldn't trust another American as long as he lived. The man who worked with my dad said he agreed one hundred percent. Not because any American had done anything bad to him personally, but because of what had happened to someone he worked with in Cuban intelligence. He said this was a man called Enrique Sanchez, and this Sanchez had been shot dead by an American agent he'd been working with during a drug raid."

She paused and took a deep breath.

Jack knew this wasn't easy.

Olivia walked over to the window and carried on. "He never knew the American agent, but my dad spoke about him quite a lot. He said my dad liked the guy. Ironic, isn't it? They must have spent quite a bit of time together, because this guy in prison remembers a lot of things about the American agent—which is why the man I saw this morning wanted to speak to me and my mom, if she was still around."

Jack hesitated to interrupt, but he was desperate for detail. "What did he tell you specifically, Olivia?"

"He told me that this agent had been working in Cuba since the war; the guy speaks perfect Spanish. He speaks Italian as well, and Sicilian, because he worked undercover in Sicily during the war. Apparently the Mafia helped the Americans when they landed in Sicily and this agent was the go-between for the US high command and the Mafia bosses. He helped plan the landing sites and supplied reconnaissance for the invasion. He was working behind enemy lines when the invasion started. If it was anybody else he'd be a national hero."

Jack was taking in all she said. "This is good, Olivia. Was there anything else, anything particular he remembered about this American?"

"The cigars," she said. "The man in prison talked to my man about the cigars. My father liked to smoke cigars, but this American agent hated smoking. And my dad couldn't understand this. The best cigars in the world are made in Havana, he told his American contact, but the agent wouldn't touch one.

"Now my dad always smoked one type of cigar—you know, the way some people only like one kind of drink. They were called Romeo y Julieta. My mom used to kid they nearly called me Julieta because of those cigars. And what happened with those cigars must have stuck in my dad's head, because the guy in prison clearly remembered what he told him.

"My dad said that the first time he took out one of his cigars in front of the American, the guy noticed the band on it—where it has the name, you know—Romeo y Julieta. He asked my dad if it was his favorite and, of course, Dad said it was. 'You're in good company,' the American told him. 'General George S. Patton took a liking to them as well.' The American said he had given General Patton a box of Romeo y Julieta cigars, which he had taken—'liberating' he called it— from a German officers' mess in a place called Ragusa. That was the day after Patton came ashore in Sicily. The agent didn't want them for himself, but he knew Patton loved cigars. My dad thought Patton was a great general. 'Old Blood and Guts,' he used to call him. I guess that's why he remembered the story."

When there was no response from Jack, she looked over and saw him staring blankly at her.

"Is there any way your man could have got that story wrong? Got the details mixed up?" he asked.

Olivia doubted it. "He was very specific. Why do you think he might have it wrong?"

"Miller," Jack said quietly, like he was talking to himself. "Miller told me the same story."

And from several years back, not long after Jack and Miller had met, the voice in his head repeated what Miller had casually mentioned, when they were talking about his resistance work with the partisans: "I gave Patton a box of cigars I'd liberated from the Kraut officers' mess in Ragusa."

For a moment Jack and Olivia looked at each other in silence. Olivia was the first to speak. "But isn't Miller the government agent you work for? The man who sends you to do dangerous things?"

"Yes, he is," Jack said flatly. "That's exactly what he is."

"My God, Jack. You know him. You know the man who killed my father."

Jack slumped forward with his elbows resting on his knees. His head felt heavy. He needed air. He drew in long, deep breaths. "I think he is, Olivia. I really think he is."

"The bastard!" she shouted. "The treacherous, cheating bastard! Where do I find him, Jack? How do I get to him?"

"Steady there," he told her, holding his head between his hands and grimacing as he tried to come to grips with what they had just discovered. If Miller had betrayed Olivia's father and had passed on the secret intelligence he had uncovered to the cartels, then what had he being doing with the information Jack had been giving him?

He felt nauseated.

"Miller knows a lot about the Sicilian families," he said, working through pieces of information, trying to get them in order. "He was there in the war, organizing them to sabotage Italian and German defenses. He played an important part in Operation Husky, like the man who knew your dad says."

"Husky?" asked Olivia. "What is husky?"

"It was the codename for the Allied landings in Sicily in 1943."

That wasn't her question, though. "No—what is 'husky'? What does it mean?"

"Husky is like when you're voice is thick and hoarse. But it also means a kind of dog. The dogs Eskimos use to pull their sledges."

"*Perro esquimal*," Olivia said. "Eskimo dog. Husky."

"That sounds right," Jack said.

"*Perro Esquimal* was the name the traffickers used when they spoke about the American agent. He just called himself Husky. They didn't know his real name either."

The sound of Olivia's voice and the sunlight in the hotel room were pushed aside in Jack's mind by fearful, agonized wailing and flashes of a dank Detroit bathroom.

"*The real name? I don't know the real name!*" Jack heard Louis Reggio scream as Joe Gordon bent over the gory face and held the knife to his throat. "*Nobody does. This fella don't use no real name. Ask…H…Hus…Hussss…Askee…*"

"Husky!" He bolted upright, damp with a cold sweat. "Jesus Christ, Olivia. Miller had my dad killed too."

Chapter Sixty

Jack had never felt more grateful to Rip Collins and the time he had devoted to Jack's training than he did in the hours following Olivia's meeting in Jackson Square.

The immediate urge to get away from the hotel, from Carondelet Street and New Orleans, to escape somewhere—anywhere—was quickly replaced with a rational analysis and a plan they would both need to follow.

"Miller has been using me, like he used your dad," Jack told Olivia matter-of-factly. He dredged his memory for recollections of what Miller had said and done in the time they had known each other.

The pieces fit. The mosaic made sense.

Miller had been involved with narcotics trafficking for two decades, or more. It could have started in Sicily during the war, or in Italy right afterward. It could have started anywhere: in Marseilles, where he busted the unions; in Cuba, when Batista was put in place—anywhere. The time and location were unimportant, the way he operated was what mattered.

To Jack's reasoning, Miller used his status in the intelligence world to mask the trafficking business in which he had become a key player. He offered occasional morsels to drug enforcement agencies, tidbits of information, low-level operatives, whatever was needed to retain his reputation as a top-level agent in the field.

Over time, Jack came to see, Miller had grown leery of old associates: *Too many of my old buddies are on the payroll. It wouldn't be good for me, or them, if we happened to run into each other.*

In that he had been telling the truth. What Miller needed was someone to do the reconnaissance for him, and who better than an unknown operator who had been specially trained with one purpose in mind—to go after the lords of the drug world and expose them to the forces of retribution, just as the man who controlled his life had laid down?

"But you told me Miller rescued you in Detroit," Olivia said.

It was a set-up, Jack concluded. Miller had wanted Reggio dead, and he ordered Gordon to kill him before he named the man who had masterminded Anastasia's shooting.

Miller also knew that the sight of the gruesome killing would disorient Jack so much, he wouldn't stop to weigh up what was happening to him. When Miller appeared at the window, just as the police were about to kick in the door, he would have looked like Jack's guardian angel.

Miller had planned the operation, but, in the debriefing that followed, he had made Jack feel kind of sorry for him. It was made to look like Miller had only been trying to do his best for Jack in sending him secretly to Detroit. And when things started to go wrong, he was seen to be doing his best by rescuing Jack from the DPD.

The police showing up. Jack guessed that was a setup too.

Making it look like Miller was rescuing Jack from Reggio's apartment was a perfect smokescreen. Miller could acknowledge some responsibility for what had gone wrong while gaining Jack's gratitude for saving him.

And with Jack's gratitude, Miller could conveniently play on his sense of honor and feeling of indebtedness, which Miller could exploit.

Lansky and Costello had also been taken in. They knew that Miller operated close to the margin of risk; that's why he had been valuable to them all this time.

In Detroit, it looked like he had misjudged the situation and the man he had sent to watch over Jack. Fortunately, or so it seemed, he'd had the foresight to go as reserve backup himself. Anastasia's friends had accepted that. Were it not for Miller, Jack might have ended his days in Detroit, either in a cell or cemetery.

After Detroit there had been no reason for Jack to suspect that Miller was anything other than what Costello had whispered to him when he and Miller first: *Three-letter guy. He's okay, but you should know.*

So much for Jack; he had been taken in like everybody else. But there was something else Miller had said recently that made him anxious, very anxious: *You can get that chick of yours to fill you in on the background to Zapata. She sounds like a smart lady.*

Miller knew about Olivia; that stood to reason. It was his linking of her with the Bay of Pigs that unsettled Jack. There was no telling how far Miller's intelligence extended on Olivia's contacts among Cuban exiles. Maybe it was a shrewd guess. After all, Miller had needed Jack to check out Zenith Technological Enterprises. Perhaps he assumed Olivia was merely party to street gossip—nothing more. Still, she and Jack needed to be careful.

"I need to speak to Lansky and Costello," he told her. "Miller knows I go see them, there's no reason for him to suspect anything this time."

"Why waste time?" she asked. "We know who he is and what he did to us and our parents. You know what to do, Jack. Why don't you go do it? Your friend Rip can help you. I'm sure he can."

"Do you know what you are asking me to do?"

"Yes," she answered. "We have found the man who killed my father and your father. So, I am saying he should die now."

"That's not what I mean, Olivia. Don't you see? There is more to Miller here. If we take out Miller now, we lose the chance to get inside what he has been working on. I want to get even with him as much as you do. But not yet. Not till the time is right. He's been using me for a long time. Now it's my turn to use him. Miller knows nothing about what we found out here. Nothing has changed for him. As long as it stays that way, you and I stay safe. We just have to make sure we keep it like that."

Chapter Sixty-One

"You're late." John McCloy sat impassively, hardly looking up to watch his morning appointment hang his coat and hat on the corner rack and place his bundled black umbrella into the stand, a deep metal thud sounding as the ferrule hit the ground. The man wore a gray wool suit with a heavily starched shirt, rigid with a slight sheen. His narrow black tie caught the light as he approached the desk. "No need for apologies," McCloy continued. "I'm sure you're very, very sorry. Traffic was a mess, and so on. Same story as always."

McCloy gestured toward the seat opposite the desk and watched as the man lowered himself into the cold leather chair. The former chairman of Chase Manhattan Bank was acutely aware of his own power and the way his demeanor forced small men to shrink even smaller. And so he drew the silence out a moment longer before finally adding, "How is our good friend, the Ambassador, these days?"

"Quiet." The two men stared solemnly at one another, each waiting for the other to crack a smile. A dim laughter slowly swept through the office, catching both men in its wake for a minute, maybe two. It had been nearly two years since a stroke left the Ambassador without the ability to speak. McCloy finally held up his hand, a clear gesture that the time for frivolities had ended and he now wanted a complete report. "He's steady. No significant change in health. Mentally, though, he's still very much aware of his surroundings. It's like he's already dead but too stubborn to quit breathing and just lie still."

McCloy sat rigidly, as if suspended by a series of carefully crafted beams and girders. "Joe Kennedy always has been an arrogant son of a bitch."

"Now do you understand what I've been trying to tell you?"

"You're preaching to the converted, son." McCloy paused, his gaze drifting off to the side. "There isn't a banker in this country or Europe who doesn't despise Joe Kennedy for what he and the people backing him did in 1929. And there's no telling how many fingerprints he left in Germany."

"You don't need to remind me. I sometimes wonder if my father had gone to Harvard, and not Yale, whether he would still be alive."

McCloy shifted in his chair, prepared himself to drive home the same point he'd already made so many times at this very desk at any of a dozen meetings almost entirely similar to this one. "Joe Kennedy doesn't give a damn where the men he's destroyed went to school. Money is all he was ever been interested in—money and power. His greed is almost impressive in its transcendence of country or creed. And now he has the Oval Office—and the Justice Department," he said. "And it was a masterstroke of yours, making Robert Kennedy attorney general."

"I hope so."

"Are you having second thoughts?"

"If the old man is proving reluctant to do what he's meant to, who's to say his boys will be any different?"

Chapter Sixty-Two

Along Carondelet Street, the streetcars rattled and rang, carrying the bustle of the city through the window where Jack and Olivia lay. Neither slept much that night. They had eaten lightly in the evening, though neither was hungry.

When his watch showed it was six o'clock, Jack got up and took a shower. It was refreshing—cleansing.

Olivia was in the bathroom when Jack pulled on his pants and noticed a piece of crumpled paper on the floor where they had been lying. He picked it up and recognized the leaflet that had been handed to him the day before by the smartly dressed protestor on Canal Street.

Jack looked at the paper before throwing it in the trash bin.

HANDS OFF CUBA!
Join the Fair Play for Cuba Committee
NEW ORLEANS CHARTER
MEMBER BRANCH
Free Literature, Lectures

F P C C
544 CAMP ST.
NEW ORLEANS, LA.

E V E R Y O N E   W E L C O M E !

It wasn't just the crude printing of the address that set off alarms. There was something he noticed about the address itself. Camp Street was where he and Rip had parked when they had gone to check out Guy Banister. The building he used stood on a corner, Jack remembered. The door to Banister's office had an address on Lafayette Street, number 531. Round the corner the same building had a door that also led up to Banister's office: 544 CAMP STREET, the door read.

What Jack couldn't figure out was why a pro-Castro outfit like the Fair Play for Cuba Committee was operating out of the same office as a commie-hating redneck like Banister. He and Olivia weren't scheduled to leave until later in the day; there'd be time enough to see what was going on.

Mancuso's restaurant was busy serving breakfast. There was a table free that gave a good view of the street, and they took it. They ordered coffee and rolls and waited to see who showed up for work at Guy Banister Associates.

The first to arrive was a middle-aged woman, Banister's secretary Jack guessed. The man himself appeared around a half hour later looking bleary-eyed. Banister spent ten minutes in the restaurant drinking a coffee before he went next door. Most of the early clients had left for work and Jack and Olivia had to give the impression of being fixated on each other to explain why they were still there.

Jack was leaning across the table, holding Olivia's hand,when he noticed a familiar figure walk by the window. He squeezed her fingers gently and moved his eyes toward the window to indicate someone interesting had gone by. It was David Ferrie.

Less than ten minutes later, Banister had another visitor. "Stay here," he told her quietly. "I'll be ten minutes, at the most."

"Where are you going?" she hissed.

He pulled the leaflet out of his pocket. "Upstairs."

The waiter showed Jack the way to the office above and he moved lightly up the treads. At the top was a door, which opened onto a hallway cluttered with packing cases. Stacks of paper and chairs lined the walls.

People were talking in an office. Two men, Jack thought. He checked another office along the hallway where some sort of machine was clunking to and fro. The young man who had given him the leaflet was working a small printing machine and didn't register Jack's presence. At the other end of the hallway was the front office, where the secretary was busy typing.

Behind the door, Guy Banister and David Ferrie made no attempt to keep their voices down.

"What I'm telling you is this," Banister boomed. "I ain't running no sideshow for nobody. I don't care how many big-shot money men are in on this deal. What do they know about this kind of business? When did any of them last shoot anything but a goose or a deer? And from what I know of those millionaire-type hunters, they miss the target nine times out of ten."

Jack heard the click of a cigarette lighter and then David Ferrie spoke. "No one's sidelining you, Guy. Can't you get that into you thick skull? This is the sucker punch, for fuck's sake. You should know that. You get them looking one way and then you nail them to the floor. Beautiful."

"And that's what Murchison and these big shots in Dallas are telling you?" Banister asked. "Something is going to happen around Thanksgiving that will get everyone excited, and while they're concentrating on that—zap!—we're in business?"

Ferrie lowered his voice. "Listen, Guy. You got that kid down the hallway set up just like you were told. Now you send him down to Mexico, where he applies for entry into Cuba. Then, Thanksgiving, here we come."

"Can I help you?" a woman's voice asked from behind Jack.

Jack turned around and smiled at her. "Thanks. I didn't know if I should interrupt."

The woman eyed him suspiciously.

Jack showed her the leaflet. "I came about this. It was given to me yesterday. I saw the address and I came to get some information about joining. What this government is doing to Cuba ain't right: cutting off baby food and all…"

Banister yanked open the door to his office. Jack whipped his eyes round inside. "What the fuck's going on?"

"I came about this," Jack repeated, showing the leaflet.

Banister's brow furrowed. "Yeah, there's been a mistake about that. They printed the wrong address."

"Do you know where I can find the Fair Play for Cuba Committee?" Jack asked innocently.

"I ain't got a clue, and I don't give a fuck," said Banister. "If you think like they do, I suggest you get out the door and down the stairs before I have to help you."

"Sorry to have disturbed you," Jack said. "Which way should I go?"

"Show him out the front way, Delphine."

The office door slammed shut.

"Thank you for your time," Jack told Banister's secretary.

"He means it," she answered. "You take my advice and stay well away from him."

"I'll be sure to remember that." He sauntered down the stairs, out the door, and around to the restaurant where Olivia was twisting her table napkin around her fingers, waiting for him to reappear.

Chapter Sixty-Three

It had been over a year and a half since the Ambassador's stroke, but he still insisted on receiving Lovall's memos. It did no harm, Lovall concluded. His advice would be followed through regardless. He had served the clan well and they looked to James Lovall to mold them into a dynasty. The closing weeks of this year were pivotal, however. They required delicate handling to ensure that Lovall's program continued to roll out as slated.

With the 1964 presidential election a little over a year away, concerns were growing about the stability of the Democratic Party vote in the South. Having a Texan as vice president should have secured the Lone Star State in particular, but infighting between local politicians had gotten out of hand; this kind of dissent, and the hemorrhaging of votes that could follow, needed sorting out. James Lovall's memo on the subject would spur the right outcome—he could count on that.

MEMORANDUM

To: **Ambassador Kennedy**
From: **James Lovall**
Date: **August 12, 1963**
Subject: **Texas**

You will forgive me, sir, for coming straight to the point. In my opinion, the Democratic vote in Texas must be secured this fall. The standing of the party is fragile in key areas of the South; we must accept this. I think it reinforces the opinion that LBJ should be replaced before campaigning begins in earnest in the New Year. At the same time, Yarborough and Connally are at each other's throats and need their heads banged together.

My proposal is that a morale-boosting presidential visit should be scheduled for the fall. Florida is important, but I would advise including Texas in our plans.

I appreciate that this is not a suitable time to raise the subject with the first lady, but if she could be persuaded to accompany JFK, her presence would be a significant asset. It is generally understood that she dislikes the campaign trail. Therefore, if Mrs. Kennedy is seen accompanying her husband on the trip I have outlined, it would send a very positive message that the current White House highly values voters in the South, and in Texas especially. In my opinion, there could be no better way of starting the coming presidential campaign.

I hope the significance of the above will excuse my intruding at this sad time. May I repeat my commiserations with you on your loss last week of the president's newborn son.

Chapter Sixty-Four

"I will give you certain telephone numbers to leave a message that will reach me—but only if it's an emergency." That was practically the first thing Meyer Lansky had told Jack when they first met at the rail station in Trenton.

It was one of those numbers that Jack had called, and now he was with Lansky and Costello back in the penthouse suite of the Sherry Netherland Hotel in New York City. Rip was there as well. Jack knew his experience in the field could be important in helping decide what they should do.

He'd had a couple of days to come to terms with the truth about Miller, but he was still surprised at the way the men had reacted to the news.

Costello scowled and sighed. "We walk a fine line. But this—I did not see this coming."

"You did well, Jack" Lansky said.

Rip Collins kept his reaction to himself.

Frank Costello lit a cigarette and paced about, deep in thought.

Lansky gave Jack's forearm a squeeze. "You did good, Jack. You kept your head when a lot of men older than you could have blown it."

The young man with them had come for guidance, but it was they who first asked him for his analysis. "You've seen all the pieces," Frank Costello told him. "Meyer and me have our own ideas, but we want to hear what you think first. How do you think they fit together? And Miller, where is he in this pack of cards?"

Jack began by taking them through his early dealings with Miller; the "setup" as he termed it. From there he reminded them what had come to light in Miami and after that in New Orleans and Dallas. The one element that was new to them was what Jack was about to describe: his recent discoveries with Olivia in New Orleans.

He told them how his suspicions had been aroused by the address on the leaflet he'd been given.

"I went back to the restaurant in the building, the place you and I went," he told Rip. "I used the leaflet as an excuse to go up and have a look around."

He saw Rip smile when he said this, but his mentor kept silent.

"I think some new organization is being put together to take over everything we've got going on," Jack told them. He'd included himself and nobody had batted an eye, but he stopped short of smiling. "Then there's Cuba. The way I see it, Castro is going to be assassinated. They follow this up with an invasion using the Cuban exiles—maybe with US help. This new organization sets up a puppet government in Cuba and they have everything in place to run drugs and weapons in and out on a massive scale."

"You don't pull any punches, kid. I'll give you that." Meyer Lansky took the same view. "That makes sense to me. This kind of business don't come together overnight."

Costello stubbed out his cigarette and lit another before sitting down on the sofa. "If what you say is halfway to the truth, we have a very serious problem on our hands."

Rip had quietly been running over what Jack had said. "You think it's around Thanksgiving that this is going to happen?"

"That's what it sounded like. Banister and Ferrie talked about something happening around Thanksgiving that would get everyone looking one way so that whatever has been planned can happen while we're all distracted."

"And you put your money on Dallas, Texas?" Rip checked.

"Murchison has got all the right credentials," Lansky cut in. "The man has personal assets of hundreds of millions of dollars—and those are the ones the IRS know about. As for his business interests, they're spread right across the country like a pirate's treasure map. Oil, real estate, insurance, railroads, construction, shipping, banking, automobiles, newspapers, water companies, agriculture—Murchison owns a piece of every part of our lives. He does business everywhere. He has contacts everywhere. If he is putting together a team, like you say, they're in for the big time."

Frank Costello stood up and crossed to where Jack was standing, pointing his index finger like an attorney in a court room. "Tell us where you see Miller in all of this."

"In the middle," Jack answered confidently. "He's the bull's eye on the target. Everything connects to him: the cartels, the dope plants in Europe and Latin America, the money from the big investors, the Teamsters, the Cuban traffickers, and the exiles running hits on Cuba. And there's the whole government intelligence network, in this country and overseas. Miller has contacts with all of them. Miller is the key to getting inside this operation."

Costello turned to Rip Collins. "You've listened to all this. Do you want to have a say?"

"Thank you." Rip leaned forward in his armchair. "The way I see it, we need to look for something scheduled to happen in Dallas in the fall, something that is going to catch people's attention. Whatever it is, it's going to need advance notice."

Costello listened intently.

"When we know what this event is going to be, Jack and I go to Dallas—two weeks before, if we have the time, to see if we can't find out what this other business is, the bit that's going to happen when everyone is distracted."

"How are we going to explain being in Dallas for so long?" Jack asked.

"That's an easy one." Rip didn't miss a beat. "Clint Murchison owns the Dallas Cowboys. And if a player like Jack Pagano wants a tryout…" He let the thought finish itself.

"I'll buy that," Lansky said.

Costello agreed.

"And in the meantime?" Jack asked. "What do I do about Miller?"

"You have to act normal," Rip said. "Behave like nothing is different. If we're right, Miller will show up in Dallas. Let him unlock the door and let you see who's inside. Then he'll give us all we need and we can take care of him."

Jack saw the look Rip exchanged with the other two.

"It will be done, Jack," Meyer Lansky assured him. "When the time is right."

Jack's curiosity had been pricked and he chanced his luck to ask, "What happens after that?"

"After Miller?" Costello asked,

"No. I mean after we find out who is in this whole deal."

"Leave that to us," Costello said. "Let's see who's involved first. When we find out who's lined up against us, we'll know how to deal with them."

It was the answer Jack should have expected, but it didn't satisfy his curiosity, or his urge to get started. "So now we have to wait to hear about some kind of public event in Dallas around Thanksgiving. Is that right?"

A month later, on September 13th, the *Dallas Morning News* reported that President Kennedy would be making a trip to Texas in November, with a visit to speak at a Trade Mart luncheon in Dallas itself slated for November 21st or 22nd.

Chapter Sixty-Five

Two weeks after the president's Texas visit was made public, Jack and his father's friends watched what appeared to be another carefully crafted move to undermine existing narcotics trafficking.

The agent of this perfectly stage-managed event was a sixty-something professional hoodlum called Joe Valachi, who was serving time for jumping bond on a dope trafficking charge in the federal penitentiary in Atlanta, where one of his fellow inmates happened to be Vito Genovese. Word on the prison grapevine reached Genovese that Valachi had turned informant for the Narcotics Bureau, and Genovese had ordered him to be rubbed out. For his own safety, Valachi had asked to be placed in solitary confinement. However, his period of protection was short-lived. The Narcotics Bureau had the Prison Bureau return Valachi to the attentions of Genovese and his disciples. Not long after that, Joe Valachi conveniently agreed to start talking to federal narcotics agents.

And once he started, Joe Valachi didn't let up.

On September 27, 1963, he went before national television cameras to give evidence before another committee headed by the old friend of the president and the attorney general, Senator John McClellan. The focus of what would become known as the Valachi Hearings could not have been more specific in targeting drug rackets nationwide.

Joe Valachi's testimony cut to the heart of existing underworld operations. Backed by detailed charts illustrating the elaborate hierarchy of organized crime families, Valachi shredded the veil of secrecy hiding what he took pleasure in calling *Cosa Nostra*. "Our thing," a riveted TV audience heard, ran a complex production and distribution chain that moved narcotics from Europe to North America and distributed them throughout the US and Canada.

Valachi's evidence was peppered with names as well. To Jack it sounded like a well-rehearsed roll call. Carlos Marcello, Santo Trafficante, Sam Giancana were ones he was expecting to hear. But the name that made him sit up was that of Dave Yaras—Jack Ruby's pal, whom he and Rip had seen with Ruby and a Cuban-looking man in the Vegas Club. Yaras was the link to the distribution arm of the network: the Teamsters. At one stage in the proceedings, Valachi was asked if there was any connection between the Teamsters and the Cosa Nostra.

"Senator, I'll tell you that in private."

Jack felt sure he would—that, and a whole lot more.

The Valachi Hearings continued until the end of October. By the time they were over and Joe Valachi had gone back to jail—La Tuna Federal Prison in Texas this time, with a $100,000 price on his head offered by Vito Genovese—his evidence had delivered a devastating blow to those he had once served and to whom he was bound by an oath of silence.

"If that hasn't fucked us all," snarled Frank Costello, "nothing has."

It looked like Jack's prediction was right on the money.

Miller gave every impression of being delighted by the revelations of the Valachi Hearings. He contacted Jack toward their end, in the second half of October. "What he told that committee will make the bastards run for cover," he gloated. "Joe Valachi has blown those drug outfits wide open. All we have to do is pick them off as they run out, like rats in a grain store."

There was more to Miller's call, though. He told Jack he had gotten wind of something sinister stirring in Dallas. "You remember those French guys Valachi named?" Jack recalled a string of men with French and Italian-sounding names who were all allegedly connected with trafficking heroin from Marseilles and around the Mediterranean.

"A contact of mine in French intelligence tells me that a whole bunch of them are going to be in the US next month, in Dallas. He says they're expected to be in town the same time as the president drops by."

Jack hadn't needed to feign astonishment. He hadn't bet on the European end being involved in Dallas. Although, now that Miller had mentioned it, their presence seemed logical. He knew the scale of the European operation from his own experiences in Sicily, and from what he had learned from Meyer Lansky. It stood to reason that the people who took care of production there would want to be represented at what was being put together in Dallas.

"That's when we plan to hit them, Jack—when the president's in town. A visit from the Bureau of Narcotics is the last thing they will be expecting that afternoon."

"That's interesting, Miller. But why are you telling me?"

"Because I thought you might like to be in on the action. You've done the leg work. This is your reward. To sign off on a job well done."

For a moment, Jack was of two minds. To hold back that he would be in Dallas anyway would make it difficult to explain his presence later on. However, he didn't want Miller to get leery.

The decision was excruciating, but he went for the first option and answered, "Do you think I'm going to turn down something like that? Think what my dad would say."

"Remind me to buy you a drink at the Carousel Club. You'll like it. It's where all the guys hang out. A namesake of yours runs it and he looks after friends of mine."

"So, I'll see you in Dallas?"

"Not if I see you first," Miller quipped. "You'll have to bear with me. I'll get in touch when we're ready."

Chapter Sixty-Six

They settled for a small hotel on Akard Street about three-quarters of a mile from downtown Dallas. It was Rip who investigated his "friends" and their favored haunt, when he and Jack went to Dallas.

The Carousel was the latest of Jack Ruby's business ventures in the nightlife of his adopted city. Billed as its "newest and most intimate burlesque lounge" when it had opened for business three years earlier, the Carousel offered its clients "a continuous girl and comedy show nonstop 9 PM till 2 AM." On the surface, it promised "beer and setup service." On the quiet, Jack Ruby made sure that his and Miller's "friends" in the Dallas Police Department received more than beer when they came by to see their old pal. Ruby also worked his old "setup service" that not infrequently involved an introduction to one of the strippers on his payroll.

Jack needed to be seen as in training, of course, which ruled out evenings in joints like the Carousel. He had been warmly welcomed by Tex Schram, and Jack was pleased with his own showing. As his strength coach, Rip had come along to watch and was impressed with what he had seen, too.

Schram and the other coaches were excited by his speed and the complexity of the patterns he was running. "It's great to have an end with handling skills like that and the speed of an outside receiver," one of them had commented.

"Best of all, he's as strong as a tackle," Schram added.

Jack Pagano was definitely leaving his mark.

After Jack's final scheduled workout, Schram led him from the field and over to a short, stocky man wearing horn-rimmed glasses and a Stetson. "This is our young Jack," he told the man.

"So I see," was the appreciative answer. "That's quite a display you put on, son. You were cutting awful hard out there. Real sharp."

Jack smiled in appreciation. "Thank you very much, Mister…"

"Murchison," the man told him.

"Thank you, Mr. Murchison. I'm pleased you were able to see me work out."

"So was I, son," Murchison answered. "Keep working him hard, Tex. Maybe we'll start to get somewhere with this kid on board." He patted Schram on the shoulder and added, "say, do you mind giving me a second with the boy, I'd like to have a word with him."

"Sure thing, boss." Tex turned to Jack. "Thanks again for coming down here, Jack. You really showed me something."

Jack offered up his absentminded thanks. His mind was on Murchison.

"That was a heck of a performance," Murchison started. "I hear you're a pretty handy fellow, too." Murchison let the words hang out there.

Jack wasn't entirely sure what to say. "Well, I did pretty well in school. My folks—"

Murchison's smile was enough to interrupt the boy. "That's not quite what I had in mind. It seems we've got a mutual friend, you and I."

Jack froze.

"Jack, Tex and the other boys are coming over to my place next Thursday. I got some business associates coming as well, and a few old friends. They'll be the usual crowd. My wife's fixed all the arrangements so half of Texas will be there, I guess. Come and join the fun," he said.

The invitation was like an electric current shooting through him, but Jack tried to sound relaxed. "That sounds fantastic, Mr. Murchison."

"Of course it's all right, son. Bring that coach guy with you, too," he said. "I'm sure Miller will be glad to see you both."

Jack had told Olivia that they would have to keep contact between them to a minimum. Instead, she was left in Haddonfield with Carmella. "Just to be safe," he had explained. But the news about Murchison's party was something she had to know. Jack found a phone booth a couple of blocks from their hotel.

To his surprise, Olivia answered. She sounded pleased to hear his voice.

"I can't talk for long," he told her.

Olivia got the message and let him speak.

"The football's going great. The crazy thing is they could even offer me a contract. How about that? Rip's checking out the guy we came to see before. Rip says he looks real busy. But today I think we got a lead on why we need to be here. Listen real carefully, Olivia, because I may not have a chance to tell you this again. Next week—the 21st. The guy who owns the business and his wife are having one of those big society parties at their place. Not only that, but he knows Miller. The point is we've been invited along with the rest of the team."

"Thursday?" Olivia asked. The telephone line was crackled and she couldn't catch everything clearly

"No, not this Thursday. Check the calendar. Check the date."

There was a brief pause. "That's the day before the president speaks in Dallas."

"You got it." Jack tried to keep his excitement in check. "I think this could be it, Olivia."

Olivia couldn't mask the concern in her voice, might not have even been trying. "You say your friend Rip is going to be with you?"

"He's coming too."

There was another silence at the other end of the line, and when Olivia spoke again her voice was anxious. "I know what I told you before you left," she said. "Now it's happening, I don't know if I was right to say that. I've got used to my dad not being around. I don't know if I could do the same if anything happened to you."

He remembered their parting, when Olivia had balked at being asked to stay in Miami to keep watch for anything developing there. *Kill him, Jack. If you get the chance, kill Miller. Please do that for me.*

Then, there had been ferocity in here eyes: hatred and white-hot anger. Now, he wasn't sure which path to take.

"Come back safely. That's all I'm asking you now."

Chapter Sixty-Seven

The gala party at Clint Murchison's home was themed as a "Night in Egypt," and images redolent of the land of the pharaohs greeted guests when they arrived and formed the backdrop to the evening.

Rip spent a fruitful evening quietly taking note of other guests he recognized from newspaper photographs and magazine articles. Soon after arriving, he had logged John McCloy, chairman of the Chase Manhattan Bank, which had backed Murchison in acquiring his share of the New York Central Railroad. George and Herman Brown, financial backers of the vice president and owners of the giant construction firm Brown & Root, were there as well. So was the fanatical right-wing oil tycoon Haroldson Lafayette Hunt.

Rip was taken aback by the next man to appear: J. Edgar Hoover, Director of the FBI. Rip was still coming to terms with his presence when Richard Nixon, Jack Kennedy's defeated rival in the last presidential election and now a senior attorney with the Pepsi-Cola Company, joined the gathering. Rip had already established that Pepsi-Cola was holding a convention in Dallas and it must have been very convenient for the former Republican candidate to drop by. However, these were two "big players" that hadn't figured into anyone's game plan.

In a little over twelve hours the president would be driving in a motorcade through the center of the city. This was going to be Miller's cover for moving on the French traffickers somewhere not too far away.

"We're ready," a voice said quietly. Jack spun round like he had been stung by a bee.

"Miller," he said.

"Who were you expecting? Santa Claus?"

"I just thought you might have been in contact sooner. I mean, it is tomorrow, isn't it, when—"

Miller put up a hand to stop him. He nodded, and then he indicated to Jack that they should find somewhere quiet to talk and led the way to a side of the room by a door leading through to another reception room where a band was playing.

"Our French boys are in town," Miller confirmed. "We're going to have the reception committee for them in place by noon. The president's party is scheduled to land twenty minutes earlier. They should be leaving Love Field a few minutes later. The route takes them down to Main Street, where they should be about a half an hour later. From there they'll wave at the crowds for twenty minutes down Main and around Dealey Plaza, close to where the French outfit are staying. Do you know where that is?"

Jack said he did. In fact, he remembered Dealey Plaza in particular because of something Rip had found out from drinking with police officers in the Carousel. They'd been talking about the Kennedy visit and the security risks in a known hostile city like Dallas. From the airfield to the bottom of Main Street, armed police would be guarding every underpass, keeping people away as the motorcade drove through. All along Main Street, every block was under the surveillance of a police inspector.

Once in Dealey Plaza, however, police cover would end. Apart from a few uniformed officers holding back traffic, no one from the Dallas Police Department and no Secret Service agents would be stationed there. Rip had been surprised to hear this, but the Dallas cops didn't show any concern. By the time the president's party was in Dealey Plaza, they'd be a bare five minutes from their destination. Besides, the big crowds would be along Main Street; fewer than a couple hundred people were expected to be waiting at the final leg of the motorcade.

Dealey Plaza. Jack knew where it was.

"Good. I want you to meet me there by quarter after. I'll come find you and take you to the stakeout. My guys are detailed to move at 12:45 precisely. You and me go in with the second wave. But let me give you this now; it's government issue. I can't be seen giving it to you tomorrow."

Jack felt something hard and cold push against his chest. He put his hand up to take it and felt the barrel of a revolver.

"Have you ever used one of these?" Miller asked.

"Rip has an automatic. I've fired that a few times."

"This isn't so smooth, but it's reliable. You can't go wrong with a .38, so long as you're up close. Still, it's only a precaution. You won't be needing it."

Jack looked like he didn't follow what Miller was getting at.

"The thing is, Jack, after what happened in Detroit, I don't want to put you in that kind of danger again. If any of those fuckers are still armed when we go in tomorrow, I want to know you got this. That's all."

It was strange for Jack to feel oddly relieved to hear Miller talking like this.

"One other thing," he was told. "My boys know you're coming along, but none of them knows who you are. To avoid any accidents, I told them you'll be wearing a light-colored jacket, dark trousers, and a white T-shirt. You got that? Wear them and you won't get hit by mistake if they're still shooting."

Jack saw Miller check the time on his watch. "It's gone midnight," he said. "I'd better beat it or I'll turn into a pumpkin. Dealey Plaza. 12:15. I'll see you there."

Then he was gone.

Jack's head was spinning. He felt like he had slipped back two months. Talking to Miller, it was like his memory had been wiped clean, like everything had been before he and Olivia went to New Orleans—before she met her man in Jackson Square. And now he had Miller's .38 in his pocket. Jack reached inside his jacket and ran his finger along the barrel.

He felt himself shudder. He knew what Albert Anastasia would tell him.

Jack was so wrapped up in his own thoughts that several minutes passed after Miller had left before he thought to check where Rip was. The party had thinned somewhat. The other members of the football team had disappeared home to bed, though some of the guests invited to listen to the president at the Trade Mart Lunch were making a night of it. Jack couldn't see their host anywhere either, but in a place that size it wasn't surprising. He fetched himself another drink and had to curb his instinct to keep touching the gun in his pocket.

When Rip did show up, his face looked flushed. "Drink up. We should leave," he told Jack with urgency in his voice.

Jack realized he wanted out of there and hurried after him. They found their car and were away from Murchison's driveway before they spoke again.

"Where did you go?" Jack asked. "I just spoke with Miller."

"Miller?"

"Yeah. He nearly made me jump out of my skin. The weird thing is, he was just like you said he would be. He acted like nothing has changed."

"That's one less thing to worry about." Rip breathed out in relief. "For him, nothing has changed."

"He told me the sting they've set up for the French traffickers is fixed for tomorrow, like he said. He says his men are going to move on them when the president is driving through town."

"Why do you think he told you that?"

"He wants me to be there; to see how they do it. That's what he told me."

"And what do you think?"

His mind filled with images of Miller and his father, of Olivia and Don Pagano, of the heroin barn in Sicily and a patch of sea that was still blood red under the Mediterranean sun.

"I don't know why he wants me there tomorrow, Rip. But he gave me this."

Rip looked across at the .38. "Show me the bullets."

Jack tipped them into his palm and held them for Rip to examine.

"They seem okay to me. He's given you live slugs."

Kill him, Jack. If you get the chance, kill Miller. Please do that for me.

Jack's fingers trembled as he fed the bullets back into Miller's gun.

"Is there any way of silencing this? Just for one shot. That's all." Jack had only been vaguely aware of the words leaving his mouth. For him, it was like hearing them from across the room.

The way he spoke carried all the meaning Rip needed to understand what he was asking. "Slip the nipple from a baby bottle over the barrel, that quiets it good enough. But it only gives you one shot, Jack."

"That's all I'll need. After tonight, Miller won't be expecting what's coming."

Rip Collins drove on in silence. He would tell Jack in the morning, he decided. After tonight he didn't know what to expect either.

His disappearance at Murchison's had been to check something he was sure, at first, he had been mistaken about. But his eyes had not been playing tricks. Vice President Lyndon Baines Johnson had arrived late to the party and soon afterward he and Murchison and the other "big players" had taken themselves away to another room, in private. There was one more man with the group. He'd arrived late, slipped in behind the others. Whereas Rip picked the others out with ease, he hadn't a clue what to make of the straggler.

The day of the president's visit had arrived. The smokescreen was being fanned. The pieces of Jack's mosaic were in place. All they needed now was the cement to bind them together for good.

Chapter Sixty-Eight

The early morning rain had dispersed and the sun was shining on a clear fall day by the time Jack arrived for his rendezvous with Miller. He and Rip had driven through here before and he was familiar with its layout.

Dealey Plaza was a grassy expanse shaped like a funnel pointing westwards. At its wide mouth stood the last of the buildings of downtown Dallas. Elm Street, Main Street, and Commerce Street flowed from there. These tapered like the spout of a funnel to converge at a triple underpass that ran beneath railroad tracks. Beyond lay the Stemmons Freeway, the Trinity River, and West Dallas.

A bank sloping down to Elm Street ran along the northern edge of the plaza. This formed a grassy knoll. At its center, the slope rose from the Elm Street sidewalk to a semicircular colonnade fronted by a retaining wall, from which a flight of steps led down to street level. Beyond the colonnade, the slope was topped by trees and shrubs running toward the triple underpass. There was a fence right along this line of vegetation, with a right-angle return that faced directly toward traffic driving down Elm Street. On the other side of the fence, to the north of Dealey Plaza, was a railroad parking lot leading to the city's railroad tracks.

At the top of Elm Street stood an austere, four-square building overlooking the junction of Elm and Houston, which marked the top of the funnel-shaped open space. As he walked about, Jack noticed workmen from the building sitting around eating their lunch.

Jack thought the DPD may have underestimated the number of people showing up to see the president drive by. There was still twenty minutes to go before the scheduled appearance of the motorcade and already people were collecting on the sidewalks and on the grassy area in the center that ran beside Elm Street. A few parents were standing with their kids in vantage points, trying to keep their growing excitement in check. Workmen from the construction site of the new courthouse on the south side of Commerce Street were gathering in little knots, looking up Main Street where the crowds packed the sidewalks five deep as far as the eye could.

In all this growing excitement, the one man Jack could not see was Miller. His heart rate quickened. Atop a building he saw a big clock strike twelve. He had fifteen minutes to go; Miller was always on time.

Jack walked from the bottom of Main Street past the reflecting pool and toward the austere-looking building, seven stories high, which faced him. This was the way the presidential motorcade would be travelling before making a sharp turn to run down Elm Street to the underpass. Jack stopped when his eyes settled on one bystander who had occupied the ideal place to see the passing procession. A man had positioned himself on a plinth beside the steps leading up to the colonnade above Elm Street. He was loading what looked like a cine camera.

A home movie to remember, Jack thought.

It was then that he saw Miller.

He was coming out of the entrance to the seven-story building talking to a man carrying a rolled umbrella, which struck Jack as kind of odd; the rain has stopped several hours earlier.

Jack didn't recognize him.

Neither had Rip the evening before.

The two men descended the entrance steps and disappeared behind the crowd that was gathering at the sharp bend, where the president's limousine would have to slow to a walking pace. There'd be a great view of President Kennedy and the first lady from there.

Miller and the other man appeared between the heads of the crowd as they walked up to Houston Street. Jack's palm was sweaty and he felt damp under his arms. If the other man didn't move soon, Jack worried that he might not have a shot.

Judging by the number of people building round him and the number of arms that would be raised when the president appeared—holding cameras, or simply waving to the man from the White House, all obscuring views and distracting attention—putting the .38 to Miller's chest and pulling the trigger would attract no attention. Jack had fitted a rubber nipple from a baby's bottle over the mouth of the barrel. In the next ten minutes, he had to trust in Rip Collins more than he ever had in his life.

In particular, he had to trust that Rip was waiting a block away on Record Street, ready to drive him back to their hotel. The instant he pulled the trigger, he would be out of there. Rip had already planned how to dispose of the gun. After that they would be driving north to Oklahoma City and flying out to meet up with Meyer Lansky and Frank Costello in New York.

For the moment, though, Miller's companion was sticking to him like glue. The two men stopped where Jack could see them through a gap in the crowd. Several people were pointing upwards to the top of the seven-story building where a couple of men, one holding a rifle, could be seen at an open window—security men, it looked like, most likely Secret Service.

Jack looked back at Miller and watched in disbelief at what happened next. It was like slow motion. The man beside Miller suddenly pointed the tip of his umbrella at Miller's leg and jabbed it into his calf. Miller looked round in horror and then began to sink to the ground, clawing at his collar like he couldn't breathe. Jack's eyes were fixed on Miller's face contorted with agony. When he looked away to spot the man with the umbrella, he was nowhere to be seen.

Jack felt dizzy. Miller was writhing and retching. Onlookers bending over him thought he was having some kind of fit. They tried to sit him upright, but his body wouldn't respond. He lay on the sidewalk, twitching and groaning, while Jack looked on feeling queasy and clammy.

"This is not how it was meant to be," the voice in his head was shrieking. "What about Albert? What About Olivia's dad? Who is going to get even for them?"

Then Olivia's voice cut him off. *"Come back safely. That's all I'm asking you now."*

Yes—that's what he had to do. Get out. Get out right away.

He couldn't fathom who had stabbed Miller, or why—that would have to wait.

Jack pushed through the crowd standing round him. Miller's breathing was light and erratic. His eyes were closed—he would never see the look of hatred on the face of Albert Anastasia's son. The sound of an ambulance grew closer, but it was clear that Miller would not be detaining the medical staff at nearby Parkland Hospital for long.

Another sound reached Jack's ears from behind him, growing louder. Like a wave surging toward Dealey Plaza down Main Street, the crowds on the sidewalks were cheering and clapping and shouting. President Kennedy was running late, but he was coming.

The waiting was almost over.

Chapter Sixty-Nine

Rip could see by the look on Jack's face as he hurried toward the car that something had gone wrong. He looked past Jack, but no one was following him. Rip started the engine, released the handbrake, and checked the traffic so that he could accelerate away as soon as Jack was in the car.

The door slammed shut. Rip hit the gas and they careered off down Record Street.

"Miller's dead," was all Jack could say at first.

"You still got the gun?"

"I got it, but I didn't need it, Rip. Someone got to Miller before me. I saw the whole thing. He's a dead man. A fucking dead man—but it wasn't me."

Rip swerved violently and nearly clipped a car driving past them the other way. The driver thumped his horn as he disappeared in the rearview mirror.

"How do you mean, someone got to him first? Who was it?

"I don't know, Rip. I never saw the man before. He was wearing a suit and carrying an umbrella. That's all I know."

"An umbrella? Why an umbrella?"

"To kill Miller. He stabbed him in the leg with the point of the umbrella and Miller keeled over like he'd been shot, only he was shaking and gasping for air."

"Poison," Rip said. "Hide a hypodermic needle in the umbrella point. It's bold, but lethal if you do it right."

"Poison," Jack repeated in awe.

"Where's Miller now?"

"They took him away in an ambulance. He looked unconscious when I left him."

Rip reached into the back and handed Jack a radio receiver. "We'd better make sure. This is tuned to the police channels. Switch it on and see if there are any reports yet of a fatality in Dealey Plaza."

Jack turned on the radio and adjusted the tuning knob.

The signal was intermittent, and with so many voices jamming the channel it was hard to make out what was being said. They picked up "Dealey Plaza." There was a garbled exchange about gunshots. Someone cut in to say they were at Parkland Hospital. Another speaker, identifying himself as a police motorcyclist, said he was in the railroad yard pursuing a suspect. The words "Texas School Book Depository" crackled through to them. They heard the names "Connally" and then "Kennedy—President Kennedy" and the words, "Head shot, I repeat, head shot. It looks fatal, repeat, fatal. Half the president's head has been blown away— It's smeared all over my windshield."

Rip slowed the car as if this would help clear the radio reception, but it didn't. "My God, did I hear that right?"

The slow motion nightmare was back. "Someone has just shot the president," Jack said. "In Dealey Plaza—right after I left. Jeez, Rip. If I'd stayed, I would have been there."

He felt the car leap forward again.

Rip was talking to him, but the words weren't making sense. Only the crackling radio reports were getting through.

"We've got to get to a TV and find out what the hell is going on," Rip shouted to make himself understood.

"There's one back at the hotel," Jack answered. "We'll catch it there."

The television coverage that afternoon was no more informative than the cacophony of reports on the police radio network. Along with the rest of the nation, they watched Walter Cronkite announce the horrifying news that President Kennedy had been pronounced dead at Parkland Hospital half an hour after the shooting. In the hotel people spoke softly, like they were already in a church. An elderly couple clung to each other for comfort. The waitress in the restaurant served lunch with tears rolling down her face.

"Olivia," Jack said quietly to Rip. "I must speak to her. She'll be worried sick."

Rip's instinct was to say no, but he saw from Jack's expression it wouldn't have made any difference.

"Not here," he whispered back.

Jack nodded and slipped away to the phone booth he had used once before, soon after they had arrived in Dallas.

If Rip had heard the relief in Olivia's voice when she heard Jack on the line, he might have relented more willingly. She was speaking quickly and not making much sense.

"You're all right. Thank God, you're all right. Kennedy, Jack. Someone shot Kennedy. He's dead. In Dallas. Dead. In Dallas."

"The other man is dead too," Jack said. "Did you get that, Olivia? The other man is dead too."

"Connally? Governor Connally is dead as well? Oh, no. I hadn't heard that."

"Not Connally. He's hurt real bad, but he's still alive. I'm talking about our man."

And the line went quiet while Enrique Sanchez's daughter took in what Jack had just said.

"And you're all right," she said. "He's dead…and you're all right." She began to sob, firstly quietly, and then louder. Big, obvious tears that Jack could hear through the phone as clearly as he could feel the warmth of her smile. Jack could have lived his entire life stuck in that one moment as she thanked again and again, finally pausing only to tell him, "I love you."

Jack did not have the heart to tell her about the man with the umbrella.

Rip was waiting in the hotel lobby when Jack returned.

"Get up to the room and get a change of clothes. I've got to check we're okay down here."

Jack was too confused to argue. He ran up the stairs, let himself into their room, and pulled off everything down to his under shorts and socks.

Rip joined him a few minutes later, locking the door carefully behind him.

Jack opened the closet to take out a change of clothing. "What's the problem?"

"Miller left you a farewell present," Rip answered coldly.

"What?"

"I caught a police radio message when you were out. An officer has been shot dead in Oak Cliff. They put out a description and every cop in Dallas went looking for a white male, black hair, a white jacket, white shirt, and dark trousers—and he's armed. Right now there is a manhunt in this city for someone wearing clothes just like the ones Miller told you to dress in today—and he's carrying a handgun. They're after a cop killer, Jack, and you fit the description like a glove."

Jack had already begun to change his clothes. As he began pulling up his pants, his legs went weak. "Are you saying this is deliberate? That Miller set me up to look like this guy who's killed a policeman."

"And a president." Rip's face was gray and drawn. "This is no coincidence, Jack. Whatever is going on here today is no coincidence. This was carefully planned. Though how in God's name killing Miller fits with it, I have no idea."

They stayed in their room for the next hour and then went down to the TV lounge to see what was happening. During that time, the predicament in which Jack might have found himself grew ever more harrowing. The Dallas police tracked their suspect to a movie theater, where he was arrested after putting up a struggle and trying to pull a .38 on the officer apprehending him.

He was taken to police headquarters for questioning and across the TV screen the cameras showed the face of the man who was already being branded as President Kennedy's assassin.

Jack thought his breathing had stopped when he saw who it was. Staring out at him were the hooded, narrow eyes of the protestor on Canal Street in New Orleans. The man his age who had shoved the Fair Play for Cuba leaflet into his hand—the man he had seen in Guy Banister's office. Set up, just like Ferrie had described.

"Now you send him down to Mexico, where he applies for entry into Cuba. Then, Thanksgiving, here we come."

The only discrepancy, as far as Jack could see, was the timing. There was still a week to go to Thanksgiving. Apart from that, whatever was happening seemed to be going straight down the line—but the events of this day had already left Jack Pagano floundering in their wake.

Chapter Seventy

The call from Clint Murchison came late in the afternoon. Jack and Rip were still watching the TV when the hotel manager told Jack there was a man on the telephone who wanted to speak to him.

Jack's pulse raced. "Did he say who it is?"

"No, but he wants to speak to you. The telephone is in the lobby."

Jack's blood had drained to his feet, or so it felt. His legs didn't want to move. Somehow he found himself at the front desk picking up the telephone receiver.

"Hello, this is Jack Pagano."

"Jack. Clint Murchison here. Things are a bit chaotic here right now, after what happened this morning. John Connally's a good friend of mine. My hopes and prayers are that he pulls through. My wife is on her way to Nellie as we speak. Could you help me out, I wonder? Miller says you're a reliable kind of a guy and I can't get hold of him right now."

The receiver was quivering in Jack's hand as he braced himself against the mahogany desk. "Sure thing, Mr. Murchison. How can I help?"

"I know it sounds kind of strange in the circumstances, but could you call by the photo laboratory and pick up something for me? I was planning to give it to Lyndon, but I guess I'll have to ship it up to Washington now. It's a terrible thing. Terrible. The last thing a go-ahead city like this needs, and Dallas has so much going for it. Hell, you know that and you've only been here two weeks."

"The photo laboratory, you say. What is it you want me to collect for you?"

"A couple of reels of film. They're a present for Lyndon—our new president. Something to remind him of the old days. Can you do that for me? I'd sure appreciate it."

Jack found his way to the film processing laboratory forty minutes later. Rip had stayed behind to keep a check on what was being reported about the assassination—and anything else that might throw light on what they were mixed up in.

An armed guard let him in.

"Since when did a film-processing lab need an armed guard?" Jack wondered to himself.

It was after hours and most of the staff had gone home.

Jack wandered down the hallway until he came to a room with a glass window in the door that gave a view inside. It was a projection room. On the wall facing Jack was a large screen, in front of which a cluster of men were bending over two projectors.

Jack watched them stand back as one of the men started a spool of film running through the projector.

It was a street scene.

In the bottom of the picture, people were standing on a sidewalk, looking toward a sharp bend in the road. Three police motorcycles slowly pulled into view and the leading machine disappeared behind a square gray object that had moved into the picture from the right of the screen. One of the motorcyclists in the second line was centered on the screen.

A dark-colored limousine, with flags fluttering either side of the front of the hood, had taken his place. A big automobile, with three rows of seats. In the third row were President Kennedy and the first lady, pretty and smiling in a pink suit and matching hat.

Jack recognized Dealey Plaza. This must have been right after he left.

Another dark automobile followed close behind the presidential limo, with men standing on the running boards on either side. A little girl wearing a red dress and white coat was running beside the limo, along the grass on the far side of the

street, excitedly waving to the first lady. On the near side of the
street, people lining the sidewalk watched the president wave to
them as his car disappeared behind another square gray object
that Jack guessed must have been a street sign.

He watched the president's limo emerge on the other side.
President Kennedy turned toward the first lady. Governor
Connally swiveled round to face the sidewalk and then seemed
to fall backward toward his wife. As he did so, the president
slumped forward and sideways toward his. In the background,
on the grass, a man in a white shirt was holding a small child by
the hand.

Two women, one in a red coat, the other in a dark-colored
one, passed by on the grassy side. The woman in the dark coat
directed what could have been a camera toward the limo.

Jack was transfixed.

He watched the driver turn his head to look behind. A thin
vapor of pink spray rose above the president's head as something
shiny dislodged from his hair at the side and appeared to jerk him
backward. Then he slumped forward and sagged toward Mrs.
Kennedy, who reached out an arm to catch him.

The next thing Jack saw was the first lady climbing out of the
back seat onto the trunk of the car. From the left of the screen a
man dressed in a dark suit appeared to get a handhold on the trunk.
The first lady was almost out of her seat and stretched across
the trunk when the man got a foot to the fender, hauled himself
aboard, and reached out an arm to push her back. Another road
sign flashed across the screen, obscuring the limo for a second and
when it reappeared it was gathering speed and heading through
the underpass, where it nearly careened into the back of a white
car moving slowly down the street in front of it.

The film finished and Jack looked around to see if anyone had
noticed him. But the hallway was deserted.

A bright flash brought his attention back to the projection
room, where the second projector had been started and the second
spool of film was running.

This was a copy, Jack decided. The footage looked identical until it came to the moment after the leading motorcyclist had gone behind the first street sign.

But something was different here.

Instead of the jump to the presidential limousine, the film continued to pan down the street where a man dressed in a dark suit incongruously opened an umbrella and then closed it again. The movement had Jack riveted, and before the presidential limousine came into view the camera paused on his face. For the second time that day Jack found himself looking at the man who had stabbed Miller.

Jack watched the frames click on, his eyes alert for any other differences between the two films. The man wearing the white shirt with the little kid was still there; so were the two women watching the motorcade from the grassy side of the street.

The driver turned to look behind, but this time Jack spotted something else. The driver was raising his left hand, pointing it over his right shoulder toward the seats behind him. And from his hand projected the muzzle and silencer of the gun he was holding.

Immediately afterward the film showed the sickening pink spray blasted out of the president's head in a shower of blood, brain tissue ,and pieces of fractured skull.

If this second version of the film contained any other anomalies, they eluded Jack, who turned away from the glass pane in the door, thinking he was going to throw up—though not from the ghastly detail of the president's killing, which was itself shocking enough.

The second spool of film rattled to its end. One of the technicians removed it from the projector and placed it in a circular canister, which he handed to a man who had been sitting between the projectors during the screening.

The man stood up, checked he had both versions of the film.

Jack recognized him immediately. This had been the man standing next to Miller, the stranger with the umbrella.

As the technician turned to walk away, the other man in the room sprung into action. With one arm he grabbed him by the head. With the other, his shoulder. Jack watched as the stranger gave a violent twist, snapping the other man's neck in one violent and graceful motion.

By the time the man turned around—film canister in hand—Jack had slipped in behind him and the men stood face to face.

If James Lovall had been surprised, he showed no sign of it. "Is there something I can do for you?" he asked.

"Like you did for this guy?"

Lovall nonchalantly reached for his umbrella. He smiled coldly at Jack before whipping his arm around and thrusting the umbrella point like a rapier.

Unlike Miller, Jack was ready.

He parried the blow, ripping the umbrella from Lovall's hands. He tossed it across the room, earning a loud smash as it sent the contents of a nearby desk crashing to the ground. Lovall took a swing, but he was far too slow for Jack.

Jack dipped out of the way.

Using Lovall's momentum against him, Jack drove the man to the ground, his knee shoved between his shoulder blades, pinning him to the ground. He reached for his face, flashes of Louis Reggio's bloody eye socket fresh in his mind's eye. Jack slipped his thumb across Lovall's face until it came to a nice soft spot beside his nose. "You arrogant son of a bitch," he yelled. "You think you're so smart, killing Miller like that with all those people around you."

Jack pressed harder.

Lovall's words were thin and strained. "You're too late. Don't you see? We've got the White House and there's nothing anyone can do about that."

Jack removed his fingers from the man's face.

Instead, he reached for his gun and aimed it at Lovall's forehead. "Aren't you forgetting something?" he asked.

With his other hand, he pulled a handkerchief from his pocket and used it to pick up the two film canisters, which lay just beyond Lovall's reach.

"You won't get away with it. The guards are armed."

Jack pulled back the hammer on the gun. "They told me, when they let me in."

The man watched with wide-eyed terror. Jack held the film canisters in front of Lovall's face. He pressed the barrel of the gun hard into his target's forehead.

He steadied himself.

And then, to his own surprise, he lowered the weapon.

Jack squeezed tight the artery in Lovall's neck, creating a shortage of blood to his brain. Within a few seconds, the man fell to the ground in a scattered heap, his dead weight producing a hearty thud.

Albert Anastasia's son was a lot of things, but he wasn't a murderer.

Epilogue

Though Jack would have much preferred to be with Olivia, his first move in New York was to find Costello and Lansky. He and Rip had wasted no time on their way to the Sherry Netherland Hotel.

Jack had been used—as had everybody else. The whole elaborate conspiracy he had carefully charted since reading his father's papers looked like a charade—nothing more.

There had been far more than a drug oligarchy in the works. More than the overthrow of some revolutionary dictator of a banana republic. What Jack had witnessed was the terrible culmination of something far more sinister and overwhelming than Albert Anastasia could ever have imagined.

"Think about all those loans made to South America," Costello remarked, unable to bring himself to light yet another cigarette. "The ones for agricultural development."

Meyer Lansky leaned forward on the sofa, his elbows pressing into his knees. "The only crop they were paying for was cocaine. And the bankers were in on it from the beginning."

"James Lovall is the banker's man," Costello said. "Always had been. And when they saw the Kennedys weren't going to fall in line on their cocaine deal, they ordered the president killed."

Jack and Rip sat silent, side by side at the table in the room. They watched Costello and Lansky go back and forth, slowly unraveling everything that had happened in an easy tone. They might have been surprised by the details, but to express as much would only have been naïve.

"And that's why the president was assassinated?" Jack asked.

"They had another reason, too. Killing Jack Kennedy was their way of getting even with his old man for the Crash. And now they control all the drugs coming up from South America," Costello answered. "And the White House, don't forget."

"When I saw those men at Murchison's party, I knew it had to be something big," Rip added. "But not like this."

An uncomfortable silence settled over the room. For as long as Jack had known his father's friends, there had been little room for silence. Business never slowed for even a second, and it didn't appear these men did, either. But in the wake of last week's events, for the first time in years, there was little more to say.

And then Costello lit a cigarette. The room remained quiet. It wasn't until he'd finished and made a move to light the next one that Jack spoke up.

"So, where do we go from here?" he wondered aloud.

Costello brought the newly lit cigarette to his lips and then lowered it again. "We're not sure, Jack. Albert tried to warn us. He did. But all we could see was Genovese shipping heroin from Europe."

"The South American cartels," Lansky interrupted. "Cocaine. We took our eyes off the ball…"

"The bankers are pulling the strings now. A new generation of players are sitting around the table as we speak." Costello turned to Jack. "The game is in their hands now. And yours."

"Haven't I always told you to follow the money, kid?" Lansky added.

Jack was relieved to spend the night at home. To his surprise, he had no problem drifting off to sleep. Olivia and Carmella were happy to have him home safe and sound. They'd left the TV off, unable or unwilling to listen to the news.

It was nearly noon when Jack finally opened his eyes again. He slipped into the shower and let the warm water rinse over him. Jack didn't know what the next move was or whether, if he did know, he would even be willing to take it.

By the time he'd dressed and made his way downstairs, he found his mother and Olivia joined by Rip in the living room. They all made their way out to the car. The sky was a flawless blue. The four of them rode in silence, making the journey to Queens amidst the midday traffic.

It was nearly evening by the time they approached the cemetery.

Olivia held Jack's arm as Carmella and Rip followed behind them. They scanned the rows until they came to the marker they'd been searching for. It read, UMBERTO ANASTASIO, 1902–1957.

As the four of them stood over the grave, Jack felt around in his coat pocket. It took him a moment, but eventually he found what he'd been looking for.

He lowered himself to one knee, the others watching him from behind.

Jack took the bullet from Miller's gun, and with his pointer finger he slowly worked it into the soft, damp turf beside his father's grave.

Acknowledgments

To my wife, Jacqueline Eve Samuel O'Halloran, and my daughter, Slaine O'Halloran:

Jackie, there are not enough words or feelings of thanks for all the support and love you gave to me in the launching of this project. Your encouragement and patience showed no boundaries, and for that I will be eternally grateful .

Slaine, your love and support during your growing years was very important in bringing this project to a conclusion. Your literary insight is amazing. I can't express enough thanks to you.

To my co-worker, Clive Dickinson:

Clive, your drive and skill were totally invaluable during the writing of this project. Thanks to you and your family for the patience to see this project through to its conclusion.

To my business partner, Mark Pearce:

Well, my friend, it has been a long and arduous road. But here we are, a few years later than we'd expected when we started. Amazingly, we are here with all the bumps behind us and we are still friends. Now the fun begins. Bravo for hanging in there through the good and bad times.

To my friend and attorney, Martin Simone:

Martin, your support and friendship throughout the years has been part of my inner strength. More than you will ever know, your friendship and counsel have pulled me through many black holes. Mere words could never express my gratitude. Everyone should have a friend of your caliber in order for their lives to be complete.

I would also like to extend my sincerest thanks to:

My agents, Jonathan Lloyd of Curtis Brown and George Lucas of InkWell Management, for all their help and patience over the last several years. My daughters, Carol Roby and Glenda Sheffield, and their families. My partner, Jay Samit, for all his help and support during the creation of this work. His advice was invaluable. My dear friend, Kathryn Autorino, for all her support in the finishing of this work. The law firm of Simone and Roos and their staff for all the tiring hours of support. My dear friend, Robert Carrozza, aka Bobby Russo, of East Boston Mass, for his friendship and support, as well as Michael Ricapito of Providence, RI; Michael Galesi of Montclair, NJ; and Vincent Amato and Johnny Boy Lapato of NY.

Lincoln Township Public Library
2099 W. John Beers Rd.
Stevensville, MI 49127
(269) 429-9575